Monsoon Country

by

Pira Sudham

Rother
Rother at Bodiam, E.Sussex
England

By the same author

People of Esarn
Pira Sudham's Best

Pira Sudham can be contacted at:

The Pira Sudham Estate
105 Moo 13
Napo
Burirum 31230
THAILAND

2

Monsoon Country

Copyright © 1993 by Pira Sudham
All rights reserved

Rothershire Edition

Published in association with
Shire Books (Asia/Pacific)
G.P.O. Box 1534
Bangkok 10501
THAILAND

ISBN 974-89067-3-6
British Library
Catalogue No. YA.1990.a.20225

First published by Rother in 1993
Published in North America by Breakwater
ISBN 0-920911-84-6 title: **Monsoon Country**
Published in French by Editions Olizane Geneva
ISBN 2-88086-062-8 title: **Terre de Mousson**
Published in German by Werner Erne Verlag
ISBN 974-89115-8-6 title: **Ein kleiner Junge aus
den Reisfeldern des Esarn**

Rother

18 Lansdowne Way
Hailsham
E. Sussex BN27 1LX
England, U.K.

Front Cover Photo by Timothy Hart

Introduction

A way with words

by Dr. J.R.L-B. Bernard
Professorial Fellow
School of English and Linguistics
Macquarie University, N.S.W., Australia

Pira Sudham, the author of *Monsoon Country,* is a most unusual writer. In the first place, although born, bred, and indeed still resident, in Thailand, he writes in English, not Thai. There can be few such.

Secondly, because his own pilgrimage through life has taken him from his birthplace, a Lao-speaking peasant village in northeast Thailand, to spend long stretches of time in cities of European culture far from it, he is in command of both Oriental and Occidental ways of looking at things. Even though these viewpoints must sometimes be at variance with one another, Pira Sudham seems comfortable with both.

A divalent world-picture is hardly unique, of course, but it is, perhaps, more unusual than it ought to be. For a writer, the double understanding it implies can be of value and Pira Sudham turns it to good account in *Monsoon Country.* In general it seems to make him more insightful, and at times it is the source of dramatic tension in the narrative.

Thus at one point Prem Surin, the principal character of the book, who also has experienced the two cultures and been drawn towards both, is made to resolve his own ultimate dilemma by choosing between Eastern personal detachment and Western

4

personal involvement.

Monsoon Country depicts the problem of social transition in present-day rural Thailand. This problem is complex and not dealt with in one incident, like Prem's choice, but a picture of it is built up cumulatively as the narrative returns again and again to touch lightly upon it.

Part of what is at issue is the encroachment of the tempting artefacts and expectations of the West upon the age-old and conservative patterns of the indigenous East. Both traditions have their attractions but it is uncertain in what way they may be combined, if at all, in the context of an impoverished peasant society. To the underlying question of what way the people directly involved should choose to act, there is, possibly, no simple answer to be given. Certainly I can read no strong attempt in this book to offer one. Rather I see the effective depiction of a poignant human situation, a depiction which draws much of its power from Pira Sudham's own dichotomous insights. He has experienced the pull in opposite directions; he has lived both lives. More fully than we who read his words in the West and more fully than those who are living through the dilemma in the East, he knows the rewards which both traditions can offer and he knows the bitter penalties which each will exact for those rewards.

We are moved to compassion as his gentle treatment, amplified with each successive vignette, builds our understanding and our empathy. We come to fear that, whatever the choices they elect to make, the foreseeable future will probably be bitter for the people in villages like Napo, that same Napo which, it is worth pointing out, is home both to Prem in the

5

book and to Pira in real life.

We should note even so that *Monsoon Country* is not an autobiography. But it is true that Pira Sudham's relationship with his narrative is a close and personal one. Only other writers who have also lived part of the story they tell themselves are as well placed as Pira Sudham to deal with their material.

Apart from his unexpected choice of English to write in and his cosmopolitan culture, there is another, a third, unusual aspect to the author of this book, and it is this aspect which intrigues me most of all, probably because I understand it least. This is Pira Sudham's actual way with words. It is like that of no other writer I know.

When one first begins to look at the writing in *Monsoon Country* simply as writing, it is noticeable that only a few sentences are "purple" rather than plain. The overall impression which the text makes is that it is both approachable and simple, the former because of the latter.

One may be tempted to see those few purple patches as mavericks which somehow escaped the pruning knife of authorial revision. But the temptation will not last long. If ever there was a writer whose every word was chosen and placed with careful deliberation, it is this one. Every word, plain or purple, is just what he intended it to be and creates the effect he calculated for it.

As the reader gradually becomes more familiar with the book and the way it is written, the feeling that the diction is approachable will remain. The feeling that it is simple, except in the most superficial sense, will, however, be overtaken by a realisation that it is both sophisticated and complex, although

6

not, perhaps, in usual ways.

It is true that the surface of the writing is most often quite straightforward, reminiscent in some ways of early Hemingway. For example, it is not difficult to find sentences which are just single principal clauses arranged in that most basic of all English sentence patterns - subject + verb + (optional) object; or even to find clusters of them. For example:

> The noisy ritual ceased suddenly. The stone, the fronds, the frogs waited. Dust began to settle. The air spoke of an intrusion.

At the same time it can be seen that the vocabulary comes typically from the standard register of the language and consists mainly of words of relatively high frequency of occurrence. It all adds up to a linear succession of familiar words in familiar places. The typical ingredients of the text are lines of prose which are not daunting. Neither are those other apparently simple lines daunting which are the ingredients of, say, a Picasso sketch.

In so much modern art a rich palette is not assembled. Modest ingredients are made to serve and used to create a whole which is vastly more than its parts. Total effects are what matter, not the nature of their constituents, and in the case of Pira Sudham, as in that of Picasso, these effects can be powerful. The few sentences quoted above, for instance, in context, shape an atmosphere of quite breathless anticipation.

Time and again as I read, I find myself pulled up to ask: 'Why was that so effective? How was that done?' The consistent cleverness of the writing forces me to pause, to savour at length and, inevitably, to ask such questions.

Full answers to them seldom come back, of course, since they are in Pira Sudham's keeping alone, but it does seem to me sometimes that very much has depended upon the choice of the *mot juste*, no matter how apparently simple a word it may have been, or more probably on the choice of several of them. Such choices are not simple matters and cannot be lightly made. They presuppose a sophisticated and unusual sensitivity to language and to its resonances.

Accordingly it is no surprise that descriptions, overt or implied, are often brief but curiously effective.

Because the writing is so graphic, though sparse, we form vivid images in our minds as we read. For example, we come to think that we know - whether we are right or wrong does not matter - what the *monsoon country* actually looks like, or more accurately perhaps, what it actually feels like. We have experienced the coming of the rain on the parched plain. We have sheltered from its searing heat by sitting under a tree, and so on.

If we seek to understand why everything seems so immediate and vivid, it may be that we should look towards the innate sense of the dramatic which seems to be part and parcel of Pira Sudham's make-up. One notes that his "landscapes" always have people and his narrative moves forward by means of the interactions of these people. His novel is evidently a work of human response, just as any play must be. But there is this difference, namely, that we do not contemplate the players as figures on a stage but somehow magically enter into their skins. We then know what they see and also what they feel as they deal with each other and with the physical environment about them. In part at least it is this which explains the first-hand quality of our impressions and why, more than in many an other novel, we have a real feeling of *being there.*

With this in mind, other qualities which we might associate with the drama come to attention. Consider the almost theatrical control of pace. At times the action moves along evenly and calmly. At other times the pace is more rapid. Usual enough, you might say. But there are other times again when the action suddenly hurtles forward, when it lurches without warning, taking the reader quite by surprise and inducing the same sort of frisson as a brilliant *coup de théâtre.* The audience in the one case and the reader in the other may be most pleasurably astonished by such unexpected and virtuoso effects, but, despite the rapidity of their happening, should not be left uncomprehending behind to wonder what has happened. Nor are they, as long as the writer knows his or her craft sufficiently well. Pira Sudham certainly knows his sufficiently well. In his writing lucidity is never sacrificed, whatever pace his action may take, unless he intends it to be.

That this may sometimes be the case occurs to us when we consider the tone of the writing. Usually it is plainly straightforward, even unremarkable. There is no use of devices like irony that I can recall and so words tend to mean just what they say. Nevertheless there is a whole crucial section in the second part of the novel which is rich in ambiguity and which operates with suggestions not clearly stated. This section corresponds to events in Prem's life which are traumatic for him and which leave him uncertain at the deepest levels of his being about the rectitude of his own behaviour, both in the particular events in question, and, to judge by his subsequent actions, in his life more generally. The burden of it all upon him is immense and, in self-defence, he veils his own mind from himself and ceases his usual patterns of self-awareness.

Accordingly it is entirely logical that we readers, who have grown accustomed to seeing the world through the perceptions of Prem's mind and to following his reactions to these perceptions through his self-awareness, should find the situation in this part of the book somehow misting over and becoming obscure. We grow unclear even as to what Prem actually did at certain critical points in the story. His actions, as well as his responses and motivations, are for the time lost to us in greater or lesser degree.

It is, of course, all intended to be so - a cunningly contrived piece of mystification for our ultimate delight. Yet it is also psychologically sound. Who among us have not known occasions when the workings of our own hearts and hands would not comfortably bear too close a scrutiny and when we have therefore simply turned from their contemplation? Prem's failure at this time to face his reality, whatever it was, does not strain verisimilitude and it is handled so that we simply become more and more intrigued. "What can he have done?" we ask ourselves, hardly daring to breathe one dark possibility which has been made to occur to us.

As might be expected, the situation becomes clearer in retrospect as we read on further - though, perhaps as in real life, not entirely clear. It is all quite brilliantly done and our respect grows for that false-simple diction of Pira Sudham with its supple power which seems to be equal to any challenge.

A weakish parallel with it might be found in the superficially plain language which T.S. Eliot adopted for so much of his play *The Cocktail Party.* Eliot's apparently pedestrian prose had within it the power to be imperceptibly transmuted into a poetic form appropriate for use at those parts of the play which called for lyrical outpouring. The parallel is poor because Pira Sudham's prose rises to its high points without apparent "transmutation". Would a better analogy be with the Thai kick-boxer whose impassivity at all times in the ring gives no hint as to when his left leg will flash around and up to deliver a stunning blow to his opponent's head? Perhaps Pira Sudham's prose is *sui generis* and no analogy is worth pursuing.

In any discussion of language use, it is unsatisfactory to divide things up so as to suggest that manner exists somehow independent of matter. It does not. Yet here, as so often is the case, this seems to have been done. Perhaps to some extent it is inevitable. But let us now belatedly turn to content, for most readers are likely to agree that the author of *Monsoon Country* is as interesting for what he says as for how he says it, perhaps more so.

Some people have seen the book as an exposé of certain aspects of Thai society. Certainly Pira Sudham does put clearly before us the plight of the peasant villagers among whom he grew up. These people seem to be as much victims of their own incapacitating philosophy of acceptance and obedience as of the cruel pattern of economic exploitation which is imposed upon them by others. The latter draws

11

strength from the former and between the two they are held hapless prisoners in a condition of grinding poverty and of deprivation, both material and personal, from which there seems to be scant hope of release.

How it all works in practice is clearly revealed to us as the action of the novel, moving rapidly over the years, impinges upon members of the Surin family, whose mental processes we come to know quite well; and in a less clear-cut way as it impinges upon the idealistic village school teacher, Kumjai. He becomes increasingly enigmatic to us as the story goes on, because Prem, through whose eyes we see him for the most part, is increasingly separated from him.

To many a Western reader these aspects of the book may well come as something of a revelation, an *exposé* if you will. At very least they are likely to cause an uncomfortable enlarging of the images of Thailand typically held in the Western mind, adding less romantic pictures to place beside those of exotic resorts like Phuket, and of golden Buddhas in scented temples.

While the revelation of this pattern of social evil has a precise local habitation, namely in and around the village of Napo, it is Pira Sudham's skill to make it not only distant and exotic but also familiar and applicable to settings we know much better. The heartlessness, and above all the greed, are the same unattractive coins as circulate in my country and no doubt in yours. As the story unfolds and they stand revealed, we recognise them as all too familiar.

This is no book of facile optimism. No easy solutions are advanced; nor is too much distraction from the problem of human evil allowed. Grim reality claims the last page more firmly than it did the first and the reader must confront it.

But it would be entirely wrong to think of this as a book of dark tones only. There is a calming stoicism in the treatment, even humour, and, anyway, human virtues are as present as human vices to warm the pages. There is kindness as well as cruelty, idealism as well as cynicism. There is love beside indifference, generosity as well as greed. They are all given particular habitation, but are nonetheless universal in essence.

In a way the book is a treatise on the duality of human nature. It addresses the question of why some human beings are "good" and life-affirming in the main, while others are "bad" and life-denying. And if its observations bring no answer to the question for the present, and perhaps there never will be one, the problem it posits remains a reality which we must all attempt to come to terms with. It may be that this book can help us, for in it the human condition is accurately, compassionately, if a little sadly, presented. As the reader finally shuts it he or she will probably have a feeling of understanding life and its complexities at least a little better.

Pira Sudham is much too wise to offer pasteboard examples of the various vices and virtues he deals with. His characters, at least the more fully treated ones, have mingling in them ingredients of both kinds, as most of us do, but of course in by no means equal proportions. Perhaps because of this they seem to have a life of their own. Whatever they may typify, whatever lesson is to be drawn from them, they are individuals in whom we believe and in whom we become very interested. They cease to be Thai or

13

English or German, as all people do with whom we come to empathise greatly, and stand before us merely as particular humans, merely as themselves. One must be very glad that Pira Sudham chose to avoid the grotesques of satire and to bring to us credible creatures whom we can get to know well as they play out his drama and bring us his message.

Moreover, these individuals, these new acquaintances of ours, especially Prem whose story the book primarily relates, are set in a plot which, while admittedly gathering its interest somewhat slowly at first, ultimately develops a powerful fascination. In time, *Monsoon Country* becomes one of those books the reader just cannot put down, more because of a desire to know what happens next than to savour any of the other admirable qualities it possesses. The story even has a denouement which, at least for this Western reader, was totally unexpected. One wonders whether it would have been so for a reader of a different background.

It is a great skill indeed to make of such compelling interest a story which has to deal instructively in weighty matters both particular and general. When one considers also that there are so many other great skills displayed in *Monsoon Country,* it seems entirely appropriate that its author should have been recommended for the Nobel Prize in Literature. It is a very exceptional book. He is a very exceptional writer.

14

Monsoon Country: A Chronology of Change

Pira Sudham was born to a rice-farming family in impoverished, rural Esarn, northeast Thailand. He made his way to Bangkok at the age of fourteen to serve the monks as a temple boy, an acolyte, in a Buddhist temple. His departure from his village is similar to that of thousands of young boys from rural areas of Thailand to find lodging and food in order to be able to attain higher education.

"If I had not left my village then, I would have been another peasant. I would have been subject, like most villagers, to the mercy of nature: floods, drought, disease, ignorance and scarcity. With endurance, I would have accepted them as my own fate, as something I cannot go against in this life," says Pira.

Of his humble background, he says, "I owe a great deal to my early village life, spending years in rice fields of Esarn, so remote and neglected. I grew up with the good heartedness, the hospitality and illiteracy of our people, as well as the selfishness, cruelty, poverty and corruption. I know the arrogance of shopkeepers, of merchants who deal with villagers, and the helplessness of the farmers. What I saw and learnt in childhood touched me deeply. I won't cut off my roots, for without them I would not be able to grow. I see my literary works as a force emerging from the grass roots, from the poor of Thailand, who had no voice before, and have been left far behind in the accelerated development and industrialisation in our cities. Now the emergence

15

of peasants has to happen."

Asked why he writes, Pira Sudham replies: "In my mind I carry memories of childhood, of life in villages, much as a pregnant woman carrying a child. Every day these images grow, and I know that one day I shall have to give birth to them through the medium of writing. Besides, I don't want people in our villages, so far removed from other peoples because of distance and poverty, to be born, suffer and die in vain. They are my impetus, my incentive to write, my life force, my source of energy and power. For so long, I have suffered along with them. An oyster, after a grain of sand strays inside and causes irritation and pain, can secrete a substance which coats the source of irritation day by day, until it becomes a pearl. Like an oyster, I overcome the source of my pains with writing, with a hope that one day, what I write may become powerful enough to change people's way of thinking."

Would we be right in thinking there was both a hint of anger and a great deal of sadness in his books? The author admits: "When I was a child in Napo Village, what I saw and experienced moved me greatly. The poverty, corruption, lack of basic medical facilities, the purchase and sale of children and also many buffaloes combined to sadden me; I was angered by the injustice and the helplessness of the peasants. I remember how I wished to tell my parents and the other villagers what I saw and felt, and what I wanted them to see and feel. I wanted to take them by their shoulders and shake them to wake up

16

and to see. But I came to realize that they would not see things as I saw them. All the while I was taught not to see, not to hear and not to speak out. Years passed and my anger and sadness gradually became crystalized. Thus I no longer harbour raw anger and tearful sadness; instead these emotions have become my resources which nurture me and from which I try to weave a rich tapestry of our village life in my writings."

In his own words, Pira explains why he writes in English instead of Thai: "As a student of English literature, I admired the writings of Emily Brontë, James Joyce, Patrick White, and George Orwell. These authors became my frame of reference, so that I determined, if possible, to achieve a certain stature in the world of English literature. Then, during those years abroad, I became aware that there were hardly any books on Thailand by Thai writers for non-Thais. People in other countries might wish to read books about Thailand, but there were very few available to satisfy such a demand. I also chose English as a medium because of the discipline of the language and the process of reasoning it reflects, in contrast, for example, to Thai, which does not have punctuation marks. Language reflects the mind, and I could see my own lack of discipline, my crippled mind, maimed for life by my background and up-bringing. I use the discipline of the English language like a cripple using crutches. Besides, I want to be able to communicate directly with English readers worldwide, without being translated from Thai, and I don't mind so much, now that my books are being translated into French, German, Japanese and some other languages. I want to speak to other peoples in various countries in a way that other Thai writers do not.

"Thailand is a fascinating country, but those who write about Thailand are generally foreigners. Foreign writers, however, inevitably look at Thailand and write about Thai people from the *outside*. To balance this, I want to be able to present this country and its people from the *inside*. At the same time, I try to look at our Thai lives through the foreigners' glasses, so that I can understand how the outsiders, the *farangs*, look at us. Fortunately, I still retain so much of my Thai mentality that I, as a person born and raised in this country, also view Thai society as an *insider*. For me, it is a blessing to be able to do both."

In his native Napo, Pira has created a 'Village Project'. Is this a way of increasing his popularity or establishing his power base among the villagers from which, eventually, he hopes to become their leader? "It is simply to do what I can for Napo. It began when more and more villagers started coming to my garden for herbs, vegetables, papaya and other fruit. If I was at home, they would ask me for whatever could be had from the property, and when I was not there, they just helped themselves. Young plants, vegetables, and herbs did not have much chance to grow since they were constantly picked and uprooted. To save them, every time I went to Napo from Bangkok, I loaded my van with young plants, herbs, mango seedlings, papaya seedlings, etc. from the nurseries en route. In the village, I gave these away to my neighbours and in this way, they can grow their own. And in this way, they had no further excuses for not having their own herbs and fruit trees. Now Napo has over 300 young bamboo groves which in two or three years time will produce shoots for eating and bamboo for making baskets and building materials. In 1993 the village has over 800 young mango trees, 500 coconut trees, and 300 jackfruit trees in addition to the ones which were already growing there.

"Then there is a water problem. In our areas, during the dry summer season, water in the ponds and rice fields dries up. In some years there is hardly any water left for the buffaloes and cows to drink. We dig for water from the dried-up swamp, but the deeper we dig, the more brackish the water becomes because of salt deposits underneath the surface.

"At the edge of the village, there is our age-old swamp which is getting shallower as years go by due to the silt brought down by streams and floods during the rainy season. It had become so shallow that it could no longer hold sufficient water to last throughout the dry months of summer.

"I talked to our headman about deepening the swamp, and putting up earth banks around it, thus making mounds which would retain rain water instead of allowing it to flow away. The headman had been elected a few months earlier (I remember him as a young boy, my junior in school, a younger brother of my friend next door.) He was most enthusiastic, and with his cooperation, the villagers gathered one day at the swamp and began digging. One dry season after another, we dig and now we have a big pond deep enough to hold water all the year round. And I have been growing trees and plants on the surrounding embankment, and buying fish fry from Korat to free them into the pond. Given some incentive and guidance, our people are cooperative, hard working and can do so much for so little.

"And I have told our good headman I would not build my power base, trying to become an MP, or the headman of the village in his place at some future time, now that I have returned to the village to live among them. I want to be just another villager, a part of our village life, living in harmony with the other inhabitants, in my retirement from active business life in Bangkok. I will write a few more books yet. I will continue being a *seeing eye* in these parts of Thailand, so I can record what I see and the changes that are taking place and to identify agents of change month by month, year by year, as I have done in my novel, *Monsoon Country*."

Monsoon Country

1

March 1954

In the Year of the Horse, Boonliang Surin gave birth to her sixth child. It was a boy. Then, following the delivery of this son, the early monsoonal rains began to give life back to the village of Napo. Summer had ended. The rainy season had commenced. The rains poured down day and night, promising and bountiful. Like most of the village inhabitants, the Surins looked hopefully and gladly upon the surrounding rice fields, which were now inundated and workable. Another rice planting season had come.

The birth of the baby was associated with a good season, so the parents named him 'Prem', which means joy.

When the time was suitable, Kum Surin went to the house of the village headman and after meekly sitting down on the wooden floor, he said:

"I've just had another offspring whom we've called Prem."

The august headman reclining on the floor, half-naked because it was a hot day, coughed spasmodically. Time seemed to stand still while he rearranged his loin-cloth. Whether he minded very much being disturbed during his nap, it was difficult to see from his wrinkled face, but he sat up now, cross-legged, and spat into the spittoon nearby. To compose himself he ran his trembling gnarled fingers several times over his face and through his grey hair.

Because the headman represented the officialdom of the world of masters, his authority commanded respect and awe.

"The other day my wife..." Kum faltered, fearing that it was not time for him to speak.

He checked himself and decided to remain silent until the old man was ready to listen.

"Bring a tobacco tray and my shirt," the old headman demanded.

This sudden order with its tone of authority startled the visitor. Someone in the inner part of the house stirred, and the wood squeaked with the movement.

"You're indeed fortunate to have another son," said the headman.

The father of the new-born child sensed that the headman's voice was tinged with personal disappointment. The headman needed a son; all he had were daughters, and now his wife had passed the child-bearing age. This was why Kum had carefully worded his message. He had thoughtfully chosen the word 'offspring' so as to avoid reminding the influential man of his misfortune. Not to have a son to carry on the family name was considered a retribution for some misdeed done in the past. For this reason Kum, who was just another impoverished peasant of Napo, feared to put himself above

22

the man who had been made a master.

The headman's wife, who had been kindling the charcoal fire in the kitchen, shook herself free of ash. Then the old man gravely donned the black cotton shirt which smelled of age and dust. Changing his sitting position, the headman took hold of the enormous census book that had been serving him as a head rest. The huge book also smelled of age. And the wizened hands trembled because of its size and weight. Now he began to thumb through it carefully, page by page. With great concentration, he bent his head towards the book so that he could see.

"Ah, my eyes begin to fail me," he mumbled.

But his official duty strengthened him. His grim countenance expressed solemnity.

"The name is Prem," Kum said doggedly, thinking that it was not yet time for him to speak further.

When the headman finally reached the page on which the name, the date of birth and the sex of the child could be recorded, Kum repeated the name and the day of birth with some confidence. He had spent days trying to commit the facts to memory. He could not read or write

But the headman could record only a few letters at a time, writing them down slowly and laboriously. Kum had to repeat the information, and restrain himself not to lean too far forward. At all times he had to check himself and remain respectful, regardless of how much he would have liked to see his child's name being written.

The headman's wife joined them, gently sat down at a suitable distance and waited. Her husband's official capacity always demanded her silence.

Time stood still. Finally the old headman spoke.

"It's a good name."

The two witnesses seemed drained.

"Being born in the Year of the Horse, in the morning, this boy will be very easy to teach and he will have a good brain, like a horse," the old man predicted.

The father accepted the prediction with a murmur as he fumbled for coins in his shirt pocket to give to the headman. Because Kum had always been a poor man, he was afraid that the sum he had to give would be insufficient, so he had brought with him a basket of cucumbers and a large gourd to compensate.

"How are Liang and the baby?" the headman's wife asked.

Her voice broke and rose, as if she had just returned to life.

"She's getting much better, and the baby is well," said Kum.

He was grateful that she had asked. Now there was no doubt of his son's existence in the eye of the law. But after leaving the headman's house, he felt anxious. He had been rather concerned because since birth the frail little boy had not opened his eyes and hardly made any movement or sound. Liang Surin, his wife, who had been confined to the fireside and to drinking hot herbal potions in order to heal herself, knew instinctively that there was nothing wrong with her baby. She had been giving him milk and warmth from her own body. He would survive and grow, she believed.

Kiang, the oldest boy, crouching next to the baby said:

"I'll call him Tadpole."

Kiang, who attended the village primary school, had read in a spelling book about a tadpole. The mother said nothing about the name until Kiang had gone away. While she was sipping the herbal tea, she saw the tiny hands stirring the air. A tadpole, a wriggling little tadpole, she murmured, as if to taste the name with her own lips. She smiled.

A few years later, when the Tadpole had become an extremely quiet and timid boy, the people of Napo began to refer to him as the Mute. Liang neither protested nor showed any objection to the new identity her little boy had acquired. She thought that such a deficiency, if it was one, could be due to the boy's own retribution or *karma*. But sometimes when she was annoyed with his silence or when there was no response from him, she would say: "You must really be a mute." How her words echoed and pierced her heart. But soon both the mother and child had learned to accept such a name.

There was only Piang, the older sister, who put up a fight. She knew that her little brother was not dumb or mute.

"Don't you call him mute, for he isn't."

"Why, Piang, he's as dumb as a tree," one girl retorted.

"Or a water buffalo," another added.

"He talks to me sometimes," Piang said, raising her voice.

For she was proud of the fact that although he did not talk to her, she understood him.

"Make him speak then," said a girl who was covered with heat rash.

Piang turned to her brother who was standing timidly nearby and asked him to say a few words.

But there was not a peep out of him.

"He's mute, mute, mute."

"As mute as a paddy field. That's what he is. Ta la la la," the girls sang and danced.

Smouldering with rage, Piang waited for them to tire of their mockery. Then she aimed for the eyes of one girl; her nails dug into flesh, and then she went at the others, sending them crying to their mothers.

Having watched the scene from her own hut, Liang tightened her sarong and came over to render justice. She grabbed her daughter and beat her.

"If you can't play nicely with others, stay away from them," she said hoarsely.

Piang did not cry, but she became sullen. Taking her brother by the hand, she led him to sit under a mango tree. Here it was cool and the ground was sandy. Piang began to scratch the sand with her index finger, making a pattern which fascinated the little boy. He followed her example and drew lines. Piang did not want to speak, for tears had welled up in her eyes. All the while she was trying desperately to remain calm. What were the sounds that she had heard the Tadpole make the other day? Was it his way of trying to tell her that he had seen spirits passing by, or something about having been an old buffalo in his previous life?

But then words did not come easily to her either. Her throat contracted and tears ran down her face. Thus it seemed that the sister was the one who needed consolation. Bruises on her arms had to be gently rubbed to take away the pain. The mocking 'ta la la la' had to be forgotten.

Kiang thought himself rather lucky to have a brother at last because three others had died in their infancy. Now he saw the little one as a future partner in strength. Kiang could not have cared less if the brother remained a mute all his life, so long as he did not grow up to be a weakling. He did not care what people said, for now he had a brother. As young men, they would be working side by side in the fields, helping one another. Each would take on a great deal of responsibility and accept hard labour, toiling on their land and looking after their parents.

There were times when Kiang looked anxiously at the silent boy, fearing that an illness or the evil spirits which had claimed the three others not long ago would take the Tadpole as well. The mute would survive, Kiang thought.

When they were alone together in a rice field, Kiang said to his brother.

"I'll teach you how to ride a water buffalo."

Prem stood close to the animal, ready for action.

By then he had learned to listen and to obey.

"Watch me first," Kiang said and jumped swiftly from the hind legs of the animal onto its back.

The docile brute showed no annoyance or rebellion. It went on grazing.

"See, you keep your legs apart and press them on the flanks, so you can urge it to walk or gallop by nudging it with your knees or toes. Like this."

Kiang's legs moved as he tried to master the buffalo. The animal pulled another mouthful of grass and snorted knowingly. Kiang slapped it gently with a rope. The buffalo jerked its head and walked. Kiang also made certain sounds to talk to the animal, which eventually stopped in front of the boy.

Kiang slid to the ground and said:

"You see, I can jump from here right onto its back." Kiang, agile and lean, paused to see whether his brother was listening. "But you'll have to hold onto its tail. Put your toes on its hind leg and pull yourself up. Try now."

The boy looked at the beast's long, sharp horns, at its great size.

"Come on, try!" Kiang said decisively. "With your right foot on its knee joint, hold on to the tail and push yourself up."

Kiang stood aside, watching.

The buffalo grazed on, unperturbed. Its black skin and coarse hair smelled of mud. The boy hung on to its tail, unsure of his own strength. Then the buffalo moved and he fell off. Kiang patted the brute and asked it to be still, helping the Tadpole to climb up at the same time.

"There you are. It's easy."

The buffalo turned its head as if to question the boy's presence; its large, protruding eyes rolled. When Kiang patted, it walked, shaking its thick head and flapping its hairy ears. Then it stopped, waiting for further instructions.

"Make it move," Kiang directed.

Because he had already surrendered, the Tadpole became powerless. How could one dare to be the master of so huge an animal? He had handed himself over to it; being now at its mercy, he could not act.

"Go on, make him walk," Kiang repeated.

He sounded disappointed. The animal went back to grazing, ignoring its burden. Kiang became angry at his brother's silence, at the face that bore no expression, at the mouth that knew no language. So he angrily slapped the buffalo's haunch. The surprised beast ran, and a second later the boy fell.

No one else was present to pass judgement on Kiang. His boyish masculinity prevented him from going to find out whether his brother was hurt or not. Instead he went after the buffalo as it fled from the scene.

"Let's go home now!" Kiang called from a distance, sounding as if no accident had occurred.

When anger and disappointment had gone, Kiang again helped the Tadpole onto the buffalo's back. Then he himself nimbly jumped up and sat behind the boy so that he had his arms around him.

Together the two brothers rode the buffalo homeward towards Napo.

2

June 1958

"We're going to have a good monsoon season this year," Piang said.

The herd of water buffaloes stirred, lifting up their heads, passing on the message, confirming Piang's prediction. Prem, who had also been close to the herd, looked for signs of the animals' understanding and sensed their elation. He looked up at the skies and knew that more rains were coming.

"Tell-tell me how-how you know-know," he stammered, squinting his eyes against the sun.

He wanted to say more but words did not come easily to his lips. It was an effort to speak, opening one's lips to make sounds for others to understand.

Piang still gazed at the clouds as if she did not hear what he had tried to say. She decided not to be disturbed while reading the auguries from the formation and shapes of clouds. She prided herself for being much older than he, and last year she had won first place in her class.

"See that cloud there," Piang said at last. "Doesn't it look like a good healthy woman? I say she's the Goddess of Rains. Over there is the Spirit of Drought who looks mean but is now weakening."

Among the grotesque forms of clouds and shadows, the Tadpole saw indescribable beauty. Could Piang read also the poetry of the skies? There was an immense electrifying power in such beauty, passing from form to form, from shadow to shadow, filling the air with its intensity. He held out his hand.

"Dooo," he made a sound which Piang thought to be 'look'. So she became silent, believing that her brother had committed an act against a taboo. For now the wind became forceful. At the edge of the forest, near a neglected melon patch which had become bare and dry, a whirlwind appeared, whirling and furling, carrying leaves and dust.

"Razor wind, please go away," Piang prayed.

For you must not dare, must not see, hear or go against evil, the Power of Darkness. So then she told him not to make remarks on such things, not to point at rainbows either, or his index finger would drop off. She became rather serious then, and expected her brother to do the same. Do not disturb evil, the supernatural, the spirits in all things; just get out of their way. Eyes were not to see, ears not to hear, and mouths not to speak against them.

Somewhere lightning struck and thunder rumbled.

"Oh, Lords and Masters, the true rulers of the earth," Piang continued praying.

Then her voice trailed off, subdued by the deafening skies. For a while she became silent. As if in a trance she closed her eyes. And when she opened them again, she began scanning the fields and shouting to other boys and girls. Then the answers came, echoing from all directions. Now it was time to get together.

The wind rose into a storm. How nice Piang looked with her thick, long, black hair flying about her comely face and head, as she waited for the rain to fall. The electrifying turbulent air woke up the whole plain now. The buffaloes began to run about, chasing one another. Many fronds on tall palm trees broke off and bats dispersed, screeching and fluttering into the darkening skies. Clouds hung low, melting into grey veils.

The boys rushed about, gathering fallen fronds to make a rough shelter so that the young ones could huddle together when it rained.

"I lost all my frogs and crabs," one little girl lamented.

"If you boys don't round up the herds now, they will run off too far." Piang seemed burdened with worries and care.

Meanwhile she tugged her little brother along and tied his palm hat tightly for him.

Then the great storm came like a million hooves stampeding over saplings and the rice fields of the open country. The rain swept and lashed at the fronds under which the children crouched. Soon, as if by magic, the boys, overpowered by the rain, took off their clothes and ran wildly, laughing, calling and singing:

> *Rain!*
> *Here comes a monsoonal rain,*
> *And I've only a handful of grain!*

The little girl who had lost all her frogs and crabs giggled at the sight of those naked boys.

"Lightning may strike them," she laughed.

"Are you afraid of lightning, Tadpole?" another girl asked after a flash of lightning had blazed.

The Tadpole opened his mouth, but with difficulty, to utter a word which resembled the sound of "Wooo."

"Yes, you are," Piang quickly said to emphasize the taboo: One must not dare. "And keep your mouth shut," she added. "It makes you look like a dum-dum when your mouth stays open."

"Are you scared of me?" Boon Srima pushed herself forward with one truncated arm outstretched like a blunt spear. Boon had been born deformed. Her hands had no fingers. Silly girl, why should you be afraid of a fingerless lass when you were not afraid of the dead?

Yes, when the old headman died, the boy went to his house to see the corpse. There was no mystery to death at all. The body was deserted, like an old nest after the birds had flown away. But he was curious though, because the headman's wife wailed so loudly that the whole village could hear.

"Nooo. No-noo afraid," he managed to raise his voice against the sound of rain and thunder.

Then he broke away from their hold on him, running off to join the other boys. The girls ran after him, shouting:

"How dare you!"

Then the boys came to his rescue, chasing the girls away. Their screams and laughter mingled with the sound of the echoing plain. How happy they were then, and their happiness marked the beginning of a rainy season.

Now that the planting season had started, the herds were broken up. The boys and the girls went to help their parents, ploughing and harrowing. As for the Tadpole, too young yet to take on hard labour, he looked after the animals when they were not at work. He was to stay close to them, taking charge so that they would not trample on seedlings or eat newly planted rice.

When one got close to a buffalo, one noticed how the big innocent eyes rolled, how they looked at things.

He had become very fond of one particular buffalo. It had long curvy horns and a wise look. He rode on this one every morning when he took the herd out from the village to graze in fallow fields, and when the afternoon sun became too hot, together they sought a tree under which they could lie for hours. The boy would rest with his buffalo, finding some comfort in silence. With an animal one did not have to speak. Words sounded crude, like rough blocks of brick which had to be put into certain places to make sense. Many a time Piang had tried unsuccessfully to drum into his skull how to arrange words so that people could understand him. But after a great deal of effort, she lost her patience.

"You're hopeless at language. People will believe that you're stupid. They'll laugh at you if you keep talking nonsense. They will. And I can't stand it," she had said moodily.

He tried so hard to please her, but without success. Words would not come easily to his lips in their proper order. They fluttered in his mind like butterflies, some of which could excape through his mouth. He could speak more and faster after he had fallen from the hut and lost consciousness. Then the sooth-sayer had to be called and they built a pit filled with burning charcoal above which a rough bamboo rack was made for his body to be laid on. They had covered him with wet clothes and they

35

prayed for his life. When he came to, they wept again and prepared food for the Spirit.

But he still stammered when he was obliged to say something to awesome people, such as the village headman or patrolling policemen or strangers who asked for directions. He would rather avoid having to speak altogether by spending more time in the company of the buffaloes on the plain.

Then one day he fell into a lotus pond outside the village. He would have drowned, if it were not for a passer-by who noticed that the boy had been down in the deep water far too long. Once more they filled the pit with burning charcoal and put the boy on the bamboo rack and covered him with damp clothes. Once again the sooth-sayer led the people who gathered there to pray for the boy's life. They believed that a Spirit wanted his life to make him one of its sons. So they begged the Spirit not to take this boy from his poor, ageing parents who needed him to work in the fields. During this ritual of bartering for a life with the Spirit, many votive offerings were made. The Surins promised that they would make 'merit' at the temple and transfer the merit gained to the Spirit, that they would prepare food for monks and donate funds and yellow robes to the temple. However, after a night had passed, the boy was still in danger and there was no sign that he would ever come back to life. The sooth-sayer said that there was only one thing left to do, and that was to give the boy up and offer him to the Spirit. Hearing this, the mother wept, for she knew that she had to comply with what the sooth-sayer told her to do. So then the old man, renowned for having grappled all his life with various kinds of

Spirits and ghosts and wandering souls, chanted the preamble to offer a life. The smoke from the charcoal fire rose, while the chanting, rich with sentiment and pathos, brought tears to many eyes. In the process, the boy became the Spirit's son.

When the Tadpole recovered and could speak as if he had never been a mute, people believed that he had been truly adopted by the Spirit who had endowed its son with supernatural qualities and who, from then on, would look after its offspring. Somewhere near the adopted one, the Spirit would be hovering, keeping an eye on him. Some people, especially children, became afraid of the Tadpole when they heard a rumour that dogs howled whenever he walked by.

"Watch out for that boy. He can speak, has a good memory, can make predictions and bring omens. Why? Mark my words and be careful," one woman warned her children.

The poor boy became lonelier than before, knowing that the others were afraid of him, and so he spent most of his waking hours on the plain with his buffaloes, and at nights he stayed in the hut. Buffaloes alone remained his source of comfort. At times, Kiang would play with him, trying to teach him how to defend himself by using fists and feet to hurt his attackers. Sometimes Kiang would teach him how to set bird traps and fish traps and how to imitate the cooing of doves. At such times, when Kiang came close, he would say:

"You smell like a buffalo. Go and jump in a pond after this."

But the boy did not mind the smell of the buffaloes, nor the mud which had dried on their skins. He was too fond of them, particularly of the wise old one with whom he had often lain skin to skin, resting in the shade of a tree in the hot afternoon, far away from human cries and company. Sometimes, with his head on the flank of the buffalo, he would softly sigh and want to join his mind with that of the wise old animal so as to gain its wisdom. He also longed to transform a child's time scale into that of the animals. He imagined himself lying inside the buffalo looking at his own life and at humanity. From within, people would suspect nothing of what he could see and understand.

There were times when he wished that most people had not treated him differently from the rest of the children. Once he had walked past the headman who had been elected after the old one died. The new headman picked up a stone and threw it at him, hitting his head. Just like that. Then the man walked on as if nothing had happened, while the boy stood there nursing his wound.

All he had done was merely to look at the man with his head slightly tilted to the right. That was sufficient to provoke cruelty.

When Piang saw the blood that had not yet dried on his face, she asked what had happened, but he said not a word. He had done nothing to deserve the blood that had been shed. If he had said to the headman that paying peasants to raise their hands to elect him was evil, it would have been a different matter because thus he would have dared to challenge the Power of Darkness. He would have been proud of the pain and of the blood that had flowed; but all he had done was to look with the eyes of a buffalo. If he told Piang the truth, she would never have believed that for merely looking at the head-man, a stone had been thrown.

He had seen how men raised their hands to vote and got paid for it. Their dumb faces shone with joy for doing something for something, with-out knowing what they were doing. To stretch their hands upward was such an easy feat to do, for ten baht, when one would have had to work the whole day as a labourer to earn a similar amount. The hand raising was done in the open, of course, at the temple ground, and onlookers, including children, could witness this election of the headman of Napo. Now the Tadpole wondered whether those who had raised their hands for money knew that they would have to pay a high price for it later. For when the man was installed in a position which bestowed on him the Master's Power, with policemen and the law on his side, he would use it for his own gain. He was known to have asked several men to play dice with him, and they had to play to lose. Some wives would never know why their husbands suddenly had to sell one or two of their buffaloes or pigs to raise money. Some had to sell a piece of their land. Some even had to borrow money from loan sharks and thus fell victim to another evil.

The Tadpole had seen how it happened. One day Kiang asked him to come along on one of his bird trapping trips in the woods. When Kiang had set a trap, he asked his brother to stay quietly in a nearby thicket to keep guard so that no one would steal the trap and the decoy. The boy enjoyed sit-ting silently in the bushes, hiding himself from all eyes, deep in the forest.

While hiding in the bushes, he heard human

voices coming from afar; and the sound of footfalls on dry leaves told him that a group of men was approaching. A minute later they came into view choosing to sit down under the very tree in which Kiang had set a trap. From where he was hiding, the boy could see that the men formed a circle and began to play dice.

As they gambled, the boy could see a few faces. Their sad eyes followed the accursed dice as if hypnotized. The tragedy weighed on them, but once in a while the boy heard curses. At one point the headman got up to relieve himself. Unfortunately he made his way towards the thicket in which the Tadpole was hiding. The leaves and branches and tall grass could not conceal him from the man. This sudden encounter made the man change his mind. He turned back and stopped the game. The men left soon after, leaving to the boy the tranquility of the forest.

3

May 1961

One morning when the Tadpole was taking the herd out of the pen, Kiang stopped him and said:

"I'll take care of them from now on."

The boy was puzzled.

"Tadpole, come up here," called the mother from the hut.

He obeyed.

Piang giggled as the mother stripped him and gave him a new pair of shorts and a shirt.

"You're coming to school with me," Piang said pertly. "Every boy and girl from seven to fourteen has to learn to read and write. You too. Now hurry up or we'll be late."

Piang sounded like a grown-up then, turning her shining head, looking so intelligent and alive. When it began to rain, Piang cut a broad banana leaf for an umbrella. He tested how powerful the rain was, lifting his hand skyward. His mind echoed: I raise my hand to the skies. He seemed pleased with the thought. He smiled at the joy so simple and yet more precious than being paid ten baht for raising one's hand to elect the headman.

Barefoot, they splashed through puddles and mud. They left the village street and turned into the temple precinct. The school building was on the temple ground. To claim it a school would be only partially true because the old thatched *sala* was also used for holding religious ceremonies. In fact it belonged to the temple and the abbot allowed it to be used for the Napo Primary School until a proper school site and building could be found. The sala was built on stilts and had no walls. Except for the teacher's desk, a chair and two blackboards on trestles, there was no other furniture. Children sat on the wooden floor according to their grades.

That morning the rain had swept in from all sides. As a result there was disorder and noise. Besides, the teacher, whose name was Kumjai, seemed too busy registering new pupils to care about the rain, the noise, and the wailing of the young ones who disliked their first day of school.

"Father's name," the teacher said.

He did not look up from his registration book while signalling the boy to speak.

Piang hesitated. Then she answered on behalf of her brother. Kumjai looked up and repeated what he said before. This time he spoke quite loudly because he was in a hurry to finish the registration.

"The Spirit," Piang replied, and she heard laughter from the classes.

Kumjai smiled for he had known of the adoption. He asked her and her brother to step aside and wait while he attended to the rest. Then he turned to the sister and the brother.

"Come here," he said and waited for them to stand in front of his desk.

"Father's name, first," Kumjai spoke to the boy.

Obviously the teacher did not want to have a

go-between. He wanted all the students in his school to learn to speak for themselves. But after a moment of waiting, the teacher had to ask the boy once more. Even then the boy's lips did not move.

"Don't you know your own father's name?" Kumjai said firmly but not too harshly.

"The Spirit," Piang answered again, determined to accept the consequences.

"Do you believe that?"

This time the boy reacted; he nodded once. And should the teacher ask who was his mother, he was prepared to nod to "Female Spirit" as well.

Kumjai sighed.

"All right, let me have your father's name," he said to Piang.

"Kum Surin."

"Mother's name."

"Liang Surin."

"Is that her full name?" Kumjai checked.

"Boonliang," said Piang.

Her cheeks paled for having made an error. She disliked erring.

"His birthday, month, and year."

"March 1954. The Year of the Horse."

Kumjai seemed pleased now with the answers, for he always required his school children to be able to speak well and without fear. He was not at all disappointed with the girl for she had been an exemplary pupil. But as for the boy, it would take some time to adjust him to the school system. Knowing this, Kumjai intended to be patient. He knew also of the boy's other identity — the village mute.

"Open your mouth, Prem."

Being pulled towards the man by an arm, the boy did not resist. He opened his mouth.

"Good teeth," Kumjai said. "But you need a good scrubbing. Any lice in your hair?"

"No, sir," Piang said, trying to protect her brother at all costs, so that he would not have to speak and stutter and stammer in front of the whole school.

But Kumjai was not pleased with her interruption.

"Can't you speak for yourself?" he talked directly to the boy. "When I ask you a question, you must speak. Speak for yourself."

The teacher had a kind, flowing voice. He was a man who had been accustomed to speaking, to putting words in their proper places and making meanings. As for the boy, he became tense and suffered the unruly, echoing words in his mind:
question ask speak speak
a question ask
ask a question
so can speak I
speak speak I so

Kumjai let the boy and his sister go at last, closed the book and began to organise his school. The older boys and girls left the sala and stood in line facing the flagpole. They began to sing the national anthem while the leader of the school raised the flag. How wonderful it seemed to hear them chant in praise of something. Words fluttered like wings of doves in flight; voices rose and tumbled, sending the flag upwards. These well arranged words of the song had been firmly lodged in their memories. And every morning of the school days this song was sung, passed on to the new ones who could hardly understand its high sounding phrases.

Then they trooped back in a single file to sit on the floor of the sala according to their classes. Roll-call began.

"Ma krup," answered each boy when Kumjai called out a name.

"Ma ka," said each girl.

Later on the teacher stood with ruler in hand in front of the class of Primary One, a new batch of eight boys and seven girls whom he had registered that day. He smiled at them; seemingly he was pleased with what Napo had offered him that rainy morning. Yes, these were the bewildered children experiencing their first day at school. And he had snatched them away from the wilderness, from the rice fields, from the Darkness. Had there not been this school they would still be roaming the plain with their water buffaloes, or working beside their parents in the paddies.

"Boys and girls, I am pleased to welcome you to Napo Primary," Kumjai said.

But to the children, his words sounded opaque, unfamiliar because he spoke in the Siamese language.

"From now on I have to speak to you in the official language of our school," Kumjai took care to speak slowly and in a kind manner.

"Ours is 'Lao', a dialect. Our village is a part of the Kingdom under the flag of tri-colours." Kumjai stopped here, pointing with the ruler towards the flagpole on which the frayed, sun-bleached flag hung limply under the fine drizzle.

He finished his talk by distributing slates and

45

slate pencils to the new pupils. Then he noticed that the boy named Prem was sitting at the back of the class, separated from the others. It seemed either he did not want to sit near the rest or that none of the pupils wanted to sit near him. Kumjai decided to act at once.

"I'll be very unhappy if anyone in this school still rejects this boy, Prem. He's one of us. There's nothing to fear about him being the Spirit's son. Who knows, it might be the kindest Spirit in the land. If you don't do the boy harm, then you won't be harmed. Now, don't let me hear either that you all call him the Tadpole or the Mute. From now on his name is Prem. Learn to call him by that name."

It sounded so strange though, that name: Prem. So new, like a new set of clothes one had to wear to go to a temple festival.

Shortly a little girl dared to sit near to the Spirit's son. Her name was Toon Puthaisong.

"Do you know how to sharpen your slate pencil?" She asked primly.

He seemed not to hear, keeping his eyes upon his own slate.

"I'll show you," Toon persisted.

She took his hand and eagerly led him away from the class, down from the sala to where the ground was dry and hard.

"Rub the writing end there, like you'd sharpen a knife," she said, watching him expectantly.

After a moment she asked: "What did that man up there say your name was? I prefer to call you the Tadpole, and I'll stick to it. Isn't he funny, that man up there? Why must he speak to us in a foreign language?"

46

Kumjai happened to hear every word the little girl said. He had noticed that the two pupils left the class without asking for his permission. So he followed them to impose discipline.

"Go back to your class immediately," Kumjai ordered. "Who said you could leave without my permission?"

The two culprits shamefacedly climbed the steps and obediently stood in front of the teacher whose voice hurt the boy more than the rod could have done.

After being reprimanded, the boy would not speak to anyone, listening only to his own longing for the plain where he could roam freely with his herd of buffaloes, for the jungle in which he could crouch low in a thicket under a canopy of branches and leaves. There, silence and stillness had brought him close to nature and to himself.

"Each of you has a slate and a slate pencil," Kumjai was saying to the class of Primary One. "Take good care of them, don't break them or lose them. To write, you must first learn how to hold the pencil."

You then learned to draw the black thing across the smooth, dark surface of the cool slate and a slightly grey line appeared. And to erase it, you used spittle or a wet cloth. The teacher wrote with a piece of chalk on the big blackboard a funny squiggle which he pronounced to be 'Gor', the first letter of the alphabet.

"This is 'Gor' or 'Gor Gai' for chicken."

Then he asked the class to copy it onto their slates. That morning they were not to do anything except to draw lines which resembled the letter

'Gor'.

So the first block of brick was called 'Gor'.

The man was obviously there to give the children education, using blocks of bricks called words, facts, and figures which were totally different from the wisdom which could be passed on from things to things, from wind to animals, from leaves to the soil.

Nature does not have this 'Gor' thing, the boy thought.

So his fingers refused to move, to make the first brick called 'Gor' while the rain pelted on the sala's thatched roof. He had surrendered himself to the buffalo and the immensity of the plain, but he could not see how he could hand himself over to this man dressed in his khaki uniform of short-sleeved shirt and trousers and a pair of leather shoes.

The boy did not trust himself to draw a little grey line to resemble the letter 'Gor'. He could almost feel the moist cool droplets of rain on his skin, and so longed for the open country on which the monsoonal rains brought joy. The rains lashed on, making his longing unbearable.

"Well, now, Prem," said Kumjai, lowering himself to the same level as the boy who sat cross-legged on the floor with an empty slate across his knees. "How are you doing? Let me see. You haven't tried to write. Why? Come, let's try together."

Kumjai took hold of the boy's right hand fingers and guided them.

"There, you see, it's not at all difficult."

He then stood to see whether the pupil would make an effort. Still the fingers refused to move.

"I've done mine," said Toon showing him hers.

"Good girl," said the teacher. "Show Prem how you did it."

When Kumjai went away, Toon moved in so close that her pigtail brushed against his face as she looked around to see whether anyone was watching. Toon had not belonged to the gang of boys and girls who had spent their days on the plain and in the woods with their herds. She had been a stranger. Now he wondered whether her name, 'Toon', like 'Prem', was merely her 'official' name . But 'Toon' sounded familiar because it was a Laotian name while 'Prem' was a foreign word heard perhaps on the radio when Kum Surin went to Muang to sell his yearly produce.

He knew that Toon's mother had died when she was very young. Then her father, Ta Sa, remarried but after having brought two boys into the world the second wife had also died. Since then no other women would marry Ta Sa, fearing that they might share the same fate because he had a black mole on his scrotum. The witch doctor said so. It was a bad luck sign, he said. And now everyone in the village knew of it, believed it. A black mole on the scrotum brought death to wives.

"I sneaked out of the house this morning to come to school," Toon was prattling on with a cunning little smile in her eyes. "I was afraid that my father might stop me coming to school because I am the only girl around to do things. I cook, carry water from a pond to fill the jars, feed the pigs and clean the house. Really, I should have entered school last year but he seemed to have forgotten that I turned seven years old and I myself did not know

49

what school was all about, not until Piang told me when we bathed together in the lotus pond. She said, 'Why, Toon, you were born one year ahead of the Tadpole and you don't go to school'. So I asked Piang what it was like to be a pupil. It seemed all fun to me to hear school children recite lessons and numbers when I passed the school on my way home from the fields. Have you ever heard this? Two times one is two, two times two is four, two times three is six. And then you'd hear a class recite some kind of wordy verses. I used to sneak into the sala after school was over. There were words written on the blackboard. I dared to sit at the teacher's desk and pretend I was him or write some squiggles on the blackboard. All the while the voices of the children rose in my mind. Two times one is two. Two times two is four. And I wondered vaguely why I was not among them and when I would be among the school children. The teacher, our neighbour, comes and goes and yet I did not speak to him. Once we came face to face on a track that leads to the lotus pond, and I was carrying buckets of water. 'Ah, little girl, why must you carry such heavy pails?' he asked. But I did not look up at him. I think he's funny talking to us in Siamese. But when he said 'Ah, little girl, why must you carry such heavy pails' it was in Laotian, our language, and he speaks to the grown-ups in our language too when he is not in the school."

Suddenly she stopped and stared anxiously at something.

"Here comes my father to take me away from the school," Toon said sadly.

Ta Sa, who wore only a loin-cloth, went to the

teacher. Kumjai had seen him coming and was ready to welcome the visitor.

"Ah, forgive me, Teacher, but my little girl did not tell me that today's the first day at school,' said the half-naked man. "She left us wondering where she was all this time. We waited for her at breakfast and we haven't eaten."

Ta Sa looked around to locate his daughter. Kumjai smiled at the helpless widower.

"Maybe from now on you should learn to cook because your little girl has to come to school every day except Sundays."

They were unkind words to say to someone who did not know a thing about education. But Kumjai knew that he had to be firm. Experience had taught him that some parents did not want him to take their children away from work in the house and in the fields. It had not been easy to convince them that education was necessary.

"Toon did the right thing," Kumjai went on. "She came and registered herself."

Because of the firm tone of Kumjai's voice and his powerful stance, Ta Sa decided not to plead for his daughter.

"It's a shame she didn't tell me. Why, she sneaked out of the house like a thief. She didn't even bother to put on a new sarong and blouse. I'm ashamed of her, teacher."

"You don't have to feel ashamed of her. She's fine. Maybe tomorrow she can put on her new clothes because she won't have to sneak out of the house to come to school."

Meanwhile, Toon did not budge. She sat there as if nailed to the floor. Though she did not say a word, she had a certain defiant air. Eventually Ta Sa left the school, walking away defeated. His shoulders drooped in the rain.

Then the class had a recess.

"Eat?" Prem offered Toon some food, seeing that she had nothing to eat.

"Go ahead. I'm not hungry," she said.

"No. Not alone. Not while you look at me."

"What have you got there then?"

The sticky rice was still warm and moist, wrapped in fresh banana leaves, and the steamed catfish was flavoured with sweet basil.

But suddenly Toon seemed to have lost her appetite. Tears welled up in her eyes. She had been thinking how nice it would be to have someone caring for her, to wrap lunch in banana leaves. If her mother had been alive, she would have sent her off to school like the others. Now *mother* was only a word. At the age of six, Toon had already taken on the duties of an adult, taking care of her father and brothers. Water had to be carried from the lotus pond to fill the jars, rice had to be threshed and meals prepared, the hut cleaned and clothes mended. Her father had become a brooding, lonely man, burdened by his own longing to have another wife; sometimes he got drunk and took out on her all his bitterness. Pain was not pain; bruises were not bruises when they were inflicted by one's father. Debts had to be paid and the last buffalo had to be sold when there was no cash to pay the annual land tax. What was the use, being a rice farmer without a buffalo? Other boys and girls took their herds out to graze on the plain. They sang and whooped and laughed, talking merrily to one another as they rode away. How she had longed to go with them, even without a buffalo of her own to ride and to take care of, just to be a part of their gang and sing along with them:

Rain!
Here comes a monsoonal rain.
But I have only a handful of grain!

She did not want to lose her girlhood too quickly, for already she had become serious, behaving like a girl older than her age. It would be nice to pretend she was frightened by the naked boys who were always chasing after the girls in the rain, instead of having to be the woman of the house looking after the father who, having lost so much at dice, would brood and curse. When she reached seven years of age, she relied on the teacher to take notice of her and ask her to attend his school. But he did not seem to see even when she was turning eight years old. Her heart sank. Well, I cannot rely on him, she thought. For Kumjai did not seem to see or to hear anything. He did not bother with gossips, whether good things or bad things were being said about him, noticing very little who liked him or disliked him. Young village girls went out of their way to please him, and yet he did not seem to see them. Late into the night he would read under a kerosene lamp which made more smoke than light, and sometimes he would shake his head to be rid of drowsiness as if to say: It's uplifting this dream of mine, keeping me alive with a will to go on.

Her father would never allow her to go to school, but between the fear of her father and the fear of growing into a young woman who could not read and write, she knew her mind. It would be a shame not to be able to read a boy's love letter and to answer with candour, or simply to write something down in beautiful longhand and then tear the paper into pieces to be blown away by the wind or to let them fall into the lotus pond to float like lotus petals when the man to whom those lovely words had been written had not yet been found.

When the day came, she had to pray to the Buddha and all things holy that her father would not see her sneaking out of the hut to go to school. If he caught her he would never let her go, and she would have to obey. Then she would be illiterate all her life. She would grow into a woman who could not even write 'I love you' on a piece of white paper.

And now she had made it! Tears welled up in her eyes once more when at last she could become a pupil of the Napo Primary School in which a little timid boy had dared to make a gesture of friendship, offering to share with her his rice and steamed catfish flavoured with salt and sweet basil.

"Ah, Toon loves Prem and Prem loves Toon!" An older girl of Primary Three gleefully voiced her discovery of the relationship.

The pock-marked girl who had just spoken could not resist the temptation to mock. She repeated her jibe and paused to watch for the effect.

"I never thought it could happen this young," the girl added maliciously.

Toon reacted. There were cries, a scrimmage, tears until the two girls were parted. Then Kumjai rendered punishment. This time it was not the palms of the hands, but on the calves. Toon could not hide with the hem of her sarong the red patches where the rod had fallen.

She was thankful when the recess was over so she could sit in the class next to her friend again. The afternoon wore on; weariness and lethargy took over when the rains ceased and the sun made the air hot and humid. The teacher looked unsettled and despondent, oblivious of the chalk dust that remained on his hands, of his hair ruffled by the wind. Primary Four had now begun to recite some wordy verses while Primary Three did sums. Primary Two had drawn a picture of an earthen jar, and now Primary One had moved on to the letter 'Kor'.

"There are altogether forty-four letters in the alphabet and each of them has a name which you must remember. Then there is another kind called vowels and there are twenty-six of those, and then there are four accent marks to make the low, high, and rising and falling pitches of each word. But just now let's try to learn and write 'Kor' or Kor Kai, an egg."

He sounded exhausted. His eyes became dreamy and sighs occurred often while the letter 'Kor' stood prominently on the blackboard. It would be alarming for a boy of seven to find certain qualities in the man of twenty-eight, traits which some people like the pock-marked girl would single out to mock or ridicule. Already the women of Napo had wondered why he was not interested in girls and they speculated about what he did in the evenings. He read, they knew, but about what they had no idea. And what else did he do, apart from reading; they really wanted to know. Because he was from a far-off town which some claimed to be farther than

Muang, Kumjai had been trying to find his place among the villagers, so that he would not remain a stranger among them. When an old man called him 'son' he was pleased, and he enjoyed invitations to parties and ceremonies in which he would sit cross-legged among the peasants even though he stood out like a red chilli among green ones. He drank very little, but for the sake of being one of them he sometimes joined a drinking bout and pretended he was terribly drunk so that he could later make an excuse to go home. He had never been a supporter of gambling. In fact he deplored the idea that some farmers might lose their property or get into debt through gambling. In the midst of miseries and ignorance, he could help them very little.

They had been kind to him from the beginning. He came to Napo for the first time one rainy day in May when the village primary school had to be set up. The old headman had called a meeting of village elders and declared that there would be a school here. "We must help the teacher to set it up," he had said, "and get our young to go to school. But first let's build him a home."

First they agreed that the old sala of the temple could be used as the school, and then decided where to build the teacher's hut. A few days later a dozen men erected a stilted hut of bamboo with a thatched roof and equipped it with a water jar stand and a chicken coop. A woman gave him a kapok mattress which she had made herself, and young girls filled the jars with water.

That year for the first time in the history of Napo, there was a school with a teacher to run it. When Kumjai opened it, there were five pupils whose names he remembered to this day: Kiang Surin, Ot Polraksa, Daeng Denudom Thong Nadee, Ood Kanueng. All boys. Kumjai longed for a bigger class to include girls also. But the Napotians still believed then that girls should stay at home and that being able to read and write and count was unnecessary for females. A few years later a girl turned up. Her name was Piang Surin, and then another girl followed. Kumjai thought he had gained some ground when a brave little girl sneaked out of her house so that her father would not catch her coming to school.

What moved him most was the death of the old headman who had been the stoutest supporter of the school. Then, when Kumjai discovered how they elected the new headman, his heart sank. Evil had been at the root of life all this time. The voters had raised their hands for the man who paid them, not knowing what they were doing and the price they would have to pay later. They elected a man in his mid-thirties who knew what he could do with power, with having the Masters and the law on his side. Take care, Kumjai had said to himself, of a man who could pick up a stone and throw it at a six-year old boy just because the boy looked at him. When he realised that I saw the act, he threw me a hateful look as well. It hurt me too, for thinking that all this time I was doing everything for Napo. A stone could draw blood from the boy, so it drew much out of my heart too. Now for the first time today I must reproach myself for pretending to check whether the boy has lice in his hair, when I wanted to see if the stone had left a scar.

The temple gong echoed. It was time for

evening prayer. It was also time to close the school for the day. Kumjai stood and announced that classes were over.

4

January 1963

By mid-January most farmers of Napo had finished reaping their rice.

Kum Surin intended to sell some of his crop to buy things from town. He filled six sacks with the newly threshed rice and hired a bullock cart to take them to the nearest feeder road where a truck would transport him and his goods to Muang. Muang, the small town nearest to Napo, boasted a railway station, rows of shops and a mill, and was sixty kilometres from the village.

The mill owner, the traders, the middlemen and the shop-keepers who were mostly Chinese had become powerfully wealthy, dealing with the illiterate peasants who squatted on their heels like beggars, watching sadly as their products were weighed and valued. When one extremely fat trader told Kum that the total sum for his rice was 280 baht, the farmer had to ask his son who had been studying in the Napo Primary School whether the price was right. Because the world had not yet devised an immediate way to punish the cheat and the wrongdoer, it was impossible to guarantee justice. At any sign of pleading for a fair price or for pity, the bloated Chinese was quite ready to yell: Take it or leave it! As he had previously shouted at a peasant who tried to haggle for more. The obese man also cursed the poor soul who dared to speak to him.

For Prem, to be asked by his father to accompany him to Muang was exciting, but to see how he cowered and became obsequious before the middlemen and the traders was more than the boy could bear. He could count quite fast, but he could not understand how the weighing machine worked and the Chinese spoke in a language which he could not understand. So what was the use of protest? All he wanted to do was to see that his father accepted the money and then left without being humiliated further. The sum of 280 baht would have to last a year. Kum spent a part of it on a kilo of smoked fish, a shirt for Kiang and a blouse for Piang, a bottle of medicine for Grandpa and cough syrup for himself. Kum was not accustomed to opening his mouth to complain. To him money was important but he would never cheat or steal or lie to get it. Money and the like are 'things outside the body' Kum had once told his youngest son. Boonliang Surin agreed. She said the most important were things people could not take from you, things you could keep inside yourself. By this she meant the richness of one's spiritual being. But because she was also illiterate, she spoke plainly whatever came to her mind. To her, life was in itself a bank in which people accumulate merit. For this reason, she offered food to the monks every morning, and went to the temple every so often to pray and to hear more of the Lord Buddha's teaching. Once a year she donated a set of saffron robes to the abbot and would continue this merit making so that she would be born with better fortune and luck in her next life. There were so many poor people in this world because they had not made merit in their last life, she believed.

Remembering his parents' words, Prem

prayed that what his father had lost during the transaction in Muang would become his merit. For he who had always been gentle and never uttered a harsh word or malicious remark against anybody, who had very little greed or ambition, he should know what contentment was. Contentment made life endurable, passing through years of plenty and years of drought, through drudgery, sickness and scarcity. Kum was easily appeased by a good season, by the respect of the young for their elders, by love and warmth among neighbours. He was always ready to be kind and hospitable to others.

Suffering too was to be endured silently. Sometimes, when the drought lingered, there would be very little rice left in the barn, let alone anything to take to Muang for cash. Once or twice Prem, like most boys, did not attend his class because he had to travel with his brother to distant villages to beg for rice. He had become a beggar, travelling from village to village, from hut to hut, with Kiang. Suffering had made the two boys less self-conscious and their begging voices had a ring of truth, even though they tinged it with pathos. They stood at the bottom of the ladders and pleaded: "Please, father and mother, may we ask you for some rice. Just a handful of rice. Drought hit us so hard this year and the last."

Only a few turned deaf ears. Those who refused their begging would kindly explain that they too were suffering with their own children going elsewhere to beg. All the while Prem thought: I shall never forget this, and shall never forget either the 280 baht a year and how father cowered in front of the fat and loud merchants. I long to give him all the dignity I can give and save him from insults and fill his bowl with rice always. I knew how much Kiang hated to beg. That was why he arranged that we took turns at every other hut. Why go to school? Once I went there after returning from one of the rice-begging trips, only to find that the school would have been empty if it were not for the teacher sitting alone at his desk reading. 'It's all right by me,' the teacher said. 'Come back to school when you can, and keep up the good work.' Perhaps I imagined that there was sadness in his voice. Teacher, teacher, why must you carry dreams in your eyes? You become dreamier as years go by and it seems that you'll never wake up to see the reality of our lives. What do you do alone in the school when there is not a pupil to teach? Maybe you should come with us as we, the beggars of Napo, go from village to village, and you'd come closer to the truth. Let tears well up in your eyes and wash away the traces of dreams. Young as I am, I have begun to understand now that we would have more dignity by not haggling for a better deal from traders, by not begging them for more. Father has a certain dignity when he is in his own village and his humility is genuine, and I understand his mild doggedness which I myself have to adopt as I squat on the ground in front of a hut of those who enjoy a better season.

When years of drought brought the family to despair, Kum had to go away for over a month with a group of men in search of new land, away from their arid plateau. But he returned severely ill. The village clairvoyant proclaimed that the spirits of his ancestors did not want him to take his family away from the land they had bequeathed him. The question of moving never occurred again to the Surins.

5

February 1965

Kumjai's life was also affected by the conditions of the village. His monthly salary and his dreams could not entirely cushion him against stark reality. He had been spending part of his income on building the school which he had moved out from the temple sala. He had forced himself to live at the same level as the villagers, keeping himself alive from what could be had in the village, enduring hunger along with his children in school. How could he take a meal in front of them? So in the hungry years he lost weight and the aura of well-being. His cheek-bones became more prominent and his eyes sunken. Drinking water became scarce, and as for bathing, he went for days without washing himself.

The new school was situated at the edge of the village by the lotus pond. Its roof had been partially thatched and it was in need of a wall. The floor was made of earth. Dust rose in dry seasons. When it rained, water turned everything into mud and slime.

Kumjai never stopped dreaming. It took him a year to save enough for a corrugated tin roof, two more years for four walls made of plaited bamboo. How long would it take him to raise the floor above the dust and mud? He had gone to the headman's house for help, hoping that the headman would call a gathering of village elders who might contribute materials so that his pupils would have benches to sit on. But everything seemed hopeless. In vain, he went from house to house talking about his plan for the development of the school. Then he realized that he had to dream on alone. So he petitioned the local education authority in the District Office to help.

When a grant from High-Above had not been forth-coming, Kumjai developed a 'self-help' scheme. He asked each of the boys and girls to rear a chicken of their own, apart from those which their families already had. Then, at the end of the season, they brought the fowls to school to be sold to the highest bidder. Money thus made went to the school fund for the tables and chairs which the village carpenter agreed to supply.

For the children's effort, Kumjai painted words on a wooden board, and nailed the board to a pole. It read: *Goodness prevails forever.*

After erecting the sign, Kumjai said to Prem, who had been elected the leader of the school:

"Supervise classes for me. Order each class to do something, watering plants around here, for example, and organize some games but not too much noise."

At the sound of the whistle, the boys and girls dropped what they were doing and rushed to form rows in front of the flag-pole. When they saw their leader standing in front of them instead of the teacher, some of them joked and made remarks. As Prem looked at them, he felt what Kumjai must have felt, saw what Kumjai had seen daily: the pitiful sight of impoverished children in rags, bare-footed. He also noticed wounds, scars, unkempt hair, running noses and unscrubbed limbs.

After testing his authority, the classes became

quiet and fell into lines. They stared at him with childish optimism. They waited now for direction. Kumjai watched from inside the school to see whether his pupils would obey and behave themselves under Prem's supervision. A moment later he went back to his task of organizing new classes.

Another term was ending, and the summer season had already come. Kumjai's thoughts revolved around his relationship with the villagers, of his standing among the poor. His was the only hut in the whole village that had an 'outhouse' as a toilet. The Napotians still went to the bushes to relieve themselves. A toilet for each home was among his many dreams. Over the years, Kumjai had become a good-hearted teacher, a money-lender without any interest (when he could spare a certain amount from his salary), and an eligible bachelor who did not seem to think of marriage.

Those who wished to return his kindnesses brought to him bananas, rice, vegetables, chickens to rear, home-made earthen jars, fish, and home-spun silk cloth and sarongs. On the other hand, ignorance also bred suspicion and arrogance. Many villagers considered him a do-gooder, a good-hearted fool, or a rival in love-making. There were a few who always saw him as a stranger in their midst, who were not pleased with what he had taught to the peasants and their children. Therefore Kumjai knew that he must be careful to maintain a harmony in living in Napo.

Now another year was passing. Ten years from now he might still be teaching in the Napo Primary School. Where would they end, these dreams? A toilet for each hut, a pair of shoes for each child, medicine and health care for the sick, a well-built dam to store water all year round, and most of all a way to protect the ignorant from falling victim to those who had been living off their hard work and their crops.

Eventually Kumjai called the classes together. They rushed to him, surrounding him, bright-eyed, and chattering, knowing that the end of the final term was at hand. Seeing them so, Kumjai became saddened, thinking that they were glad to leave him and the school.

He felt sadder, standing there to enact time and time again the last day of school. For how long had he been dreaming of tables and chairs, so that on this day, all of his pupils could sit properly instead of squatting or crouching on the ground looking up at him, making him too tall and too isolated?

"I'll announce the results of the final examinations," Kumjai said.

They squealed, squeaked and applauded, never for one moment suspecting his weariness and despair. He began with Primary One and rewarded the top three in the class with prizes. Before announcing the results of Primary Four, he took time to make a speech, saying that those in Primary One, Two and Three would be returning to school the coming May and those who had passed the examinations would be moved up to Two, Three and Four. "I'll be looking forward to seeing you back. There's a plan we'll be working on together. We'll keep hens and plant vegetables, making use of the land, here, just behind the school. We'll build a chicken coop and sell eggs. We'll also sell vegetables, and we'll use the money to pay for tables and chairs."

Kumjai paused; then he went on to say that for those who passed Primary Four, he would follow their progress in life with interest, and if any of them could afford to further their learning in another school, he hoped that they would do so. "Education improves the mind. It is light to show the way in darkness."

Kumjai stopped. He was becoming rhetorical, speaking for the sake of speaking, to an audience of forlorn children of the poor. He felt the hollowness of his words, their emptiness and uselessness. It was unnecessary to be so flowery with words in a little shack called *school*. Kumjai swallowed the rest of what he wanted to say. Yet in a fleeting glance, he understood the effect of his speech on his pupils. He saw that they were waiting, not for the beauty of his words, but for the break-up of school. He knew it! Their eyes gleamed with anticipation. Kumjai suspected that he was merely keeping them from going back to the natural course of their lives. Soon they would return to the rice fields, to the wilderness, to ignorance — the Powers of Darkness. They would grow quickly, the bright young ones with not so much of a future, and the thick-headed fools with life and time to waste.

"Here are the examination results of Primary Four," Kumjai said, raising his voice.

He read in a rapid succession the names of those who had passed and those who had failed. Then he went on to give prizes to the top in the class.

Prem, who was at the top, appeared amid applause.

He would continue with his studies after finishing this school, Kumjai believed. Prem bowed to pay respect to his teacher and received a book of poems and a cake of soap.

"The second prize goes to Panya Palaraksa."

Another boy came forward, a comely lad who was musically gifted. The teacher gave him a bamboo flute and a cake of soap.

"Toon Puthaisong is third."

There were loud cheers and applause for the popular girl. For Toon, who had had the courage to come on her own initiative and attend the class on the first day of school, Kumjai had searched high and low for a book entitled *Lives of the Greatest Heroes and Heroines of Our Time.*

The parents of these prize-winning pupils might be aware of their talents, but if Kumjai told them that they ought to send their children to a secondary school in Muang, they would come up with reasons why they preferred to keep them at home. After all, they had raised their young to work and to look after them in their old age. What good would it be to have an artist or an educated person in the house?

Intelligent or stupid, diligent or lazy, they had eventually left the school, leaving Kumjai alone. Suddenly he felt quite empty, gazing towards the sun-burnt plain. For him it would be a long span of summer until the school opened again in May.

In April, the hottest month of the year, the water disappeared from the marshes. Millions of fissures appeared where water used to be, venting the spirit of the earth. The horizon, once framed with vegetation, melted and evaporated into the shimmering haze. The plateau seemed endless.

Having reached its zenith, the sun mercilessly burnt the landscape.

To survive, the buffaloes constantly moved in search of grass and rice stubble; their skin which once glistened with health during the monsoons was now the colour of the brown landscape. They moved slowly so that no blade of grass would escape their eyes. The herdboys too moved with their animals, but took to the shade wherever possible.

Because of malnutrition, at eleven years old Prem had become skinny, barely reaching five feet in height. Like his herd, he looked dusty and weary. Under the roof of the school, cared for by Kumjai, he had had a better chance to grow. His intelligence could develop. But on the barren plain, in the wilderness, the primeval forces became paramount. He did not realize then that when he left Napo Primary School, he was saying goodbye to a life of an intelligent child protected by the teacher; now he was entering another life — that of a youth destined to follow the path of a peasant dominated by scarcity, superstition, floods, drought, sickness and dire poverty.

Meanwhile he submitted himself to the leader of the herdboys whose name was Peng. Peng was fifteen and proud of his prowess. No other boy could climb tall palm trees as fast. When the Napotian gang of herdboys came across a group of boys from another village on the plain, Peng would be the champion of Napo and challenge the leader of the other gang to a boxing match. But in school Peng failed his examinations every year.

One day Peng caught Prem reading a book of poems as he rested with one of the Surins' buffaloes under a tamarind tree. The former was full of primeval bitterness and the urge to destroy, while the latter seemed vulnerable and defenceless.

"Why, Mute, you're no better than anybody. Don't try to put it over on us that you're so different from the rest of us. Everybody can read and write. Why do I always see you with this buffalo? You love him so much, eh?"

Prem got on his feet to face his leader, putting his book into the cotton bag his mother had made for him to carry his food and water. The buffalo rose too, and Prem gently patted it as a warning to avoid human conflict. The old friend took the hint and walked away, but from time to time, he turned his mournful head to look at the unprotected boy.

Peng began to prance with clenched fists. "Come on, let's fight."

The poetry reader went up to the bully to appease the brute force by his own submissiveness. Peng hit him hard many times in the face until blood began to flow from his lips.

Other boys, too far away to see the mighty blows of their leader on the former prize pupil of Napo Primary School, began to gather fallen fronds of palm trees and drag them over the parched gravel soil, hoping that they could trick the frogs hiding in their dark holes or in the grass into believing that it was the sound of a monsoonal rain. As they ran, they sang:

> *On ancient stones*
> *and ground dry as bones*
> *we drag fronds to make grating sounds*
> *of pelting rains and thunder hoping*
> *to deceive hibernating frogs*

in their hiding holes
to ferret out their croak
of cheer and jubilation
but it is only our fantasy
to imitate the vibration of monsoon
for monsoon is more
is dust swirling
   cool wind blowing
   foliage singing and furling
   storm and lightning
   fish migrating and spawning
   buffaloes running and coupling
   roofs shaking and leaking...

Peng laughed and ran off to join the other boys, leaving his victim alone to nurse his wounds. Prem wiped the blood off his face with his hands. Tears came to his eyes. He wept not because of the pain, but for hearing the song which he himself had sung so many times every summer when there was nothing better to do on the plain. He longed to be able to put into a poem the beauty of sounds and images and feelings that the monsoonal rains aroused in him, to give songs for the herdboys to sing. Already in his mind strings of simple words were forming.

Then one of the boys saw someone coming across the plain, one of their grown-ups perhaps, or it could be a stranger traversing the country.

The man who was approaching turned out to be Kumjai. The noisy ritual ceased suddenly. The stones, the fronds, the frogs waited. Dust began to settle again. The air spoke of an intrusion. For the man held an official position which made him distant, mysterious, venerable, and forceful. Seeing him coming across the plain at that time of the day was a mystery also.

After discarding their fronds, the boys went to Prem to join him under the shade of the tamarind tree. Sweat ran down their faces; they trembled as if they were still school children under Kumjai's care. They waited anxiously, not knowing what could bring authority down upon them. But having sought the company of the one who had been the cleverest in school, they felt safe under Prem's protection.

Peng too joined them and kept his mouth shut.

Finally Kumjai reached the tree.

"It's really a hot day," he said.

He knew the plateau was theirs, and he was an intruder, an alien in their domain, impeding the flow of their life. But seeing Prem there, he decided to be with them for a while, sitting on a gnarled tree root protruding from the earth.

"Where have you been, sir?" Prem asked.

The other boys shifted uneasily.

"I've been to Baan Wa to see whether a man there would sell me some planks. The school needs to be repaired."

The merciless sun had drained him; his voice cracked like dried leaves being trodden on. Kumjai wetted his chapped lips with his tongue, wondering whether he should talk of his new plans for the school. But under the weight of the arid land, of this wilderness, he felt that the boys belonged to another school, to another force.

After a moment of silence, Peng mumbled that the buffaloes had roamed out of sight; he stood and

73

went away to search for them. At first the champion walked slowly away; then, at a safe distance, he ran, as if he had been freed, to flee across the plain. His loosening turban flowed in the wind.

Another boy said he should go too, and ran.

So from the teacher, they fled, one by one until there was only Prem now. The vacant space where the other boys had been became a gulf. Then Kumjai noticed the tip of the book in the boy's bag.

"What have you been reading?" he asked, glowing with interest.

"The one you gave me," Prem said, tugging at his bag.

And perhaps it's the only one he has ever had, too, Kumjai thought, hiding his pleasure in seeing proof that the boy kept on reading even though he had already left his school. He smiled and said happily:

"Ah, it's cooling off now. I'll rest here for a while. Perhaps you'd better go along with your friends. They'll be waiting for you."

The boy got up and bowed. The wind, the sun, the shadow of the leaves intermingled and made patterns on his bowing form. The foliage of the tamarind tree stirred in the desultory breeze.

Facing himself, Kumjai looked inwardly towards the heart of his loneliness. He had been longing for company in which he could confide, with whom he could discuss the welfare of the village. Living the life of a single man among the poor peasants had brought him such grief, that he could only speak his mind to the passing wind.

After having stretched himself flat on the soil for a while, he fell asleep. He dreamed, seeing himself walking across a strange country. When he reached a lonely tree under which an old man was resting, Kumjai said:

— If you don't mind, I'll rest with you here.

— Please yourself, stranger.

— Are you always by yourself on this plain?

— Most of the time I'm alone, tending my herd. When the sun is low and the heat lifts from the air, I round up my buffaloes and take them home.

— What's the name of your village?

— Ngingota.

— Ngingota! So I'm at last near the border.

— Only half a day's walk. To the west. A small stream runs there, at the foot of the hill. On a cliff stands a sentinel.

— A sentinel! Why?

— Often there are travellers and defectors using the pass. I've seen them sometimes crossing this plain. Besides them, it's very rarely that I speak to anyone.

— How peaceful it is.

— Yet sometimes the day can be rather monotonous. The sun keeps me under a tree and the air is so still.

— But consider yourself fortunate not to be involved in conflicts and change.

— Ah, young man, I've known conflicts and change too. Once in a while bandits rob me. This is no man's land, child. The robbers kick and hit me in the head for having absolutely nothing worth taking. Then I suffer a seasonal change. When the north wind blows, the chill bites through

75

my thin cotton clothing, and at night I curl up by the fire-side. Rice becomes yellow and ripe, then the harvest begins. Hard work comes and again I'm released by summer. The wind changes its course. Drought comes some years, hand in hand with illness.

— What hope have you then, old man?

— Well, I hope for a better life after my death.

— Why don't you hope for a better life in this life?

— For something better in this life?

— Yes.

— You're teasing me, young man. It's a sin to jest with an old man.

— I'm not joking. I know for sure. I have read many books about people in many countries.

— Where are these people who enjoy a better life in this life?

— Those who are enjoying material comfort are near and far, races apart, living in both east and west. When I was young my parents taught me well, and I went into a city to learn more, to read books. What strikes me most is that there are races of people who believe that men have the right to govern themselves, to speak truthfully without fear, to discuss ideas and cultivate their skills and excel in their work. You'll be surprised to realize how much they know about us.

— What do they know about us?

— They know that we're infested with worms

and other diseases, that we're undernourished and corrupt, that there are conflicts among us, that our wealthy men are extremely rich and our poor are frightfully poor, that there are thieves in high places as well as low. Knowing this, they send us experts, money, and materials to help us develop ourselves along their way to success and material wealth in the name of modernization, progress and industrialization.

— What? When have they been doing this? I've never seen anything coming my way. If ever I get their money or their help, what will they take from me? My rice, my land, my buffaloes?

— I don't know for sure, but the aid is believed to be free.

— Free!

— It's ignorance on our part, perhaps.

— These foreigners must be very rich then?

— I know something about their concept of values, their way of life. They have cars and good wide roads, hot and cold running water right in their houses. In cold weather they put on warm clothes and have fires or heaters inside their living quarters. They have radios, televisions, telephones, and refrigerators, which have become their basic necessities.

— These things you've just mentioned are beyond me, except for the radios. I've seen one. Some traders who came through the pass brought one. This radio thing has caused a big stir among us. I can't believe that a tiny thing like that could speak and make music. But then a gang of bandits came and took that radio away, killing one of us. And you said the foreigners will give us all the things you've mentioned?

— All of these and more have come our way, and reached our cities and towns. One day soon they will come your way. It may not be only the foreigners who will directly bring them to you...

— Oh, child, say that you're only teasing me. I beg you to be careful of what you say.

— For that matter, I seek only peace on this plain, and look for a place where I can hear songs sung freely.

— You may have to walk a great distance. But come, young man, the sun is yet high. Share with me my drinking water. When the sun is by yonder tree tops and the birds begin to return to their nests, you may come with me into the village to make my hut yours for the night.

— This solitude, Kumjai murmured.

The cool evening breeze woke him. But his dream did not dissolve immediately. Kumjai glanced at the spot where the old man could have been in his dream, and thought: Change is inevitable and the agents of change could come in many forms, visible or invisible. Sometimes they come with a young man or girl wearing jeans, after having been to a city, or with a movie van, or with colours of plastic utensils or plastic bags, and sometimes with guns and grenades, the brutal change.

He thought of the children with whom he had shared the shade, believing that in the course of their life, the winds of change would come and touch them, dictate to them. Will they give up so easily the old for the new? Kumjai trembled, thinking that he had seen a lot of change taking place in Napo since he arrived.

From now on, thought Kumjai, I shall make my pupils aware of the change which has already taken place and of the change to come, to know that which is to be cherished and that which should be altered.

This new scheme for his school brought him joy, adding one more dream to his life. Kumjai continued to sit there, contemplating his new dream, exploring all its avenues. In so doing, he saw himself traversing the highways and byways of the dream, alone as always.

Kumjai saw that his work so far had been limited to fighting illiteracy and to building the school. Should he add more? How about building up a person? He had always left it to hope that the parents of some of these intelligent pupils might understand how education could benefit their young, and so would send them to further their learning in secondary schools and colleges. But in vain. After only four years with him in the Napo Primary School, the Lord of Darkness took hold of his students once more, and he felt the emptiness of the speech that he made at the end of each year. Next year he might not bother to say that education improved the mind; he might just say: Goodbye now, it's nice to have had you with me for a while. Go out and face the world, now that you can read and write. But then he knew that he would not say such a thing; he would have to hang on to the idea that 'education improves the mind' until he could find a better phrase to use. His high-sounding speech would remain hollow and meaningless unless he could do something as an example for parents to follow.

Could he afford it?

To build up little by little a floorless, thatched shack without any wall until it could be called a school had been a preoccupying dream, leaving him very little room to think of anything else. Now the idea of building up a person entered his head. He was surprised that he had not thought of this before. To give a kind of scholarship, to support a student and send him to a secondary school, and later to a university should not be too heavy a burden or too complicated an involvement for him when, in so doing, it would encourage some parents to give the chance of a lifetime to their children.

At this point Kumjai considered the expenses involving school fees and living costs. Then he compared it with his own past. He had stayed in a Buddhist temple where he sought free lodging and food by becoming an acolyte to serve a monk so that he could attend a city school. In this way, it cost his father very little. Apart from the expenses for clothes and textbooks, there was hardly any need for payment unless an illness occurred.

Resolutely Kumjai stood, and strode off as if his feet did not touch the soil. He seemed as light as air, embracing his newly formed dream as he followed a path towards Napo.

In the evening, after having had his dinner, Kumjai visited the Surins. Boonliang Surin welcomed him, spreading a bulrush mat and then fetching a bowl of water and a tray of tobacco. In his polite gentle manner, Kum Surin asked the teacher about the school. Kumjai talked of his plan to ask for help from the men in the village to repair the thatched roof and the bamboo walls, of having a chicken coop built within the school compound.

"I also have a plan for your son, Prem," Kumjai said in a firm tone. "He is one of the brightest pupils in the school. I think he should have a chance to further his education."

"We're proud of him too, honourable teacher. But we don't have any money," responded Boonliang.

"I see a way which will not be too costly to send Prem to a school in the city," Kumjai replied. "I can take your son into my care. Then, with your permission, I will support him to go to a school in the city. There's a temple where he can stay as an acolyte."

Kumjai wanted to talk to the boy's parents of his plan, of his purpose and the boy's future. His voice rose as if he was reciting a well-remembered poem kept so long in the heart.

No one interrupted him. His listeners seemed to have fallen under the spell of his recital. After a while, Kum coughed and Boonliang shifted. Then before anyone could say anything, Kumjai took his leave, saying that he would call on them again when he returned from the city.

Rains began to come. Soon the villagers would be working in their fields. Prem, along with Piang and Kiang, would take on a man's duties. But then Kumjai returned from the city, saying that a monk had agreed to accept Prem, that the boy must leave for the temple the next day.

At daybreak the teacher came to the hut to accompany Kum and his son to Muang where they would put the boy on a train. The neighbours gathered to witness the departure. When Boonliang began to weep, one woman said:

"Let him go. What's the use of keeping any of these hungry children? If only I could sell one or two of mine!"

"Farewell, Tadpole. If you make good, don't forget us. Farewell!"

With mute acceptance, Toon watched the scene from afar.

The train was loaded not only with human beings but also with bundles of possessions, implements of various types, and bags of fruit and foodstuffs. How fascinating it was to feel the speed, to see the landscape, to watch the vendors at various stations selling iced-coffee, bananas, boiled eggs, peanuts and fried rice. Beyond the mountains, the monsoon season had already come. The landscape here was a flat, alluvial plain; the language was foreign. At the stations on this side of the hills, the food hawkers called out in the language of another country.

After his arrival at Wat Borombopit, Prem lay with fever in the darkness of a tiny room. A temple boy came to give him an old mosquito net and a mat.

"What province have you come from?" the boy asked.

Prem struggled within himself, trying to speak, to reply in Siamese.

"Can't you speak Siamese?"

Silence.

After the boy had gone, Prem shuddered and longed for home. He saw in his mind's eye his father and Kumjai standing at the lonely railway station. I shall have to be worthy of them, he thought.

The next day he went out from the monks' quarters, following a stone path. A few steps led up to the circular platform where a large flock of pigeons swarmed. The walls and pillars glittered with a gentle touch of sunlight. Towering above everything was the gigantic golden pagoda. In front of the chapel he stood in awe of the splendour of the door intricately inlaid with mother-of-pearl.

"Are you the new boy?" a young monk asked.

The door rattled as it was pushed open to allow him to enter. Then the monk switched on the lights, revealing the sublime interior. A gold image of Buddha in the sitting position presided on the lofty throne.

Presently a guide led a group of tourists into the hall. These must be the *farangs,* Prem thought, taking to a corner to make way for them. Kumjai had told the classes of the *farangs.* Now they were right in front of him, perspiring, taking photos. Suddenly, one large *farang* came forward.

"Hello," she greeted him.

Perspiration ran down her oily face.

"Hell-o," Prem tried to respond. She smiled broadly and gave him a coin. Avoiding the woman's wish to prolong their encounter, the boy quickly disappeared.

Later he came across an older acolyte.

"A farang gave me this," Prem said.

The two boys examined the foreign object.

"What is it?" Prem asked.

Having been to a secondary school where English was taught, the older boy read slowly: L-I-B-E-R-T-Y.

"You can have it," Prem said.

But the other boy laughed.

At the suggestion of the older boy, they went to the nearest money changer to find out the value of the gift.

The foreign coin seemed worthless to the money changer.

"You can throw it away. It's worth nothing," said the obese Chinese.

"What is LIBERTY?" Prem asked his new friend when they returned to the temple.

"Don't bother with a farang word. Learn to speak Siamese first."

Later on they told each other about their birthplaces. Rit, his new friend, came from the north. Rit had a fair complexion and fine features.

In the afternoon Kumjai's friend came to visit the Venerable Brother whom Prem served. After the formal conversation was over, the man took the boy out to the nearby shops to buy school uniforms, a pair of shoes, and two pairs of socks. Prem was thankful, for Kumjai's friend had spared him from being ashamed in front of the shopkeepers by not asking whether he had seen socks and shoes before.

This friend of Kumjai seemed to have acquired the taste and air of those who belonged to a big city.

Prem could see the veneer glazing over the man's northeastern features. It must have been such a friend who advised Kumjai to give up his dreams, his dedication to the rural farmers, for a city way of life.

Prem sensed also that this man would always remain a stranger to him since he could not feel close to those who had taken on a new identity and were ashamed of their origins.

Glad to be alone now in his room, the boy put his new clothes away, folding them carefully so that they would remain neat for the first day of school. The little room had a narrow window, resembling a prison because of its iron grill. Despite its stuffiness, crumbling walls, and cockroaches, it meant privacy and he was grateful for that.

Suddenly Rit appeared at the window.

"What are you doing?" he whispered, looking about him as if to make sure that he was not seen by anyone.

"Nothing in particular," Prem said from the darkness of his cell. The rusting iron grill separated them. Now Rit seemed small and pleading, clinging to the iron bars, lifting himself up to the window.

"I'll come out and join you in a second," Prem said.

Together, the two boys left the monks' quarters and entered the compound of the 'Chedi'; then they sat on the concrete circular border built to protect the trunk of a frangipani.

Rit became silent, looking down at his feet. Prem could not think of anything to say. When they first met, Rit had seemed big and fair, with fine complexion and graceful movements of people

85

from the north, full of gaiety and a sense of superiority because of his age and height and the years he had spent in the city. But now Rit appeared dark and brooding.

Time dragged painfully on as the bells tolled for evening prayers.

"Have you heard what other boys said about me?" Rit said at last.

What could other acolytes say of Rit? Prem asked himself. Could it be something shameful, so that Rit had to go about in his daily life like a wounded dog, fearing the abuse and accusations from others?

"No, I haven't heard anyone say anything about you."

"Oh well, you'll hear of it in time," Rit sighed.

As if by magic, four senior acolytes appeared and closed in on them. It was Rit who was at bay, target for an assault.

"So here we've got Rit the Red and his victim," one of the four mocked.

They towered over the sitting boys, and by the power of the Right, they seemed solidly united.

"Be warned, boy," the second member of the Right said for the benefit of Prem." This 'Com' here likes to prey on new boys to poison them with dangerous ideas."

"Why don't you try to do it to us, Rit the Red?", the third sneered.

A jet of spittle shot out and hit Rit in the face. The liquid dripped down his chin. He got up then, and walked away from his assailants. Not once did he look back to see how his new friend had taken the confrontation.

To meet Rit afterwards was difficult. Prem wondered whether their future meetings would have to be on the sly, and how he could bring himself to ask why the other boys treated Rit so badly.

Later it was Rit who made a new approach: "You've been trying to avoid me."

"You're wrong to think so," said Prem.

After that they did not speak for a long while, as they walked away and left the temple. Beyond the temple wall, they followed the Lord Canal. This time Prem sought Rit's hand so that their alliance could be reconfirmed. They reached the northern edge of Pramain Ground, bordered by tamarind trees.

By the Chowpraya River, the two sat on the embankment as the sun was setting beyond the City of Thonburi. The sluggish river reflected the mellow mood of such a time of the day while sampans and rice barges eased their way up or down the channel. Rit's fairness turned golden with the touch of the setting sun. In such a moment, it was possible to ask:

"Rit, why did they treat you so badly?"

For a long while Rit did not speak; it seemed that he had not heard the voice of his friend as a long-tail boat sped by. Then the older boy lifted his head. A nervous and poignant look came over Rit's countenance. It was this serious expression which startled Prem. Then, despite the mellow evening and the soft reflection from the river, the air seemed heavy and tense. With a tone of someone who harboured both love and hatred in his heart, Rit spoke:

"This river flows from the north, as you might

know, from the hills of my home. There, the water runs cool and clear. Time and again I slid down its banks to bathe and to swim. The men brought their elephants down to drink after a day's work in the teak forest. As a little boy, I was always afraid of the elephants, of their great size and trunks and tusks. Until one day my father took me with him into the log-yard across the river and I saw the elephants at work, moving the logs alone or in teams. How they exerted their muscles and obeyed the men who commanded them with a sharp metal stick. It was frightening to realize how we could inflict pain upon other creatures as big as the working elephants. I was impressed by their strength. And once I rode one of them, trekking through the hills to a new log-yard. I remember the motion of its gait, its sighs and the way it swayed its huge head, snatching leaves with its trunk along the way. Now over a decade later, I often long for the elephants' capability to endure pain. How could I have known that someone would spit at me and slap me in the face or kick me in the groin for being different, thinking different kinds of thoughts. Because I serve a monk who is said to be dangerous to society, I suffer as if I had caught a dreadful disease. I don't know what actually are his views. I really don't. I merely catch from time to time during his conversations with other monks some words about 'an inquiring mind' or something about 'conscience' or 'corruption' which I don't understand. I try to retain these words in my mind so that one day I can find out what they mean.

"What others think of him and their condemnation and their punishment of me don't alter the respect I have for him. He was born in the same valley as myself and one day he came back to the valley for a visit. When he was ready to return, my parents gave me to him as his acolyte, to serve him, because his former one had left him. That was how I came to be in this city. Here they won't let you forget your birth, that you're not one of them. They are doing the same to you too, Prem. You may laugh about it when other acolytes shout at you: Buffalo! Buffalo! And you continue to laugh as if they have said the funniest thing.

"How I long for the elephants' capability to endure pain, so that I could exist and be strong in this hostile place. I never feel at home here, Prem. My home will always be among the hills and the cool clear streams of the north. If you had ever been there, you would know why. We are quiet and enduring people, not used to scheming and calculating and cheating. My father may hit the elephants hard with sharp metal prods to make them work at the teak yards, but never because of hatred or sheer brutality. The elephants know that. That's why they work hard for the men. In the evening when the work is over, both men and the elephants know that they become human and animal again, one needing the other, going to the same cool and clear river together, bathing and feeling good.

"Here, the river has been made dirty. I feel sorry for it, knowing how it is so clear and cool and wonderful in the north. How these people have been abusing it. It breaks my heart to see how dirty it is now; how broad and impersonal it has become once it reaches the Central Plain. And that goes for me too, being abused and made profane and humiliated. I would rather have an elephant's water on me any day, rather than the spit from the rascals in this city.

"Mother always took good care that I was well scrubbed. She used cloth soaked in warm water to rub me over the chest and behind the ears on chilly days when the mist descended on our valleys."

Now there seemed to be a mist coming over Rit's eyes. And then silence followed. Walking back the two boys held hands and took a different route. When they entered the temple gate, they separated and said no parting words for fear of being heard and seen by other boys who might suspect a friendship that had been forbidden.

Knowing now the dangers of their friendship, Prem became anxious of the hostility which he himself would have to suffer along with Rit. If Rit can endure, so can I, the boy thought as he lay down on the mat to rest in his little room. He thought of Rit's yearning for the elephants' ability to endure pain and of his own longing for the protection of the thick skin of a water buffalo and its enduring nature, for the wide plain, fresh air and the placidity of rice fields. He recalled a lullaby:

> *The mud-dotted frog is tired*
> *of wandering, and now the water is gone.*

The acolyte tossed and turned, thinking of the grandfather whom he had lain beside since childhood.

> *Where have you been all day long?*
> *What have you done wrong?*
> *Come, come rest by my side.*

He thought of Toon, of an afternoon when he hid among the rice as she walked back from her fields. He surprised her and they fell together onto the ground; she was full of rice pollen and self-defence. And now that he had discovered his manhood, he longed for her more than ever.

A rat gnawed at his toes which protruded from the mosquito net. He quickly sat up with a fright and saw only darkness. Later he crawled out of the mosquito net and started his chores. At daybreak the monk's saffron robes seemed brighter than gold against grey houses and the shabbiness of the market places. The monk carefully trod his path, his eyes observed only a few feet ahead and stopped at the spots where people were waiting to offer him food. Then the monk bent his head as the donors lifted up their bowls of rice, slightly tilted so that the contents would be tipped into the begging bowl. Following in the footsteps of the monk, the acolyte carried a container in which he would collect the curries and fried food. Meanwhile the monk progressed on his way, and by the time they turned back to the temple, the sun had risen high and the populace and vehicles had begun to fill the streets.

In their living quarters, the acolyte emptied the contents of the begging bowl and the container and put them into dishes for the monk to eat. Then the boy would sit quietly nearby, always ready at the monk's beck and call. At such a time there were moments for thinking one's own secret thoughts, while the temple bells tinkled in the breeze. He wanted to know what kind of beliefs made some people think that Rit's monk was a danger to society. Perhaps one day Rit would be able to tell him.

When the monk finished his morning meal, the boy ate the left-overs and did the washing up and general cleaning of the quarters, before going to school. If it was a Sunday, he would fetch a rake or a broom to sweep the temple ground so that the public and the tourists would see that it was a well-kept place of worship. Here the coming and going of people, especially the foreigners, attracted him. Often he caught their attention too; some of them took his photograph or said something to him. And he gladly posed for them with the golden pagoda shining brightly in the background.

All the while he suffered along with Rit since they could no longer keep their alliance and friendship secret. Once he wrote to Kumjai and told the teacher about Rit and Rit's monk, about his own desire to know what were the thoughts and convictions which could be so forbidden and considered so dangerous to society, and which caused such misery to oneself and to others.

My dear Prem, Kumjai wrote in return, you may be experiencing a difficult time right now. But because you're intelligent, I'm sure you can adapt yourself to new surroundings. Be alert and keep yourself open-minded and never judge a fellow man unfairly. Be tolerant of others and try to understand their habits and ways of thought. Then you'll find life there easier and endurable and enriching. You'll also be home-sick, but don't let it discourage you. No matter how difficult your time may be, remember that it's a sacrifice you're making, so that you can improve yourself by learning and experiencing while you're growing up. Your people at home are all well and they send their greetings and their love...

Kumjai collected the files and books, putting

the chalk boxes and pencils into large paper bags. It was once again the last day of school. Come April and I'll turn thirty-four, Kumjai was thinking to himself. Sometimes he felt so old, as old as a weary buffalo. Now after the school children had left him, he was thinking of how to pass the time during the summer. At this point, he thought of Prem. Then he decided to make a trip to the city and to see how the boy was doing.

That evening, he paid the Surins a visit.

"I'll be leaving for the city tomorrow," Kumjai announced as soon as he sat down.

Kum Surin coughed and cleared his throat in an effort to form words; his wife appeared dazed by the news. Piang Surin who had been listening in the dark said:

"Toon may have a letter for Prem, so I'll go to tell her."

"Are they in love, these two?" Grandmother asked ponderously.

"Since their school days," said Piang as she went down the ladder to the yard below the hut.

Toon, who was so happy with the message, had to keep her joy from the eyes of the members of her family who were then resting and trying to sleep. After lighting a kerosene lamp, she took out her unfinished letter to add a few lines to it. After Piang had taken it from her, she extinguished the lamp and tried to sleep, thinking of the man who would make her his woman one day.

In the house of the Surins, Kiang was chosen to write to his brother. When he did write, Kiang tended to be philosophical and at times attempted to use words or phrases which he himself did not

93

quite understand though he remembered them well from books read at school. The brother resorted to such eloquence because he knew that Prem was more learned and clever than he who had not done so well in classes and had never been to the city.

Normally Kiang would try to avoid writing to his brother even when his parents asked him to do so. But now he appeared quite willing, getting paper and pencil out from boxes and turning up the kerosene lamp till it produced more smoke than light. At times he wrote stealthily, bending his head low, looking over his shoulder to see if anyone was watching. For now he came to the part mentioning his desire for an underwear that Prem could get for him. Kiang had never before needed such a luxury, but one day he saw Kumjai by the edge of the lotus pond preparing himself for a swim at the end of the day. The teacher was the only man in Napo who wore shirts and trousers; the village males went about half-naked in cotton shorts or loin-cloth, or sarongs. When Kumjai undressed by the pond, Kiang saw for the first time in his life the underwear which the teacher kept on while swimming. Since then he became obsessed with a longing to own one of his own, so that he too would be able to take a bath in the pond or the common dam without being embarrassed by the glances of passers-by or the teasing comments of cheeky boys. At present, like other men of Napo, young or old, he was either naked or wore his loin-cloth when bathing, and afterwards he had to put up with wet clothes.

So Kiang wrote and added a postscript repeating his request, so that his brother would not forget to ask the teacher to bring it on his return.

Before the departure the next day, Kumjai stood in front of his hut saying farewell to the Surins and a few old people who came to wish him a safe journey.

Kiang saw the sense of well-being the teacher radiated; his holiday clothes were well pressed and clean, and his whole demeanour told of cleanliness and good health. Kiang secretly longed to be like Kumjai. How wonderful would that be to have fine clothes, clean fingernails, neat and well-parted hair, a handsome face, instead of the smell of mud and sweat.

Kiang could no longer bear such a longing, so he walked away from the crowd. As he went back to his hut, sadness weighed heavily on him. In his life, Kiang would never have the chance to know anything except the existence of a peasant tied to the land.

From the hut, Kiang fetched an axe and left for the plantation where he would clear the land to plant jute. Before leaving for the work, Kiang stopped to drink. While drinking, the water in the bowl reflected his features. Kiang saw the image of a stern, savage face, in contrast to that of Kumjai's. How ridiculous it seemed now to want an underwear!

Kiang could not laugh at his own folly, so he brooded as he strode across the fields, trying to ease his heart with a song but his voice failed to rise above the mocking cries of the mina birds on the bamboo trees. Then the soft morning sunlight brightened the landscape of tall grass wet with dew. It seemed not so long ago that, at this very spot, the Tadpole had fallen from the buffalo on the day he

95

first learned to ride. Kiang recalled his anger at his brother's silence, at the face that bore no expression and at the mouth that knew no language. Thinking of their childhood, Kiang could smile. He never thought that the Mute would grow up to be an intelligent young man, so far away from home. All he ever wanted for his brother was to survive and grow into manhood so that they would work together in the fields. Now Kiang doubted very much whether the Tadpole would retain the memories of childhood and of all that they had shared.

Meanwhile Kumjai skirted the fringe of the forest, progressing towards the outer world. In leaving Napo where the role of the school teacher had weighed heavily on him, he felt lighter. Soon he would be a stranger among strangers in a crowded bus and later in the streets of the city. In Napo, he had been called Son, Guru, Brother, or 'that good-hearted fool', by different groups of villagers. But he was not there to run their affairs; therefore he had taken care not to step on the toes of the new village headman who had been trying to build up his power base.

Somehow the villagers began to turn to him for help, not only in financial matters but also for advice regarding land disputes, divorces, land tax and sickness.

Kumjai sighed, and the leaves in the woods surrounding him seemed to stir and heave along with him. He stopped now, having arrived at the bumpy, dusty road where a bus would pass on its way to Muang. At this meeting point, there was a group of villagers waiting for the same bus, squatting around a crudely made narrow bamboo bed on which lay a woman's body.

"Where are you going?" Kumjai asked in a way of greeting, and went closer to them.

"We're taking the patient to the Health Centre in Muang," the oldest volunteered.

Trying to sound as friendly as possible, Kumjai asked them about their village, and about the distance they had had to carry the sick woman. The answers they gave were short, coming from laconic men, shy with strangers. So in silence they waited for the bus to come. And when it came, bringing with it clouds of dust, it was loaded down with passengers as well as with farm produce, including cages of pigs and chickens.

Now the old man was begging the driver to allow him and his sick wife a free ride because they did not have money to pay the fare.

"We're suffering from a very bad year of drought," the old man pleaded.

"Everybody has to pay," the driver shouted mercilessly.

The driver spat the dust out of his throat. The old man wailed for sympathy. It was his own dear wife who was near death and the eternity of suffering had reduced him to shamelessness when he had to beg for sympathy and kindness. Watching them, listening to them, Kumjai suffered for his knowledge of human tragedy. Day in, day out the driver had to go through such a scene, so often that nothing moved him any more. Finally the dilapidated bus began to move, but then Kumjai stopped the driver, indicating that he would pay the fare for the group.

Only then the men could load the woman at

the back of the bus. The sick woman, supported by the old man, opened her eyes briefly and coughed. Closing her eyes again, she seemed to surrender herself to the will of others, to the dust, the rough ride and fate. Kumjai could envisage the end of the trip where the Health Centre would be overcrowded with patients and their relatives who could not meet the bills. And there would not be too many good-hearted fools to pay for them there.

Now, as the bus ran along over the stones and pot holes, the old man turned to Kumjai to thank him, mumbling words of blessing. In swaying to and fro along with the motion of the bus, most passengers seemed lifeless; suffering was trans-formed momentarily into dumb endurance. Look-ing at them, Kumjai seemed to know them all so well; he could recreate vivid images of their huts, their activities, and their expressions. He thought: As long as I live in the area, I cannot blot these people out of my mind; I cannot pretend I do not see the sickness and hopelessness and poverty. How much can I give, and for how long can I go on giving? All the time it's giving, and giving, and giving, and there is very little coming back to nourish me. One day I will be drained and spent. What will I do, when one day I wake up and dream no more? With what strength and power and method can my teaching be made more effective? Now it has already begun, the unexpected, the thing that I dread — the feeling that futility is in all things; that I have been making an idealistic approach to life. I might as well tell the boy, Prem, to wake up. To say to him: you're a part of my dream. Wake up and be practical. Would the boy gaze in silence at the end of the dream? I have always been afraid of his gaze, of his eyes. They say more than his lips. Would he say then: Dream on, teacher, dream on, and I shall dream along with you. Yes, I am a part of your dream.

But it is not altogether a happy dream; its road is rough and dusty, paved with coarse sand and loose stones. It has taken years to convince the people that the school should be independent from the temple. The old sala is good but classes have to be closed every time a ceremony is to be held. It takes a year for the roof, two years for the walls to be installed; two years for chairs and tables, crudely made from bamboo for every child to dream upon. They follow the dreams, raising chickens and keeping hens for eggs. But at night thieves come not only to steal the eggs, they take the hens away as well. You should be lucky they do not burn down the hen house. And you in this fretful dream could merely preach that there are some people in this country who have no conscience; they think only of their own gain, their own power bases, without caring for the good of all. You hope that the wind would carry every seed of your words to land on a fertile ground from which ideas could grow. In this barrenness? How could a shack with thatched roof and bamboo walls withstand the ferocity of a monsoonal storm? The old sala of the temple won its round that year when the roof of the school gave in and the walls were blown off and the flood drove the children back to the temple sala. I really could not take it, this defeat. For days I tried to borrow money from friends in the city but they would not dream along with me; city life has made them tough, practical, and selfish. Kind with advice though, which I do not need. I need money and help to rebuild the shack to call it school again, not empty words of advice. Words are more destructive than a thousand storms. Beware, they said. Don't be too unrealistic. Whether they used the word 'idealistic' I am not so sure now. Why make a sacrifice when one should be thinking only of oneself? You should build your own power base, like the headman, or team up with him to fleece the peasants, to cream off the budgets, the relief funds, the road construction money, etc. You'd be rich!

I should not have gone to the city to seek their help. Cold, destructive words. They made you blush with shame. It is a shame for leaving the school in ruins from the flood. The children were draining the building for my return, making the dam from mud surrounding the shack. So with my own hands, I mended the roof and remade the walls, but I am not a carpenter or a builder. It takes months to put the roof and the walls together, while pretending not to hear the mocking laughter from some quarters: 'When he's busy, he's harmless.'

I was right to believe that Prem would continue to read after he finished his Primary Four. I saw him with the Book of Poetry on the plain one hot afternoon when I came away from Baan Wa. And I was right with Toon too, though the front cover of the *Lives of Great Heroes and Heroines* has been torn off by her half brother who fancied the photo of the red-headed, buxom woman with a tiara on her head. Yes, I must look for a book for her while staying in the city; she could read when alone in the hut or in the fields.

What else could one do in the city? Kumjai asked himself. Whenever he accepted hospitality from someone, he could never feel as comfortable as he would be in his own hut in Napo. It was not his nature to take. And city life was not for him. The buses were overcrowded. The streets were noisy and dirty. The dust and fumes from automobiles suffocated him. Then once more his so-called friends would offer their advice — the cold water of empty words to wake him up from his dreams. Words could be more destructive than a thousand storms. "How dare they tell me to give up the school and join them in the city for opportunities, for the wealth and power which come to those 'whose hands are the longest'. I never want more than I have now, and I can never see myself accepting bribes and commissions or stealing from the funds or charities meant for the poor and the needy."

Kumjai saw that he would dream on alone for a long while, there in Napo. Meanwhile the bus rocked and jostled him, bringing him into close contact with the peasants crouching next to him. The sick woman moaned now and then and the worried old man, her husband, tenderly watched over her.

When the bus finally stopped in Muang, Kumjai assured the old peasant that he would stay with them, and he hired two pedicabs to take them to the health centre. Once there they joined a large number of people waiting. Because it was not graded as a hospital, but only a third rate health care centre in a poor district, there was no chair anywhere. Patients and those who accompanied them had to use the rough concrete floor; some had to lie down;

there were those who were so ill that Death came to them while they were waiting for treatment. There was a man whose axe had slipped while cutting a tree and badly cut his calf. There he lay among others moaning and displaying his horrible wound. Then a bullock cart arrived from a distant village to deliver a man who had been shot and stabbed while attempting to protect his wife and children from robbers. When relatives unloaded him from the cart they discovered that he was already dead.

Sitting among these people, Kumjai seemed resigned. He was crestfallen, thinking that such a scene would happen every day here. Time seemed to have no value or meaning. Only pain, disease, and death existed.

When it was the turn of the sick woman, Kumjai helped the old man carry her into the examining room. The medical officer was a young man who had not yet learned to assume an air of compassion. All one could see from his face was the impersonal officiousness with which he treated his patients, case by case. Kumjai had no way of knowing that years later this officer would have made himself so popular that he was elected as a member of parliament from his constituency. After that the sick and the poor of Muang and surrounding districts never saw him again.

Meanwhile Kumjai reproached himself for all the years spent in Napo, believing that he had fortified himself against pitiful sights; but now that great miseries confronted him, he wept inside. What could he do then but to put some bank notes in the old man's hand and say a few words to comfort him. So it was Kumjai who suffered all the more as he walked away towards the town centre. Having missed his train, he went to an inn to spend the night and to wait for the morning train.

6

August 1973

Each year when Kumjai closed the school for a vacation, he made a visit to Wat Borombopit to see the monk and Prem. His stay in the city was spent mostly with his young friend. Together, they looked into bookshops to buy a few books for Toon and for the boys and girls who were top of their classes. But one night, in August, Kumjai arrived at the temple to see his friend, the monk, looking furtive, haggard and weary. There was something very odd about the arrival, which prevented Prem from asking any questions. After the monk had opened his door and invited Kumjai into his room, Prem went outside to see if there was anyone waiting for the teacher in the alley. But he saw nothing in the darkness. Back in his own room, Prem waited for Kumjai, trying to stay awake. However, after a long time, he finally fell asleep. In the morning he discovered that Kumjai was gone.

"Kumjai left in the night," said the monk, who assumed an air of complete detachment, making it difficult for the acolyte to ask questions.

But Kumjai's short, unexpected visit and his departure without a goodbye were puzzling. Prem finally found a chance to ask for an explanation.

"He needs help," the monk explained. "Not only that, he wanted to tell me something. When you haven't done anything wrong, but certain persons try to make it seem as if you had, you need to tell someone so that you'll be understood and believed. I believe him. And that's what he needs. It's important to him."

A week later, Kiang's letter came. 'Teacher Kumjai has run away,' Kiang wrote, 'and it seems he won't return, ever. Perhaps you should come back and help me with the work in the fields.'

Kiang did not provide any information regarding the cause of Kumjai's flight. Prem knew that it would take more than a verbal threat from the headman to drive the teacher away from Napo. But Kiang, who always believed that it was a waste to follow Kumjai's dream, sounded pleased and jumped to the conclusion that his brother had no better things to do than to return to Napo, now that the teacher was no longer there to impose any obligation on the Surins.

Without support from Kumjai, it would be difficult to continue his studies and enter university. Must I strive for higher learning? Prem asked himself. What a pity to go back to the darkness after having done so well in the high school examinations. "I have come this far," he reflected. "Alone I boarded that train to come to the maze of this city. That's bravery. Now am I afraid of going further? I could not stop that train then as it took me away from Father and Kumjai. My journey must continue."

So he sat for the university entrance examinations and passed them with flying colours. But instead of joy, the success brought worries and new financial needs for uniforms, books, tuition fees, and pocket money.

The monk was aware of his acolyte's dilemma.

"Kumjai may not disappear for long," the monk said. "But I can see you're worried. To replace the support from Kumjai, I'll try to find another source of income for you. Don't despair."

It was not despair that he had to carry so painfully in his heart; it was the fact that no one, not even Kumjai himself, had thought to let him know the reason for the disappearance. What had Kumjai done? Since the monk chose to say nothing about the subject, the acolyte had to endure his doubts and anxieties in silence.

"But being young," the monk continued, "you are likely to be prone to sorrow, worries, defilement and impurities. You should learn to face life in all its changes with a calm and clear mind. I'd advise you to follow the Eight Precepts."

"Yes, I'll observe the Eight Precepts," he said resolutely.

The venerable monk re-arranged and tightened his yellow robe and then asked the acolyte to cup the palms of his hands in readiness for the bestowing of the Precepts:

— You shall not kill.
— You shall not steal.
— You shall not commit adultery.
— You shall not lie.
— You shall not take alcoholic beverages and drugs.
— You shall not consume any meal or nutritious drink after mid-day until the next day.
— You shall not apply scent, talc, or cosmetics to your person to make yourself attractive and you shall not attend performances and other forms of entertainment.

— You shall not rest or sleep on comfortable
materials.

"Perhaps you can also undertake meditation.
Meditation or Vipassana is a form of mental culture
to achieve mindfulness, clarity, and knowledge.
When you're mindful, you know what you're doing.
You're mindful of your actions, your words, your
thoughts, and you see things clearly as they are."

"Yes, Honourable Brother, I shall follow the
Eight Precepts and undertake Vipassana," said Prem
obediently.

To earn money, he learned to produce temple
rubbings for sale to tourists who visited the Wat. In
his old school uniform, he looked much younger
than his age. The foreigners would think that he
was only twelve or thirteen, making it easier for
him to arouse their sympathy and to sell them his
works.

"Temple rubbings, sirs. Only twenty baht
apiece," Prem approached the tourists. "Only twenty
baht a rubbing," he persisted. But they pretended
not to hear or see him. He had to walk backward
when the two *farangs* would not stop.

"Pai! Mai-ow!" one of them tried to get rid of
the hawker by speaking loudly in Siamese.

The rejection went deep, hurting the boy. But
temple rubbings must be sold so he could go to
university.

Despite the rude remark made in Siamese by
one of the visitors, the other *farang* seemed kind,
paying attention, not to the products, but to the
seller. This particular *farang* looked quite like a
movie star. Yes, the short hair-cut and the features
reminded Prem of Glenn Ford.

107

With a slight sign of friendliness, the temple rubbing seller offered his handiwork once again.

"They are very beautiful. Good for framing. Only twenty baht apiece."

His English sounded fluent and innocent. But the *farang* who could speak Siamese decided to get rid of the nuisance once and for all by saying loudly in Siamese that they had come to the Wat to see the temple not to buy temple rubbings. That hurt the boy the more, but still the two men were from another world. To the rubbing seller, the blue eyed, fair skinned people remained merely cardboard figures, for he had no real awareness of their life.

"They're truly fine rubbings. I make them myself," Prem pleaded.

"You make good rubbings, eh?' the *farang* who looked like Glenn Ford turned to acknowledge the boy's existence with a teasing smile. It sounded like a joke. So Prem smiled too, and was rather pleased with being nicely spoken to by this Glenn Ford look-alike.

"Good rubbings, sir. Only twenty baht a rubbing," he firmly said, displaying the products piece by piece.

This time, the *farang* who could speak Siamese had to tell the boy to get lost. Prem's aggressiveness had its limit. Knowing that they would not buy anything from him, he went on to offer other services:

"May I be your guide then?" he said expectantly, determined that if he could not make any money from them, he would practise his English.

"No!" said the man who could speak Siamese. "I live here, I know this country far more than you!".

Obviously the man killed two birds with one stone; he managed to get rid of the hawker of temple rubbings and at the same time he impressed his guest. To prove his point the long-time resident began to show the visitor the temple.

How could the man know more of my temple than I? Prem stood there, dumb with amazement. He was proud of his temple of which he had become a part and which he knew so well.

Nevertheless, the contact with the *farangs* did not cause too much pain. He watched the two men going away from him. But then the *farang* who looked like Glenn Ford turned and came back towards the seller of temple rubbings. He smiled, and before his friend could stop him, he touched the boy's shoulder, squeezed it gently, and then put a one hundred baht banknote into the boy's shirt pocket.

Fortunately, the monk whom Prem served had found a source of income for his acolyte. He gave the boy an address with some advice:

"Take good care of your appearance. Put on clean clothes when you go to see them. They're rich people known to the Lord Abbot himself. I don't know them personally. And before you leave for their residence, go to thank the Lord Abbot first because it's he who asked the laymen on your behalf for the job."

The bus carried him away from the old part of the city to the residential area in which his prospective employers lived. The mansion was completely protected by high concrete walls of which the tops were covered with broken glass and fenced with barbed wire. After ringing the bell, he waited, facing the immensity of the walls. Footfalls on the driveway and the barking of dogs told him that someone was coming. A small opening in the huge iron gate revealed a face. The eyes searched for the caller.

"I've come to give tuition to the children," Prem told of his reason for daring to press the bell.

The face quickly disappeared from the square hole in the iron gate which still remained secured and closed against his intrusion. A few minutes went by while the caller had to be cleared with the owners of the mansion. He patiently waited, tolerating the formality and the sniffing of dogs. When he was allowed in, Prem quickly looked to see whether the two great Alsatians would do him harm. He observed that the driveway was lined with urns of frangipani on one side and porcelain jars of cultured trees on the other. Green, well-manicured lawns spread out like carpets; monstera vines climbed up the trunks of the coconut trees; varieties of ferns grew thickly around boulders and rocks; flowering orchids were kept in the shade of trees; bougainvillaea flowered profusely upon traceries under which potted plants were hung. At a glance, he could see trees and flowering shrubs he had never seen before. Then the two-storied mansion loomed over everything. It was designed to be modern and solid. The great house boasted of its opulence.

"Take him to the swimming pool," the lady of the house told the housekeeper. The tone of her voice encompassed all the prerogatives of her class and wealth.

There were several deck chairs by the swimming pool as well as a glass-topped table and four white wrought iron chairs.

How still the pool seemed. Without a breath of air to ruffle its surface, the blue water seemed so inviting. At the farthest end, a few white frangipani flowers were afloat. What a perfect image of heavenly luxury! In truth he had once imagined what Heaven would be like. A place like this house and garden seemed perfect for angels and supreme heavenly beings. Perhaps it was after a place such as this that the city was named the City of Angels.

He could hardly imagine that a section of the community lived in such a state of perplexing wealth. He knew that there were rich people as well as poor people, but no one in Napo would believe him if he could describe this mansion and its garden to them.

The lady appeared in her flowing long dress. It was sleeveless, in lime-green, designed for grace as much as for coolness. She arched her soft graceful neck to watch her steps, lifting her skirt slightly away from the path as she came up to the poolside. One could see that she must have been very pretty in her youth. The aura of splendour and power was as subtle as her perfume. He stood up in awe.

"Sawasdee krup," he said as he lowered his head to meet the tips of his fingers cupped together in the 'wai' gesture.

She waved her dainty hand as a command for him to sit down. For herself she chose a chair on the opposite side of the table.

"When will you start going to the university?" she asked in a rather severe tone of voice reserved for strangers, especially those under her command.

"In a month's time, Khunying," Prem answered in the mannerism of an exemplary schoolboy; he brought his knees together on which he laid his clasped hands. She saw that he had an honest, pleasant and intelligent face, and was pleased with his mild and courteous manners.

"Which is your best subject?"

"English, Khunying."

He suffered a slight block in the throat, making him sound rather hoarse.

"How about Maths?' she pursed her pale pink lips, in her usual habit of rendering a voice of nobility.

"My second best," he said confidently.

"Good. The children, especially the boy, need to be coached in English and in Maths. We're thinking of sending him to study in a public school in England. Have you been to London?"

As if anyone could whimsically fly off to London, Paris or New York.

"No, Khunying."

Then she went on, saying that she herself was a graduate from the Faculty of Arts of the same university of which he would become a student, that she had no head for Mathematics but her French was excellent. She indicated that it was her mother who went to the Wat and knew the Lord Abbot.

At that moment she saw a gardener pruning too heavy-handedly the shrub of a variegated kind. She lectured him in a less noble tone of voice, as if she intended to make the gardener never do that again. The wretched man stood there taking the scolding with his meek, cowered stance. Then she ordered him to fetch one of the servants.

When an elderly woman came, Prem was surprised to see that the servant squatted neatly on the path at a respectful distance to take orders. But then he quickly accepted this as a way of behaving in such a grand house.

"Go and help the nursemaid set up the nursery for lessons and prepare the children to meet their tutor," the mistress gave orders.

The harshness in her voice previously meant for the gardener had been slightly toned down, and the temperament which the temple boy saw flaring up a moment ago had disappeared from her gracious features.

"Would you like some ice-cream?" she turned to ask the tutor.

"No, thank you, Khunying. I'm holding the Eight Precepts."

Impressed, she asked:

"What for?"

"For being an obedient temple boy," he said.

Not only being impressed by his practice of the Eight Precepts, Khunying was charmed by his pleasing manners.

"It must be quite interesting to live in a temple," she adjusted herself, shifting for more comfort from the iron chair.

"For an outsider, it may seem so, but there's no luxury and entertainment for us at all."

"And for you no dinner." She smiled at her own witticism, looking kindly at him. The smile refreshed her face, which looked younger and more beautiful while the smile lasted.

"Would you care for tea or coffee then? I'm sure your Eight Precepts don't stop you taking tea.

Monks do, don't they? They like tea, so my mother told me."

"No, thank you."

He studied briefly her painted toenails protruding from the fringe of her long dress. Then the children came out and they did the 'wai' to greet their tutor. Tid-Toy was a boy of ten, and Nid-Noy a girl of eight. The children looked fresh, clean and active in their crisp white shirts and, for the boy, white shorts, and for the girl, blue jeans. They embodied good health, loving care, and good diet. How intelligent and lovely they looked! Prem remarked to himself, reflecting on his reckless, impoverished childhood. They were like two beautiful plants growing in fertile soil with loving care and plenty of water. They also surprised him with their knowledge of the English language, for it had not dawned on him that certain kindergartens in the city taught it along with the mother tongue.

Because of the contact with the Phengpanichs, Prem made a decision, a month later, that after graduation he must become a rural school teacher to replace Kumjai. It was not for him to remain in the city, teaching the children of the rich.

He began to make friends in his first year at the university. When a government grant was announced, he applied for the scholarship to study in England. As a candidate among almost a thousand students vying for the award, he passed all the written examinations and was on the short list for the final test, an interview. That morning, before leaving the temple for the test, he knelt before the Honourable Brother. The monk blessed him and added some words of advice:

114

"When you speak, speak clearly and calmly. Weigh your words carefully. The Vipassana will guide you. You'll know what you're doing; you'll be mindful of every action, everything. Look them in the eyes and be honest."

The people to whom the monk referred were a panel of judges made up of seven old sages: three professors, two departmental heads of a government body, a psychologist and a *farang* man who acted as an adviser to the Siamese government. Sitting in front of these men, Prem Surin felt an invisible hand touching his shoulder. Prem thought he heard Kumjai saying: I'll be your guide and your strength. I'll always be with you.

"State your name, age, and parentage," one of the judges began the interview.

"Prem Surin. Born in March 1954. The second son of Kum and Boonliang Surin, rice farmers in the village of Napo, Burirum, Northeast Region."

Confronting their cynical eyes, Prem visualized the armies of forlorn children of Napo, the children in the school which Kumjai had built. He also recalled memories of the vast tranquil plain shimmering under the sun, changing its various moods: green and gold during the harvest, smouldering in summer, cool and inundated during the monsoon season. It was made up of layer upon layer of poetry so sublime and ancient, of age-old wisdom, of misery, drudgery, happiness, and of the simplicity of rustic life. Parts of all these had become parts of him.

"Why do you want to study overseas?" an old professor asked.

It's a sacrifice your're making, Kumjai whispered. The candidate remembered those words so well.

"I've risen from the mud, from a mire of ignorance and darkness, to catch a glimpse of light to free myself and to walk in daylight. I was, and still am, that buffalo boy who alone boarded a train bound for this city in May 1965 so that I could go to a secondary school. Now eight years later I am ready to brave the flight towards an unknown country to encounter all sorts of new experiences, to learn, to hear more, to read more, and to look from afar so that I may see my own country in a truer perspective. When I achieve my goal, then I shall return to help my country and its poor."

Was he trying to fool them or to impress them? The *farang* adviser to the Royal Siamese Government smiled.

"Have you a girl friend?' asked the psychologist.

Prem became aware of the silent presence of Toon Phuthaisong, and in his vision, he and she, two children of the plain, were skipping along over the fields, laughing and singing. She came to him now in her full form of womanhood. How he longed to create a poem to celebrate her beauty.

"Did you take part in the October 14 Uprising?" one of the Departmental Heads asked.

"No. In the morning of October 14, 1973, I remained at the temple where I live, learning to read a Pali script with the monk whom I served as acolyte. He can vouch for that."

In the morning of October 14, just before Prem would be ready to go to the university, Rit turned up and urged his friend to join the protest staged by a huge mass of students on the university campus. But the monk forbade his acolyte to leave his quarters. I know what's going to happen, the monk had said. You must not go. I forbid you.

That fatal day hundreds of students marched out of the university. Many were killed by troops shooting from tanks and helicopters. Rit too fell and died with his skull broken. Rit had at least spat in the face of a well-armed soldier, while I stayed safely in the darkness of my room. When I learned of the massacre, I wanted vengeance. I wanted to rebel against everything that made me a Siamese, against the life of an obedient boy who had to behave, to be there at the beck and call of Masters. On the other hand, I was still alive because I had been obedient, obeying the monk's order to stay away from the students' mass protest, and also because of my own lack of critical thinking and any form of political thoughts. Come with me, Rit had said, and you'll know what 'LIBERTY' on a foreign coin means. But then Rit died along with hundreds of students, shot by troops and tanks and helicopters.

"No, Sirs, I did not participate in that Uprising, on October 14, 1973," Prem said to the judges, and thus he appeared absolutely harmless.

Walking along the pavement back to his class after the interview was over, the hopeful candidate for the scholarship sensed his new strength. He was aware that apart from Kumjai and Toon and his parents, the forlorn armies of the children of Napo too had been his allies, that in order to survive future massacres, he must learn how to keep his ideas to himself when he had a chance to develop his critical thinking.

One day Kum Surin came to Muang with the year's crop for sale. There were times when he missed his boy, the Tadpole. Then he felt sad and alone and unprotected on such a journey. When the Tadpole had been with him, the boy would talk to him, keeping him company, squatting closely by his side as they waited for the goods to be weighed and valued. When I'm old, too old, Kum thought, I'll not be able to come to Muang any more. Kiang is useless, and soon he'll be married and leave me to go to his wife's home.

The old man became more pained at the thought.

The transistor radio in the middleman's shophouse was loudly broadcasting the news. At first Kum did not pay much attention, until he heard that a student by the name of Prem Surin had won a scholarship to study in England. But even then the old man was not so sure of his hearing. Perhaps he imagined that he had heard his son's name because he had been thinking of the Tadpole. Well, if he wins anything, he'll let us know, the old man assured himself and put the small amount of cash from the middleman into his shirt pocket. With his greying head bent to the ground, he trudged wearily to the shops where he would buy a few items for which his wife and daughter had asked and cough syrup for himself.

As the father had expected, a few days later Prem turned up in Napo.

However, Kum Surin could not possibly have known what the scholarship meant. He thought that whatever it was it would be still the same departure, that his son would not be with him for a long

118

while. Even now the father was not certain it was the right thing to do, allowing his own son to go away. Nevertheless, the father responded to his son's urgent need:

"We can sell one or two buffaloes, so we can raise the amount of money you need."

Unfortunately Kiang had wanted to sell one or two buffaloes to make two thousand baht in order to get married. Kiang gave up his wedding plans without a word of protest.

What Prem asked for was around three thousand baht to have a suit made, to buy a suitcase and some shirts and trousers. And for such goods, his old friends, two buffaloes had to be taken from their home by a buyer, to be resold and carted away from the village by a truck for delivery to a slaughterhouse in the city.

In the evening the air became cooler and the half-moon rose. Boonliang Surin concentrated on feeding her silk-worms in their large bamboo trays. She seemed quite absorbed in scattering the mulberry leaves all over the tray resting on her legs as she sat on the open porch near her son who had come home.

"Why did Teacher Kumjai run away?' Prem asked when he saw an opportunity.

In the stillness of the night, the words echoed louder than intended. She did not answer as quickly as she should have done. Her lips twitched and her throat contracted when she spoke: "He's run away because he's a communist, so people say, hiding with a band of men in the jungle somewhere. He's put our village under the watchful eye of the law."

Boonliang faltered a little in her effort to speak

of a subject so foreign to her mind, a hap-pening which, she herself sensed, was tinged with danger.

"Kumjai became a communist?" Prem sat up in surprise.

The mother spread the mulberry leaves faster over the silk-worms, for suddenly it seemed that obscure shapes and forms in the darkness had ears.

"Kumjai, being honest and dedicated, made trouble for others. When the grant to build the school finally came, he found that the sum was much less than the amount printed on the paper. When he asked for an explanation, he was told that some money had been spent on the costs of obtaining the fund, for this and that. Then Kumjai determined to make a case of it. For this he wanted to go to the city to consult his learned friends. Many of us, old people, asked him to accept things as they are and not to go against the evil. The abbot, too, tried to stop him, telling Kumjai that in a country where mosquitoes are a part of life, there is no need to point out that the insects suck blood and carry dis-ease, as if it had just been discovered. Some of us who were fond of him tried to warn him of the danger, but he did not listen. So when he returned from the city, Kumjai became a stranger among us.

"We were told that he intended to claim the ownership of the public land on which his hut was built. The fact that he made a fence and planted trees on it proved that he intended to own the land. Yes, it is true. He planted a lot of trees there and put up the fence. Kumjai himself said to me one day when I walked by on my way to our rice fields that the fence would protect the young trees and plants from the cows and buffaloes. When his

120

flame trees began to flower, Peng turned up with his gang and destroyed practically everything which Kumjai had built and grown. Yes, Peng and his gang, former pupils of Kumjai, armed with axes and knives to cause so much pain to the man who once was their teacher.

"Piang said that she saw Kumjai weep for the fallen trees as he gathered them together in a pile behind his house. He had given so much attention and care to his garden. You could see how much he liked growing things. He brought from Muang various plants and cuttings, and in his garden frangipani, bougainvillaea, hibiscus, jasmin, palm trees, cashew nut trees, and mango trees were thriving. During the drought, when every drop of water is precious, he would still try to save his plants and trees from being scorched. He would go for miles to fetch water.

"I asked myself why he could not own that little patch of land if he wanted to. It was a waste land by the swamp until he turned it into a proper garden. Every rainy season he added more trees, plants and shrubs. In the afternoons when he finished teaching, and on weekends, you would see him tending them, watering or pruning. One day he came to our house to ask for some buffalo dung, and I offered to help him gather the manure into a pair of baskets. He said he was going to start a compost heap. I had not heard the word 'compost' before. He told me of a simple way to make fertilizer: 'To put some goodness back into the soil' said he. That made me think a little, when for hundreds of years we have not done anything to put 'goodness' back into the earth. We have always lived off it, taking the goodness out of it. So I went with him to his house on the pretext of helping to carry the baskets of buffalo dung, when in fact I wanted to see how he set about making the compost.

"It must have been the compost made of buffalo manure, leaves, coconut fibres, and twigs left for a while to rot that made his garden rich with growing things. He was a keen tree planter and gardener all right. You could see on his little plot of land young fruit trees, plenty of plants both flowering and variegated kinds, nicely spaced with a little walkway winding around them. He often came back from Muang with some cuttings and potted plants for his own garden and for giving to his neighbours to grow. But it has not been our way to grow plants just to look at. That was why some of us laughed when we heard that he actually shed tears for the chopped trees. They did not know or understand why Kumjai lost his heart after Peng and his gang ruined his garden. Well, I said to myself, if some people want to make the teacher feel that even his own students have turned against him, they made a good job of it. He hardly spoke to any of us and we felt uneasy speaking to him seeing how sad and disheartened he looked.

"Some people who were in the know said that he sent letters to various people in the city and to newspapers to make trouble. Then there was a rumour that Kumjai had been financially supporting the communists in our area. Strangely enough the authorities seemed to have some proof, a piece of paper on which the list of names and the amounts of money were recorded. 'But that was the list of donations towards the temple at last year's temple fair', Kumjai said as he went from house to house when he wanted to tell us the truth.

"But then armed men came to our village to take Kumjai away. Luckily Kumjai escaped, or perhaps they let him get away to make it ring true that Kumjai is indeed a communist.

"The abbot tried to keep the school going for a while, getting the children back to the sala, which is closer than the school, so that it would be easier for him to keep an eye on the pupils. But he could not keep the school going for long. Besides, the headman said that we did not need the school at all. He said, what was the use of having a teacher who considered himself better than everybody else? What was the use of being able to read and write? It only made the children think that they were better than their parents. You had no need to be able to read and write to be farmers. You could not eat books, he told us."

Boonliang paused for breath and assumed a haughty pose. Mimicking the headman, she rounded her lips to say:

"Reading and writing don't make you happy. Happiness for us is eating and making love."

Her courage to taunt left her then and she appeared fearful, turning around as if to see whether the awesome headman was near, observing her making fun of him.

Piang, who was dusting the wooden floor of the sleeping quarters, giggled at the mimicry.

But Kiang did not laugh; instead he corrected his mother, saying:

"You got it all wrong, Mum. The headman did not say 'happiness is eating and making love.

He said 'happiness is eating and.... He's not *that* polite."

Kiang laughed at his own contribution. Kum Surin coughed with some authority to assert that such talk should end. The old house became silent when Kiang left to court a girl in the village.

Having spread a mattress for her brother, Piang came out to sit beside the Tadpole who seemed to be drowning in the stream of his own painful thoughts. Should she disturb him?

The Tadpole could not speak though he wanted to say something to be a part of his family. He would very much like to say: Yes, it is easier and safer to lead a quiet life, seeking happiness from the pleasures of eating and sex, from being silent, and from being considered 'harmless' in a village where there is no room for Kumjai.

Since no one was speaking, Piang decided to tell her brother something which their mother had omitted.

"I could not believe that Peng and his cohorts could tear down the teacher's fence and axe his trees. They, all of them, were his pupils. How could they. But at the time, I did not know that Peng and a few friends of his had become the headman's hangers-on, waiting for tit-bits to be thrown their way.

"Yes, the abbot moved the classes back to the sala, then Toon and I went to help him. We had not altogether forgotten how to spell, to add, subtract and multiply. So between Toon and I, we kept the school going for some time, hoping that Teacher Kumjai might return. But we have not seen him since. The school was left empty. Soon some people stole the walls, the roof and dismantled the chicken coop."

"The children..?" Prem tried to speak. His throat would not open.

"The children have to go to the school at Baan Wa for the time being, but since our headman does not like having a school teacher here, the kids may have to continue going to that school even though they have to walk a long way."

After a moment of silence, Piang ventured to add: "For what he did for Kiang, we could not repay him. If we did, we would have to sell our land, our house and our rice fields. It happened one afternoon when Toon came to tell us that Peng and his gang had got hold of Kiang and some other people to gamble. These days the gang has been so blatant, being protected by some influential men in uniforms, that they did not bother to go to the woods anymore to commit such an evil deed. It took place at the edge of the swamp near Toon's house. To save Kiang, we sought our teacher's help. Walking behind Kumjai, I felt the fear of evil as we went near to the gamblers who were so absorbed in their game, sitting on the ground, that they were not aware of our approach. The teacher had to say quite loudly: 'Kiang, come away with me now.'

"Kiang looked at the gang with some anxiety while the men gazed at the teacher with amazement. They seemed stunned at the audacity of the teacher who was unarmed, with two young girls tugging behind him. Kumjai dared to challenge them and their protectors. 'Kiang, for the sake of your parents, come with me,' Kumjai said firmly.

"Peng got up to meet the challenge, maliciously eyeing me and Toon. 'You can go with these

125

'women' when you pay what you owe us,' Peng said to Kiang, aiming to hurt Kumjai as much as possible. You could see his fangs sticking out of his thick dark lips, as he said that. After a quick look at the crestfallen Kiang, I knew instantly that he had lost money. How much? My heart beat so fast I couldn't breathe. 'How much did you owe them, Kiang?' Kumjai asked, trying to keep himself under control. When Kiang did not answer, Peng said indignantly: 'Fifteen thousand!'

"I put my hands over my mouth so I wouldn't shriek. Oh, the price of evil! And Evil itself seemed standing by with a taunting smile on its face as the teacher and his former pupil stared at each other. 'I'll pay,' Kumjai said, stretching his hand to pull our brother up, but Kiang seemed to have shrunk to the ground into the arms of evil. So I stepped in and pulled him away from the gamblers. For the first time in my life I lost my respect for our older brother, but I didn't regret it. 'Fifteen thousand you owe us, and if you don't pay us today, I'll tell our Bosses to take it out of the School Fund,' Peng cried after Kumjai.

"Despite a rumour that Kumjai disappeared from Napo with the School Fund, I have always suspected that the Masters and their gang took the money which was meant for building the school. Otherwise, they would have been making our lives so miserable that in the end we would have to sell our house, our buffaloes, and our land to pay them. Greedy as they are, they would never let us off so lightly," Piang concluded.

A great knife was being twisted inside the young man who could not speak. Sensing that her

126

brother was upset, Piang suggested that he should go to sleep on the mattress prepared for him.

Prem thought of Kumjai: You should be careful in giving out books of poetry, and you should not tell everybody that they must try to reach for the light, for the height of learning. Words cannot be eaten; they are not as good as making love. You don't go about telling the beasts that education improves the mind. But year after year you sow with every passing wind, playing your unweary flute to the ears of buffaloes. Today, I stood in the ruins of your school, looking for the little wooden board which bears your words of 'Goodness prevails forever'.

Where is that dreamer now, the dreamer who suddenly saw reality when a band of his own pupils, armed with axes and knives, woke him up from his dreams?

Years it took him to build the school. He spent a year to replace the tattered bamboo walls with a wall of sturdy planks. Years went by and his plea for help fell on deaf ears. He became more sullen and severe. He seemed no longer to be the benevolent teacher among the impoverished village youngsters, but a lonely man looking drawn and weary. He spoke to himself rather than to the classes, scattering words of wisdom to the wind. I looked about me and saw only the dumb faces of the children who had no clue to what he was saying, but every breath of wind carried seeds of hope and seeds of bitterness. Should I allow them to grow in my mind? One year a storm blew away all the mouldy and moth-eaten bamboo walls and the roof, and the school was flooded, forcing us to go back to the old sala. It seemed that not only human elements were against him but also nature. I could see that he began to harbour more and more bitterness in his heart as he became cynical, seeing the futility in all things. Our way of life reminded him: You cannot go it all alone, against the forces of the land. Let go of all your dreams. Be like everybody, live like everybody, and accept the belief that poverty is a divine measure to keep the peasants and the ignorant submissive. Suffer not when you see how they are cheated and exploited by the tradesmen and the officials. You canot spread your arms far and wide to protect them all.

I was frightened by Kumjai's single-mindedness and his fight against corruption and injustice and ignorance. I was afraid for his sake when he spoke out loudly to us, his pupils, about the state of affairs, reminding us time and again that if our bodies were infested with worms which usurp nourishment from our food, we would remain undernourished and suffer from malnutrition. He said that the country is in the same state when there are too many thieves in low and high places, making use of their power, their positions, their cunning, shamelessly, without conscience, but with great capacity for avarice, to work only for their own advantage, and for their families. These people are like worms in our bellies. And like our bodies, our country would always remain impoverished and its growth would be stunted as long as we harboured such parasites.

Words. How many children could understand his words? And he went on to say that the village was the best example. If our headman and his group

128

took half or three-fourths of the relief fund, the foreign aid, the budgets for road construction, for building dams, then very little could reach the people, very little could be done to improve the roads, to build the reservoirs, to fight disease and to lessen the hardships of the people as a whole. Their greed became an obstacle to the well-being of the people. At that time, while Kumjai was speaking, the headman walked by within earshot, and I feared that he might have heard Kumjai and want to do the teacher some harm. What could the teacher achieve by telling us, dumb children of the poor, that our leaders were stealing, building their power bases, and using their positions for their own gain. After all, the men voted for those who paid them.

In our village, unfortunately with my own eyes I saw how our leader cheated us that year when the drought hit us so badly that a charitable organisation from a foreign country sent us a supply of rice and powdered milk. The leader took three-fourths of the shipment and sold it to a Chinese shopkeeper in Muang. It so happened that father and I had gone to Muang to barter mother's silk materials for rice. There, we came across our leader, and I saw him selling the rice and powdered milk. Young as I was then, I knew that this was the emergency food sent to be distributed to starving people. Our leader had never set foot on a rice field to till the land and grow rice. Yet he had bags of rice to sell. When I pointed him out to my father to take notice, he warned me: You see not, hear not, speak not, and the evil won't do you harm. Obeying my father, I turned away from the scene. For thinking of the scar on my head from the wound caused by a stone,

I prayed that the man would not see us, the witnesses of his deed, for fear that he would find a way to silence us.

And the teacher dreamed on. He kept himself busy by adding new walls and repairing the school. After four years with him, I was no longer one of his pupils. But then he still represented a dream for me. Remember, it's a sacrifice you're making, he wrote once. Now he will come back to save us with arms, so they said. Could it be that he would be arming himself with truth, to speak truthfully on our behalf without fear?

Liberty is a foreign word, found on a coin a foreigner dropped in the palm of my hand, but it has taken me years to fully understand its meaning; it has taken the death of Rit, a fair boy from the North; it has taken the disappearance of Kumjai. Liberty! When I go to England, there will surely be more words to understand and to remember. It seems that each new word takes me farther afield, always away from Napo. Even my illiterate mother could foresee that, and she said once: "It will come to no good, this reading of yours." But I read more and more.

Meanwhile I shall try to keep reciting the litany: 'One year for the roof, two years for the walls', and '280 baht for the rice crop of a whole year' alive in the depths of my heart.

A few days later, when the acolyte had returned from his village to the temple in the city, the monk talked to him: "Soon you'll be far away. In years to come, when you are educated and become an important man, don't forget your origins, your parents and relatives and friends. Gratitude is the mark of a good person. Consider how fortunate you are to have this chance. Make use of it to learn. It may seem easy for sons and daughters of the rich and the influential to go overseas for their education and training. But for you, or someone like you, it is a chance in a million. Concerning Kumjai, you must understand me for being silent or secretive when it comes to talking about his disappearance. I am a monk and cannot act like a layman. I cannot tell a lie and speak ill of persons. You must not harbour bitterness in your heart. It was I who stopped you from joining the Uprising on October 14, 1973; and perhaps I saved your life. You must understand also that Kumjai does not contact you because he does not want to cause any repercussion on your future.

"As for me, Kumjai's misfortune touches me. As a monk it should never be able to move me, for I should be detached from the world of the living, believing that suffering is universal, caused by deeds or *Karma*. But knowing Kumjai since childhood, I am not surprised by his actions. He has been accusing me, saying that I became a monk to close my eyes, to cut myself off from the world, from reality, living within the walls of the Wat. Once he directly insulted his city friends, who asked him to give up the life of a rural school teacher and come to the city for more money, by saying that he would rather become a monk and choose a Wat in the city where it would be less painful not to see, to hear about the suffering and injustice done to the people in villages. One by one he cut his friends off, and if I were not a monk and his childhood friend who provides you with shelter, he would have cut me off too.

"Farewell then, my acolyte. Some day we'll meet again."

7

November 1974

Kiang could hardly visualize life in the world far beyond his district, but he kept thinking of places and people with whom his brother was coming into contact. I would be lost anywhere except in Muang, Kiang admitted to himself.

He worked on, reaping and advancing farther than Piang and his parents who worked at a much slower pace. Kiang stopped and sat under the nearest tree to roll a cigarette. Out of the corner of his eye he saw his mother. How small she seemed in her dark clothes under an old palm hat. He pitied her for her age and for the hard work she had to do. I'll write to the Tadpole to please her, Kiang decided.

At home, in the evening, Kiang wrote:

2 November 1974
105 Napo, Buddhaisong, Burirum

My dear Tadpole,

We've just begun harvesting. Everyone is in the fields. At a time like this I miss you so very much. We talk about you more often now since you've sent us letters, postcards, and photos of your new place and strange looking people. Nearly all the villagers come to our hut to see the photos and to read your letters. It's a pity that our mother cannot read. She always urges Piang or Toon to read them to her again and again, in case I did not read the real account of yourself, hiding from her news of your problems and illness. She must know the truth. If you're sick, she demands to know it, so that she too can suffer along with you. She just can't take it that you must face your problems all alone in such strange surroundings and among the foreigners who are so different from us.

You know she never wanted you to go away at all. Now in her old age she suffers, waiting for the day to see you come back to stay, never to leave us again. She does not sleep well, and often tells us in the morning that she has had a terrible dream.

I've tried to understand why you stay away from us and the work in the paddies. I do not want to think that you went away because you disliked working in the fields. It was Kumjai, wasn't it, who took you away from us? Now he's no longer here, you can come back if you truly want to. You always tell us in your letters that you miss us and think of the village and the animals. This gives me a hope that one day you'll come back and help me with the rice planting, harvesting, and tending the buffaloes. The land and the herd need you, and I need your help most of all.

You may be glad to know that we have three new buffaloes. But the mother of the herd died of old age a few days ago. She had served us for a long time. When you and I were small boys we used to ride on her back together and urge her to run through water in that shallow stream near our paddies, remember? She is the one you learnt to ride; she pulled the plough and the harrow over the years till her neck became hardened and finally broken.

Well, she has done her task. May she be born again in a better form and so be happy and content. I buried her in the mound near the sluice where she liked to wallow in the mire. Father keeps her long horns in the rice barn as a token of good luck.

This animal has given me an insight into the duty of each life. When we are born, men or animals, we have our duty to our kind. Those timid buffaloes, though they are whipped and killed, never revolt. They give their service in silence and with endurance. When they die, they leave their hide and horns for men to use. Then life has meaning: living to serve. Mine is a son's duty. I may live long yet, and endure hardship and discomfort and scarcity, for it is my turn to take care of our parents, respecting them, seeing to their needs. I listen to them and obediently follow their advice and their tradition. It is my gratitude.

You talked of your 'goal', your intention to be highly educated, of your magnificent future, which are all beyond me. There is one thing I know though: that life is still good in our village. We are quite content and our daily existence is endurable; though we don't have much money, there is this hut and the paddies to till. I'm not ashamed just because some people see us as ignorant and poor, as downtrodden, impoverished, without dignity. I also don't fret about whether we get anything from the wonderful promises of the Master. I don't care if there are a lot of people who grow richer from our hard work, as long as this piece of land is ours, and the hut still stands.

You've been away a long time now, Tadpole. Here another season is passing. The rice is now ripe for the harvest. I'm proud that these golden sheaves we are reaping are the result of our hard work, my vow to the land. The grain is life and gives the promise of plenty.

One day you'll return, I'm sure. You'll learn perhaps that there's no other place that can give you more comfort than your own home, among your own people. I remember so well our boyhood; you used to be rather frail and timid, hardly spoke a word. And I was so afraid that you might not make it when you were drowning or when you fell from the hut that time. We had to put you on a bamboo grate over the charcoal embers. You recovered and have grown up. No one could imagine that it would be you who are now better off than any of us, going into the world.

There are only Piang and myself now to shoulder all the heavy responsibilities. Father and Mother are getting old very fast, but they still try to help as much as they can. I have to turn away when Mother gazes hopefully across the wide paddy fields to where you might suddenly appear before her weary eyes.

Hope you continue to keep well. We are well. With love from all.

Kiang.

The effort to finish the letter was quite a strain on Kiang, who had to grapple with the thoughts he wanted to put across to his learned brother. Kiang wrote painfully and slowly, trying to be clever and philosophical because he did not want to sound like a simpleton compared to his intelligent brother.

Having extinguished the kerosene lamp, he gazed idly at the stars thinking of the distance his letter would have to cover before reaching its destination.

Kiang tried to fathom that distance but could not. He also tried to put himself in the Tadpole's shoes, should he be so intelligent and fortunate. Then he shuddered at the thought, fearing the departure from Napo, the life among strangers in foreign countries, and the difficulties in learning. Kiang dreaded the school and the disciplines Kumjai had once forced upon him.

So now he would be content only with being what he was, hopefully aiming to find his wife very soon. As for Piang, the village life, compared to the life in Muang or in the city, never made her discontented with her lot. She endured and carried on her responsibilities as she grew into a fine young woman. She said she should not get married until Kiang found his wife first. For this reason a few suitors had been turned down and at the same time she pressed her brother to try harder looking for a girl to marry. Piang felt that as a young sister, she should wait and stay single so that she could take care of the parents. Kiang did not want to be in the way of his sister's happiness. Besides, young Bae appeared on the scene and frequented the Surins' hut, helping Kiang in repairing the thatched roof, in threshing rice and occasionally bringing fish and game. Bae is diligent, Boonliang observed.

Kiang began to be extremely serious about his marriage. But when he wanted to think seriously, he discovered that his mind became vague an listless and flitting. This frustrated him so much that he gave up reaping half-way through, and left the paddy with an excuse of going to shoot down a bird or two to make a meal. He carried his bamboo blowpipe, striding across the plain towards the woods. Once he was far from all eyes, he discarded the pretense and sat under a tree, trying to think. However, thinking aggravated him further for he could not concentrate or reach the heart of the matter. So he drifted; then he remembered the image of the Tadpole as a young boy running against the rain, following the buffaloes. Why must the Tadpole go away? Kiang asked himself. What makes men go from place to place? There was no answer to this, so Kiang went further across the plain, burdened with questions to which he could not find any answers. At the same time he suffered the feelings that lonely men experience; but then Kiang did not know it was 'loneliness' for he had never called it that.

Aimlessly he moved on, hearing neither bird calls nor the bellowing of buffaloes. He wanted to get away from Napo, from people, from himself. He missed his brother now, wanting to be told of life elsewhere, to know a little more. He came to a stream shaded and cooled by a leafy tree. Under the tree he stood mindlessly looking at his reflection in the water. The slightly distorted picture told of leanness; it was all limbs and no flesh. Kiang wondered what he looked like to others. Taking off his baggy shorts to bathe, he thought of Kumjai because of the underwear which had lost its original colour and become frayed and grey. It took him back to the day the teacher had brought a few pairs for him from the city.

The one he had just taken off would not last for long now. When the elastic around the waist finally gave out, he would have to throw them away, and he would have to go back to the old days when he had done without. Such a train of thought saddened him, and he knew there was no hope of getting any others.

But now, looking at his nakedness, he became aware of his need as a man for a woman who would bear his children. Only then could Kiang be serious; he decided that when the harvest ended he must find a wife.

Toon too was deeply concerned with her marriage. It had been generally known among young men that she was one of the very few girls in Napo who did not respond to their calls and the playing of flutes or the *kaen* by her house at night time. Normally she retired early and did not come out to spin cotton yarn on the porch, inviting the men to court her.

Nights without the men crooning from the dark pleased Toon for she held nobody else in her heart but the Tadpole. But Toon's nightmare remained, for it could be any evening now when some senior members of the community would call on her father and ask for her hand on behalf of some brute she might not even know or like. In the case of marriage by proxy, it was a matter of the amount of money the suitor's family would offer. Not so much following her own will and choice, she must obey her father's wish.

Toon curled up at night fearing the thought and wishing that the Tadpole would return and save her from such a marriage. Why did he have to stay away so long? What was it that he had to learn and what would become of him? Such questions came to her mind night after night.

Sometimes she wept quietly in the dark when the ache and longing were more than she could bear.

Prem knew too that Toon had been waiting for him. Yes, he would marry Toon when he returned one day. He had been aware of her love and her longing. She was among those upon whom he had inflicted pain by his departure. How could he show much of what he felt and suffered? Sometimes he wanted to let them know how painful it was to him to be away from them.

There were times, however, when he felt happy to be in England. Being both physically and mentally outside the border of one's country, he enjoyed a sense of freedom, a feeling that he was free, free to act, to speak, to be an individual, to be different. In London, there was no one watching him, putting a limit on his reading, policing his thoughts.

On some Sundays, when the weather was encouraging, he went to Speakers' Corner in Hyde Park to listen to people from all walks of life calling attention to their ideas, grievances, outcries, accusations and affirming their rights, airing their views, expounding solutions. This kind of freedom fascinated him, for he had lived nearly twenty years under martial law.

He recalled a phase in the history of Siam when the Prime Minister of the time with his wife and their entourage had toured Europe and North America. While in London the party must have visited Speakers' Corner because on their return to Siam the Prime Minister introduced 'Hyde Park Speaking' to the public, allowing the speakers to use Sanarm

Luang to imitate London's Speakers' Corner. Enthusiasm for it was so overwhelming that crowds gathered at the little park. But Sanarm Luang could hardly boast the same tolerance which Hyde Park enjoyed, for the authorities at the time did not share their English counterparts' attitudes. Moreover, it was difficult to accept that there was corruption, social injustice, poverty, and selfishness. Therefore to talk openly of these matters in a public place was outrageous. It was indeed an extremely grave mistake to import the theory and practice from abroad. How dare the people criticise and speak about all that had been kept in the dark? Suddenly the Siamese 'Hyde Park' became a place of mass arrests, and was eventually banned.

How free and happy Prem felt now, thinking that if he had died in the October 14, 1973 massacre, he would never have experienced this sense of freedom. His understanding of the word 'Liberty' rose like a bird, gliding with the wind. He became convinced that his effort to get out of his own country had been worthwhile.

His bed-sitting room in Elia Street, Islington, required that he should be self-sufficient. It was the first time in his life he had to live on his own, in his own place, fending for himself, living on his own resources, solving problems, facing himself in the narrow room he learned to call, after the fashion, 'the flat'.

The pleasures of being on his own and the happiness from the sense of freedom lingered on. Many a time he sat, contemplating the growing collection of books on the shelves and on his desk. No matter how keen he could be, there would still be

141

more and much more to read and more pleasure to be had from reading. Names flashed through his mind: Fielding, Richardson, Shelley, Johnson, Gibbon, Crabbe, Blake, Wordsworth, Coleridge, Byron, Shakespeare, De Quincey, Keats, Hazlitt, Sidney, Donne, Jonson, Pope, Burns, Spencer, and Milton. For now the Autumn Term of University College had begun.

For a long while he sat, listening to his own thoughts: Alone, absolutely alone here now, in a country where Kumjai might not have to disappear, where Rit might still be alive.

Meanwhile a young man by the name of Paul Manning who lived in the flat above him started to pluck at his guitar. Tucked away cosily from a main thoroughfare, Elia Street was quiet; his flat was at street level, he could hear footfalls or the rolling of beer bottles on the pavement when some drunks kicked them out of the way. Paul's guitar sounded tentative, as the fingers groped for the notes. Was he alone too? Yes, I might have been dead, Prem thought, on October 14, 1973, if the Honourable Brother had not prevented me from going to join the demonstration with other students, showing solidarity for the need for a constitution, the right to vote, for freedom, and for the abrogation of martial law which had been enforced for over twenty years. In his life he had not known the meaning of 'freedom', 'liberty' or 'democracy', until he reached England.

While Paul was strumming on his guitar, Prem was searching for words. He had always longed for their deliverance in a poetic form:

Otherwise it is a sacrifice
in living among foreigners
the life of a crow in peacock's feathers
learning to read lips, forming
words in parrot-like mimicry
gaining new gait and a pair of new eyes

Paul's telephone rang and when it was answered, the Siamese put down his pen, waiting for the guitar to be strummed again. But then Paul gave up his effort and went out.

What shall I do with these words spilled from my mind? Prem asked himself looking at the sheet of paper upon which the ink had dried. He thought he heard chuckles from those famous, well-loved English poets on the shelves!

So he put the paper away.

November still had some bright and dry days. Taking a walk in a park or along the Thames was a change from the classes, from being confined in the flat, and from reading. To feel the crisp wintry air, to witness day by day, week by week, the change of colours on leaves in autumn was comforting and stimulating. At the end of each day, it was possible to think that he had survived the departure, and stayed alive, and that 'staying on' in England was enriching him. For he had been avidly drawing impressions, making observations, and gaining experiences from each day.

His first summer and autumn in London had passed, and he had been ill. Rains made the shortened days sombre, putting the need for winter clothes and an electric heater at the top of his want-list. Books still had priority, and hunting for more volumes in various bookshops in the West End soothed away the loneliness.

In the streets one shivered with cold. London had seen too many pitiful beings to spare sympathy. The teeming millions moved to and fro, filling and emptying the streets. He looked at the faces and saw the landscapes of many nationalities, at paintings and sculptures in museums and perceived a beauty far beyond what his mind could hold, making him long to be able to conceive and create a beauty of his own. He gazed at merchandise in shop-windows and longed to possess certain materials that would bring warmth and comfort, that would make the dreary flat more cheerful. He longed for an encounter which would bring friendship or familiarity.

Shaftesbury Avenue led him into the throbbing heart of Soho. Allowing himself to be exposed to the night of longing, he moved along the small half-lit alleys, lured into sex-shops, accosted by painted faces. But it was not the prostitutes, the pornography, and sex objects which he was looking for. Eventually he entered a Chinese restaurant where its peculiar smell and the Oriental faces of the customers and waiters brought home closer. A young Chinese waiter came to take his order now. Prem's choice was fried rice and he took care not to say 'fly lice'.

One could be easily comforted by the seemingly universal Chinese, by the voices and the faces of these Orientals. So he took his time, eating his dinner.

Outside, darkness had fallen, and with it came a drizzle. Where could one go now? He dreaded an

144

evening alone in the flat, with only the company of poets and novelists. But it was no fun either to be lost in the narrow streets of Soho in the misty night with a fine rain to give one the death of cold. So he hastened to get out of the labyrinthine alleys.

"Hey, Chink!" someone shouted at him from across the street.

Three men in leather and jeans closed in.

"Wait a minute!" one of them pushed the Siamese against a wall.

They had bet among themselves, so one of them said, whether he was circumcised or not. A knife flashed. First the plastic raincoat came off, then jacket and the shirt.

"Down with your pants!"

"You'd better do what he said, Chink," sneered the second man with mock seriousness, playing on Prem's bare chest with the knife. The third man stood apart, waiting for the scene to be over. They could see he was just a lamb, an easy prey on their way to bigger things. It was all for fun, and a little profit from his wallet which did not contain much. In backing away the Siamese fell over his trousers. This comical, naked situation succeeded in giving pleasure to the audience of three. Then they moved off, kicking his scattered clothes out of their way.

The poor Siamese could stay down on the pavement counting grains of dirt and the rough bricks where he fell. If there was a desire to get up, it was because he was shivering with cold, and then because another person arrived to look upon his nakedness.

This man at first appeared rather reluctant to interfere and to be involved, but then he stooped to

145

pick up the scattered clothes and the emptied wallet from the street. Prem could see the figure towering over him with his clothes in his hands was not another thug or sadist to inflict further injury upon him. It was an Englishman in a thick tweed coat, who turned away to be polite, while Prem put on his clothes.

What could one say in a situation like this?

The Siamese quickly dressed, ready to move off. And it seemed that the two men would have gone their separate ways if the Siamese had not happened to go the way where the Englishman had parked his car.

"Can I give you a lift? the Englishman said across his parked car.

Despite the deep voice and the kindness, the *farang* cannot reach you now, not when you have already withdrawn deep within your old sanctuary, lying in wait inside a water buffalo, there on the wide plain of Napo, leaving behind the interplay of coarseness of the leather and jeans and the gentility, between the cockney and this smooth-faced Englishman who could be from a breed known even in Siam as the English upper class.

"I've just come out from a theatre near here. It was a tremendous play. Do you go to the theatre sometimes?" the man asked, turning to look at his passenger.

You have not learned much, lacking an understanding of most things English, still trying hard to mimic the Queen's English. When you round your lips to say 'here', 'there', and 'everywhere' and keep the upper lip stiff, you have some qualms about it, for it would sound unbecoming for a buffalo boy

146

to have the accent of the English upper class.

"Operas, Concerts?"

You have only vague notions about these. Operas are beyond your reach and understanding. Concerts? You once invested two pounds just for an experience of a 'Prom' concert at the Albert Hall, but that was last September and you have not been to any since. The name of the conductor was Wilhelm Hagenbach.

"My name is Charles. Charles Tregonning."

What is in a name? You are still the Tadpole, the Mute, the Obedient, the Acolyte, the Impoverished, the Buffalo Boy.

"My name is Prem. Prem Surin. From Siam."

Should you invite him in? It would be most out of place for the man, who speaks upper class English, who drives a Rolls-Royce, who wears an immaculate blazer.

Here, in this room he had been trying to hide from all eyes an attempt to create beauty of his own through poetry while the famous poets of England watched from the shelves. Now the flat had never seemed so drab and bare, exposing its needs to the substantial figure of the Englishman who was going grey at the temples, whose hair, kept slightly long and wavy, was neatly parted and combed towards the back of his head where it became more curly. What would this man be doing in a working class street of Islington? His Rolls-Royce parked outside 21 Elia Street appeared as out of place as its owner in this one-bed, one-chair, one-man room. The expensive gold watch, the gold signet ring on the little finger of the left hand, and the shiny metallic buttons of the blazer jacket spoke a sublime and rich language of their own against the loud jabbering of an old narrow bed made up as the settee in daytime and the crude little chair newly bought from a second-hand shop in Upper Street. And when Mr Tregonning produced a packet of cigarettes and a gold lighter, there was not a single ashtray in the place for him.

The host remained standing, looking about at a loss, fiddling with the cup and the saucer.

"Will this do?" Prem asked and offered the saucer to his guest as an ashtray.

The visitor was adjusting himself in the wooden chair which squeaked a little under the moving weight. Would an English gentleman ever dream of using a saucer as an ashtray in his castle? Charles Tregonning accepted the offer with a mild smile on his smooth face.

As a result the host could not offer a cup of tea since there was only one cup and one saucer in the flat. He had never thought that he would have to entertain anyone. No, he would not offer tea.

"Sorry. I haven't got around to buying another tea cup," he said.

Among thousands of things he had not learned was the mechanism of social grace and the art of making conversation. Worse still, he had allowed a stranger to enter this private world which he had kept alive with his longings and dreams, with the creativity that gave birth to poems. So now it would be safer to talk of Siam, its tourist attractions, answering questions with short or elusive remarks.

And equally this suave, reserved Englishman promised no more than one could see from outside, should you be window-shopping for intimacy.

8

December 1974

"It's only for the time being," said the Student Officer from the Royal Siamese Embassy who had been coaxing Dhani Pilakol to accommodate another Siamese who had been living alone and had fallen ill.

While showing the room which the sick student could use, the host-to-be resented being asked to shoulder a responsibility which was not really his, to provide an easy way out for the official who exploited one's sense of being from the same country, using his meek grin and sweet words. Dhani was, on the other hand, angry with himself for not being able to say no.

"Very good then," the Siamese official concluded. But seeing that Dhani looked gloomy, he suggested a benefit to be gained from accepting a house-guest:

"He could be a good companion. At least you won't be too much by yourself. From the records, he came out top of the final examinations for high school certificate."

So what, Dhani thought. They learn by rote anyway.

"He's so bright that you won't need any light here at night!" the Official laughed at his own remark.

But Dhani did not laugh.

Eventually, the grinning man, who did not

bother to take off his overcoat, knowing that his mission could be quickly accomplished, left the flat with relief and warm feelings because of a good deed done for all parties, himself included.

Once he was alone, Dhani admitted that the situation was his fault, because he always pretended to be gregarious. Often he was flippant in the company of his countrymen, laughing childishly, speaking Siamese with gusto. All for the sake of protecting himself from being condemned as 'un-Siamese'. So he blamed himself for his false gregariousness, his simulated flippancy, his apparent conviviality, his luxurious two-bedroom flat in fashionable Hyde Park Square. 'Danny's flat', as it was known among groups of Siamese living in and around London, provided an ample place for students and non-students alike to come and cook and have a good time together. They used the well-equipped kitchen and the foodstuffs supplied through diplomatic bags by Dhani's influential parents for parties, and his spacious, tastefully decorated living room as their meeting place. Some of his visitors claimed they had travelled from Oxford, Cambridge, Birmingham, or Exeter, so he could hardly turn them away when they knocked at the door unannounced any time of the day or night. He had to put up with the general untidiness, the rigmarole, the ruined privacy, and the lack of sense of ownership. Some of these guests took advantage of him, looking into drawers and without saying anything claimed his socks, underwear, shirts, handkerchiefs, or shoes. The kitchen would be strewn with rubbish and unwashed dishes after they had eaten all day. Then at night he went out with them, a pack of grinning children with group strength laughing at things English.

What is this poor child's name? Dhani thought of his new house-guest. Prem Somebody. Typical of these young students coming away for the first time, dying of home-sickness or from the English food and climate. To survive they have to cling together in their dingy flats, living out of each other's pockets and each other's minds, cooking their smelly foods, speaking Siamese all the time, defending themselves from things foreign.

Absentmindedly Dhani went about his rooms adjusting the furniture, savouring the last moments of privacy. Being methodical and tidy he kept his flat on the fifth floor extremely neat and clean. His love for wall-to-wall carpeting, for old English and French furniture and art objects from Siam had transformed the flat into a blend of East and West. Most of his collection of Siamese treasures such as the blue and white porcelain, images of Buddha in various sizes from different periods and in different styles, ancient religious manuscripts, carved ivories, the Swankaloke and Benjarong pottery, the Ban Chieng pottery, some rare brocades, were some of the items he had brought out of Siam. Being the only child, Dhani had the pick when it came to 'gifts' from the house of the Pilakols.

While the material wealth from Siam reminded him of his former identity, the English secretary and cabinets, antique armchairs, Queen Anne dining table and chairs, as well as the library of books and records kept in alphabetical order, and the crystal and silver, told of his growing up in Europe. His knowledge of English, French, and German was equal to that of his own language, if not better, because he left Siam at the age of ten. His father, Dr Prakarn Pilakol, had strongly felt that his son should be educated as early as possible in a European country. He could not have chosen a better place than Lausanne, Switzerland to start his son off on an academic career suitable for a future leader of Siam. At the age of twenty-six, an Oxford graduate in Mathematics, now reading Economics at the London School of Economics, Dhani's quest for higher qualifications seemed endless. At the same time, he enjoyed living outside his own country. His manners were refined; he liked things English, French, German; his wardrobe was largely from Savile Row. Dhani Pilakol had everything going for him. No doubt his parents had his life mapped out as well as choosing a young lady of noble birth to be his wife. Dr Prakarn Pilakol meanwhile had become Siam's foremost minister controling the country's finance, industries and natural resources. His wife, however, could not claim a prestigious official background but certainly she belonged to one of the richest and oldest Chinese families in the whole Kingdom. So Dhani or Danny, as he was endearingly called by his friends and colleagues, was the offspring of a marriage of extreme wealth and great political power.

After having parked his car in front of 21 Elia Street, Dhani emerged, surveying the location. Dhani quickly observed the buildings, cocking his handsome head. At the same time he seemed amused at the thought that here in this quiet little street a Siamese lived. Look at this, his very name, P. Surin, managed to insinuate itself among the

152

English: P. Manning, D. Davies. A short unSiamese-like name. Hardly intrusive.

Dhani pressed the bell and waited; his lips tightened as he tried to compose himself and present an indifferent air to the person whose nationality he shared. Surin? Dhani focussed on the name at the door. It reminded him vaguely of something simple and rustic, an echo from another country.

Then the front door opened and a boyish, closely shorn head appeared. The two Siamese awkwardly made the 'wai' greetings.

"Is that all you have?" Dhani politely inquired, looking at the suitcase and a carton of books. He did not really care, wishing that the scene at the door would be over as soon as possible so that they could get away. Seeing so much of the 'Siameseness' in the boy's face and manner, hearing his Siamese voice, Dhani's resentment arose, remembering that he had been forced into the situation and into housing this stranger who came from the land in which he was born. (Wasn't it for this that they held the right to claim so much from him?)

"There're two more cartons of books already outside," Prem said and vaguely indicated the boxes on the pavement next to the black iron railing.

Whether the younger Siamese was momentarily blinded by the daylight or the princely aura it was quite difficult to tell, but he busied himself loading the car with his belongings. Though he felt very weak from the fever and his hands and legs trembled, he would rather perform this manual work himself.

Dhani drove the car away from Elia Street. Looming ahead was his dread of having to converse

153

all the time in Siamese with this stranger. But then the stranger did not attempt to speak, to seek immediately an alliance for being from the same country, no jolly outburst of chatter or presumptuous remarks based on their patriotic brotherhood. Instead, Dhani sensed the distance, the barrier which had already been drawn solidly. With a certain degree of curiosity, he took a quick glance at his passenger and saw the crew-cut schoolboy. Another victim of culture shock, Dhani concluded.

"It might be a help if you and I spoke in English."

Dhani managed to glaze his voice with a thin veneer of sympathy.

By now the boyish looking Siamese had huddled tightly within his plastic raincoat. Silence could be counted as consent.

"How old are you?" Dhani tried in English.

"Twenty."

The buffalo boy felt that his response in English was too abrupt. So he added:

"But I'll be twenty-one next March."

They entered Edgware Road now. Being more relaxed Dhani thought of more to say. English somehow put them on a neutral ground, a basis on which they could behave towards one another like two human beings, if not two Siamese.

However, the gap between twenty-six and twenty, the distance between Hyde Park Square and Napo, between the landscape of Germany or Switzerland or France and the plain of northeast Siam, between the glory of the House of Pilakol and the poverty of the Surins was immense. Fortunately the caretaker of the building was there to help them

154

unload and carry the boxes of books to the lift, and from the lift into the flat.

"You should have some fresh air for a few minutes," Dhani said, opening the windows of the guest room. "How do you feel now?"

Kindness when it was genuine seemed embarrassing. Dhani felt he should do something physical like bringing a glass of orange juice, closing the windows again, touching objects in the room. For at present words were still jarring. Outside, a London taxi droned and the bare branches of the sycamore trees in the Square cut sharply against the grey English skies.

What part of London was this? In coaxing Prem to move, the Student Officer had said: It's one of London's best addresses. But instead of gloating over such good fortune, the weary guest bore the adverse effects that the wealth of others could have upon him. The room was full of things and the owner's voice.

Having appeased his host by trying to rest in bed for a while, Prem got up and staggered against a chair from which a small piece of paper fell on the carpet. He picked the paper up and read: Bought at Sotheby's; 12 July 1970, two George III mahogany chairs, moulded backs with serpentine toprails and pierced waisted slats, tapering legs, £55 the pair.

Somewhere in discreet places, all of Dhani's material riches might be priced and labelled. These Siamese things — the images and ancient scrolls could have been taken from some temples. Strange though that they should have been brought out of the country to a place so far and foreign, Prem thought as his eyes roved around the room. These blue and white urns and bowls too might never return to Siam for they held an air of permanency here. Like Dhani. That Englishman, Charles Somebody would look suitably at home and relaxed in this chintz-covered, high-backed armchair.

To the host, evenings were still full of restraint, when he came back to the flat to face the house-guest. Mornings tended to be easier when conventional greetings could be resorted to before they went their separate ways. This particular evening, Dhani made up his mind to be more hospitable than before. The warmth of his flat had already brought back a healthy glow to his features.

"Really, it's so cold outside," said Dhani when he came face to face with his guest.

Then he took things out of two large shopping bags which he had carried home. He loved buying things, and on arriving at the flat, he immediately unwrapped them so that either he could use them right away or could find a place for them.

"Now we can make proper cocktails," he said as he showed Prem a silver mixer which represented both practical value and an investment. How Dhani glowed towards the silvery thing, narrowing his dark eyes in examining the hallmark.

"Let's have a cocktail, Prem."

Their activities managed to draw them closer. Having asked his flatmate to squeeze a few oranges for juice, Dhani went into his bedroom to change, to comb his hair and refresh his skin with eau de Cologne.

"Excellent!" Dhani said, coming to the kitchen as if he were very pleased with the orange juice.

Then from the selected bottles, Dhani measured the ingredients. "How was your day?" Dhani asked as he put ice-cubes into the mixer, glancing at his assistant. A curious fellow, Dhani judged, all screwed up in knots inside himself, unlike most Siamese. What has he got to hide behind those big round eyes? Something dark and piercing lurking there, but you've got to catch it quickly.

"It gets on my nerves a bit, having to speak and listen to English all the time," Prem said.

"I've good news for you then. We're invited to the Residence for dinner this evening. You can speak and listen to Siamese there," Dhani said; and with a cheerful expression on his face, the cocktail maker vigorously shook the mixer.

"It's called Blood and Sand," Dhani said and poured out the frothy, ruby coloured liquid into two chilled cocktail glasses.

"Ugh!" Prem made a sour face. "It tastes like blood."

"I didn't know you drank blood," Dhani said sulkily. "Don't drink it if you don't like it."

He left the kitchen for the living room where he hoped to be soothed by the music. Prem thought he had made a mistake, but it was not with malice, or an intention to disagree, for peasants tend to speak what comes to their mind. The Blood and Sand was perfect. Dhani's annoyance was the fault of the boy from the rice fields who had not acquired a taste for sophisticated drinks.

"I don't want to go out tonight," Prem said, following Dhani into the living room.

"Please yourself," Dhani said, not turning to see the buffalo who was making a revolt. "They're expecting us both, that's why His Excellency told me he would bring a letter from the Embassy to give to you there."

Dhani put on a record, then with his drink in hand he sat in his armchair, elegantly crossing his legs. 'Parsifal' would be ideal to calm his ruffled mood.

"What letter?"

"I don't know. How would I know? A letter from your folks, maybe?" Dhani said ruefully.

Their visit obviously pleased His Excellency and his wife. Being a close friend of Dhani's mother since childhood, the Ambassador's wife had been treating Dhani as if he were her own son. She graciously extended her attention to Prem due to his pleasing manner and good appearance.

"Does your mother write often?" She asked Prem during dinner.

He could not give an immediate answer. However the lady was prepared to wait. She knew of him from the official sources.

"My parents cannot read or write," Prem said and took a quick glance at the faces around him as if to see whether they might laugh at him or not, then he admitted further that the letter was written by his older sister.

They let him alone for a while as he seemed to concentrate on his food. Being grateful for the fact that they did not try to prise more out of him, Prem gradually went back over Piang's letter.

> Kiang and I are both married now. Kiang moved to his wife's in Baan Wa. Bae, my husband, moved in with us, taking on Kiang's responsibilities and he's very dili-

158

gent. Father and Mother think well of him. Now I'm with child...

Imagine Piang with a child!

"What are you laughing at?" the hostess inquired gently, for she had been observing him, wanting to give more attention to him. Her soft kind eyes shone with tenderness.

"Oh, at what Danny was saying," he replied.

"What did I say that was so funny?" Dhani stopped talking to the Ambassador.

Once again they gave him the attention which made him clumsy and ill at ease. "You said that Robert Halsworthy's books have been banned in Siam since he said we smile like the Cheshire cat," said Prem.

"I've just been informed that the author has also been expelled from Siam as a result," the Ambassador punctuated their conversation and gave a signal to his wife that they should have coffee now, in the living room.

"I think Prem would do all right," Dhani was saying to the Ambassador as he gently swirled his cognac. "He's very perceptive and very sensible. He studies very hard, could not care less about going to movies or wasting time like most of our students. The only problem is that he's overly sensitive."

Dhani seemed pleased with his remark. Mentally he was rubbing his hands with a certain pleasure that accidentally a child of monsoon country had been put in his hands, like some soft clay for him to mould and remould to his own desired form.

With this in mind Dhani said forcefully, after

arriving back in their flat:

"Prem, I've poured us some cognac."

"I don't drink," Prem said but relented as he met Dhani's commanding eyes.

So then they sat on the settee side by side going over Dhani's photograph albums, revealing Dhani in various places and stages of growth. They began from photos of small, smartly dressed Dhani standing in front of the great house of the Pilakols, much more opulent than that of the Phengpanichs, with the parents who appeared so loving and watchful, the old grandmother seen through the side windows of her limousine.

"I left home when I was ten," Dhani told his friend, remarking on another phase of his life. The photos told of his schooling in Lausanne, riding, playing piano, posing with his friend Reinhard von Regnitz, cycling, *Auf Weihnachtsurlaub in Bayern.*

"Believe me," Dhani continued as he carefully swirled his drink. "I too experienced homesickness. Nothing could be more lonely and boring than a cold and wet Sunday afternoon in a boarding school when nobody came to see one, and when there was nothing to do. Worse still, it was painful to see other boys' parents come and spend time with them. But looking back now, I am thankful for the experiences and for the change. Ha! I could be easily hurt at the critical remarks people like Robert Halsworthy, or the lecturers, or other students made against us, criticising Siam. Even though they do that academically. How I used to defend her in those days. The blind patriotism! It seems now that I've removed the blindfold. I can see her in a true perspective."

160

Dhani paused. Clearing his throat, he decided to fire the bullet which he had reserved all these years:

"You see Prem, I could hardly blame my parents for sending me here when I was so young. Gradually I got over my homesickness, and finally I came to an understanding that I must do everything in my power to ensure that I developed my faculties to the fullest. If one society denies me the right, I must seek another that offers the favourable environment and the intellectual freedom. I will not tolerate a society which impoverishes and deforms me."

After Dhani had taken a sip of his cognac, he said further:

"I dare say that your departure from home and your experiences in England will broaden your mind."

Afterwards, in his bedroom, Prem reflected: How lucky it was for Dhani who could prevent himself from being mentally crippled by leaving the country at an early age. As for me, at the mercy of the brute force and the evil of the land, blood had flowed from my mouth and my forehead. But still I was more fortunate than Kumjai and Rit and hundreds of other students. Knowing the price so dear, one should learn to be prudent. And an album of photographs would be a useful way of presenting oneself to strangers. Besides, it was an easier way than to say: Look, I've put myself in a nut-shell....

Otherwise it's a sacrifice

to live among foreigners
like a crow in peacock's feathers
learning to read lips, forming
words in parrot-like mimicry
gaining new gait, new pair of eyes
I now suffer the life of a man
so much for himself within himself;
often I try to piece together
the sound of monsoon and the laughter
of children from the wind
and my own need to grow old among kin
but my cause has become doubtful
looking back now I see no landmark
of my beginnings and my track
cannot be retraced
for the wind has erased
the impression from the sand.

Yes, he would rather have several albums, borrowing Dhani's technique, to show to others: a boy riding a water buffalo, toiling in the rice fields, learning sums in a shack called Primary School of Napo, faces of other children, old people, young girls doing their silk spinning, Kumjai giving prizes to the top of the class. These would be his facades, and the words must remain unspoken, for he had not yet been able to create a mechanism to turn bitterness into wisdom, or the skill to transform childhood memories into poetry.

Meanwhile he strung bitter words together and in the enclosure of his mind, a substance was secreted to coat, like mother of pearl creating a pearl, the source of pains:

I've heard this warning

162

since childhood
but pale as grass growing
in darkness,
vindicated by silence, I
live a lenient life
to survive.
In vain.

Decades have gone yet I await
the coming of the brave, of men
who dare to speak their mind,
of reasons worth reasoning,
of truth acceptable to lying men.
Must I take a soundless flight
when time lapses into silence
as another decade has gone
or wait still until they come,
the thick-set thieves, to hurl me
into this fearful abyss?

Outwardly Prem appeared quite healthy. The central heating in the flat sent out warmth twenty-four hours, day and night; there was always plenty of food. But to live with Dhani one had to be reasonably presentable.

"Prem, I can't take you anywhere, not in those clothes and that plastic rain-coat!" Dhani had voiced his disapproval. "And by the way, I've never seen any underwear of yours in the laundry. Haven't you got any?"

Following Dhani's taste and guidance, Prem's wardrobe began to collect the famous names in fashion including several pairs of shoes, gloves, and ties. Since Dhani would not accept payment for the room and the food, he requested that his house-guest spend his allowance on clothes and help with the laundry and general cleaning of the flat. Their togetherness had smoothly settled into a pattern. They took turns in cooking. Prem offered to do the ironing on Sundays. By now a year had gone and it seemed most natural to speak to each other in English. By and large living in a luxurious flat in Hyde Park Square put one on a map of respectability. Here, the buffalo boy from Napo was in constant touch with sophisticated and wealthy people, the intellectuals and music lovers whom Dhani kept as friends.

Initially he allowed himself to be influenced by Dhani's style and taste, blindly aping his mannerisms. In Dhani's eye, Prem had improved tremendously. Perhaps, it was due to this improvement that Prem took the initiative and invited a young lady from his class to dinner.

On this occasion, Prem imitated Dhani's courteous and refined manners. As Dhani would have done, Prem courteously opened the lift door for her to leave first, unlocked the door to the flat and asked her to enter.

"What a super place!" Elizabeth Durham cried in awe of the splendour of the East and the wealth of the West that characterized the furnishing of the flat.

It was a pity that Dhani had had to go to Munich, for he would have been pleased to observe what his understudy could accomplish in so short a time.

"All yours?" she asked, poking her head into the living room.

"For the time being, yes. Let's put everything in the kitchen."

He dropped a bag and the fresh mushrooms scattered on the carpet of the vestibule.

"There goes our dinner," the host said and hoped that the situation would still be under control.

He would like to play it the way he had planned, the way Dhani would have done: To put away what they had bought and then progress to the living room where he would ask her to be at home, serve Blood and Sand, and turn on classical music.

"You must be a millionaire," Elizabeth said while gathering the mushrooms from the floor.

"My flat mate is the one who has loads of money."

Blood had flowed into her face; her breasts heaved when she stood up, then he lost the air of being the master of the situation, stuttering in bad English:

"While I take care of these dinner things, why don't you go into the living room and make yourself at home?"

"You want to get rid of me," she babbled into his ear and bit it.

Forgetting to behave like Dhani, he suddenly became himself, a buffalo experiencing an elation from a monsoonal rain, skin-soaked, tongue testing drops of rain, the eyes blinded by the electrifying speed and flashes of lightning, the ears deafened by the thunder. His heart was beating strongly and fast with the rhythm of the magical monsoon.

After Elizabeth Durham had left, he thought of their male-female interlude. Words began to form in his mind:

My lips must pluck each petal
and savour the pollen
to make the flower my new word.

He sat still for a long time, listening to the flat, to the vibration of London. Later, he wrote:

"From here my journey will be lengthened into another year with a faint hope of finding you..."

Not having a clear cut image of who the 'you' would be, he stopped to ponder. Would 'you' be Elizabeth Durham or another English girl? Elizabeth had made no bones about love. To her 'love' was so Victorian. 'What is it, but a neurotic affectation', she had said. 'People have confused it with sex. Sex is healthy and normal'. He could never be her only man, for when it came to men, she liked them mature, middle-aged, and preferably married so that they would not bother her so much with the question of ownership, marriage and jealousy.

So instead of the intention to 'lengthen the journey into another year with the faint hope of finding you', he crossed the last two words out, and replaced them with 'reading more, seeing more, hearing more...'

Then he got up from the desk and began to walk the floor, going into the living room, staring out vacantly at the park below. He was bored with his high sounding ideal after having fully gratified himself with sensual pleasure.

It was very well to admire an orchestra conductor who held so high a stature as a musician, a well-known name, standing on the podium rendering beauty through music, reaping success after success, ovation after ovation. It was all very well to long to possess the gift of a great poet, skilfully creating images and structures out of his private logic and perception. But at present the would-be poet seemed to draw images and structures from the thin air and emptiness from his crippled heart, still learning to perfect his skill, aping the mannerisms of the West, when the bitter litany of 'one year for the roof and two years for the walls', and his own begging sound of 'please give us some rice', rang on in the mind.

Would he now be satisfied with being just a graduate, returning to be another Westernized scholar in a university back in Siam? Originally he only wanted to be able to give Toon a poem to celebrate her beauty, to uplift her weary heart from the drudgery, to point out simple things which were beautiful, to give a few ballads and songs to a gang of herdboys so that they could sing to praise the powerful and magical monsoon. Now he held a lot of conflicting ideas and had not been able to create those songs except bitter words in a foreign language to celebrate nothing but the pain and despair in his own heart.

Yes, it would be difficult now to go back to the room and his writing desk to face that piece of paper on which words of high ideal had been arrogantly written. What could one do with the mumbo-jumbo of words passed off as verse?

He quickly sensed that he was drifting into a rather destructive stream of thoughts. Pulling himself together, he put on a record of classical music. Then Dhani rang from Munich:

"How are you? I can't possibly come back till mid January. Hate to think that you'll be spending Christmas and New Year by yourself in the flat. Come and join us. You might find old von Regnitz a little tiresome because he's been very sick. There are lots of rooms in the house and plenty to see in Munich. We might go skiing in the Alps. Come as soon as you can. Phone me after you've booked your flight. I'll meet you on arrival at the airport. Close all the windows and check the gas. Make sure it doesn't leak. Turn off the electricity too. At the main switch. Use the money we keep in the drawer for the airfare."

Germany? It sounded more foreign to him than England.

At Munich Airport, Dhani and his friend, Reinhard von Regnitz, met Prem at the exit. The blond and blue-eyed Reinhard whom Dhani called 'Reiner' stood slightly taller than Dhani; his stern and disciplined manliness struck Prem as the image of a typical young German hero in war films.

Reinhard drove them away from Munich in the family car, a white Mercedes, at high speed once they got onto an *autobahn*. The salt spread over the road had melted the snow into sludge. Alone in the back seat Prem looked in awe and wonder at the snowy landscape, at pine trees drooping heavily from the weight of snow. A few hours ago he had closed the door of their London flat, taken a taxi to Heathrow Airport under the grey and bleak English skies, but now it was the whiteness of snow all over, silently holding its mysteries from him who came

168

from a tropical country. Now and then Dhani and Reiner conversed in German. Not being included in the conversation, Prem concentrated on the sound of a foreign language. The snow and the peculiarity of the German language held equally awe-inspiring qualities. At the same time, Prem marvelled at Dhani's linguistic ability. At one point, Prem closed his eyes, listening to the two friends, and believed that two Germans were speaking. It dawned on Prem that Dhani was in fact a *farang* in the guise of a Siamese.

On approaching Heeringen, the car slowed down, edging along a narrow road to bypass the town centre. Houses became fewer. Then the car veered off and entered a cobbled driveway into the courtyard of a grand two-storied Bavarian mansion.

Reiner unloaded his guest's suitcase and offered to carry it into the house. At the staircase, Dhani took over, taking the visitor to one of the rooms upstairs.

"I used this room a lot when I came on holidays," said Dhani.

The room was rich in dull gold, carpeted with shaggy Greek wool; the eiderdown-covered bed promised the comfort that Dhani had enjoyed.

"Make yourself at home. I'll wait for you in the living room. I think Reiner is getting coffee for us. See you in five minutes," Dhani said.

Turning towards the windows, Prem wondered whether he would have enough time to experience Dhani's European childhood and the differences in the four seasons seen through the panes of this bedroom. How fascinating the silent snow seemed.

The stairs were of thick dark wood, partially carpeted, leading down to a spacious vestibule and then on to the living room in which Dhani and his friend were putting out coffee cups and saucers on the low table.

On the same table there were candles surrounded by fresh sprigs of pine and painted pine cones and colourful Christmas decorations. Dhani lighted these candles, making the white porcelain and silver service on the coffee table come alive.

The living room of this old Bavarian house was spacious and called for stoutly upholstered armchairs and sturdy side-tables. At one end, further from the doorway, stood an immense writing desk and cabinets which displayed a large collection of cut crystal and silver and porcelain pieces.

"Gemütlich is a German term for having coffee and cakes in candle-light before Christmas," Dhani explained.

Everything, including the white shiny cups and the silver spoons and golden pine cones, made quite an impression on the Siamese who had never taken part in the rite of Christmas.

Reiner and Danny wore identical black turtle-necked cashmere sweaters and grey flannel trousers. Not only did they dress alike, their alliance seemed solid.

The darkness which was quickly descending upon them softened the edges of the bulky furniture, and reduced the generous room into a microcosm of which the burning candles became the centre.

Were it not for a keen eye, Prem might not have been able to detect how displeased Reiner could be, having to wait for his father to join them. Nevertheless he poured the coffee into three cups while Dhani brought in the cakes. A few minutes later, Herr Helmut von Regnitz made an appearance. Because he moved rather slowly through the dark passages of his great house, the three young men did not hear or see him until he was ready to sit down with them. After a rather brief and formal introduction, Prem made a quick study of the father. Helmut von Regnitz, a composer, had not quite recovered from his recent illness. His eyes had deepened in their sockets; however, there was a sign of life in them as they flickered against the dancing candle-light. His thinning hair looked as white as the snow outside. Once an upright and proud man who upheld his righteousness and the glory of Germany above all things, old von Regnitz did not succeed in controlling his sinewy hands from trembling.

They were obliged to speak in English which sounded jarring and broken. Eventually they decided to talk in German.

"Die Christlich Soziale Union," Reinhard was saying for it seemed they were discussing politics.

As the father and the son and the Siamese son, Dhani, seemed to hold quite different views on this topic, an argument arose. To them, to be aggressively putting one's idea across, to express one's viewpoints with a sheer conviction, seemed normal, but to Prem they were clashes of words, vexing the soul. Moreover the sons should never behave disrespectfully towards the father in such a loud and aggressive manner.

Feeling quite embarrassed and upset, Prem got

up, taking cups and saucers and coffee pot and sugar bowl and jug of cream to the kitchen where he remained, washing the dishes.

To restore peace within himself, Prem sought the refuge of his bedroom. After a while, he went downstairs and let himself out into the yard. Standing a foot deep in snow, the elated Siamese stretched out his arms skywards to welcome the falling snow. The flakes came down falling on his hair, melting on his face. How one could exult in the experience! The Siamese went farther from the house and looked back, seeing the glow of the living room through the frosty window panes behind which sat Reiner and Dhani listening to a recording of an opera. In the next room, the old father pensively worked at his desk.

Nobody seemed to pay any attention to the falling snow which silently and secretly gathered, piling up, flake by flake, encroaching on everything. He took a handful of it, making a ball to throw at the vanishing line of the trees but decided not to disturb the perfect silence. Standing very still for a long time, the man from Monsoon Country tried to be at peace and in harmony with the white night. He might have achieved such a tranquil state of mind if he had not caught sight of Herr von Regnitz moving curiously about his study. It was a movement of a man in pain, staggering and stumbling and falling. Coming closer to the windows, the observer saw that the composer had lain on the bed gasping like a stranded fish.

In the next room the two men were still listening to the opera. Should he voice his discovery? Prem did not know what to do. He tip-toed into the house and went back to his room to change his trousers which were dripping at the legs. When he returned to the lounge he said nothing of the experience. Reiner looked up as he came into the room. How blue were those eyes. Dhani was too busy pouring Sekt to take notice of Prem's re-entry.

"Zum Wohl!" Dhani toasted with a German sparkling wine.

"Zum Wohl."

Each, with a glass of Sekt in his hand, sat solemnly listening to the recorded opera. Only Prem Surin, who did not share their musical knowledge, stayed for the sake of the others.

When the opera came to an end, Reiner and Dhani agreed that they would prepare dinner. They discussed what they should have, and who would do what, in a brotherly fashion.

"Can I do anything?" Prem asked.

"Nein," Dhani said. "Just relax."

Alone in the living room with his glass of wine, Prem wanted to know what had actually occurred in the next room, whether the old father had been very ill and perhaps needed someone to take care of him.

Meanwhile Reiner spared a thought for his father and went into the study. After a few minutes, he returned to the kitchen, telling Dhani that old von Regnitz would not join them for dinner.

"If he's sick again, we can't go skiing," Reiner said nonchalantly.

They had dinner in a cheerless frame of mind. The composer locked his door against any intrusion and turned in for the night. Prem made an excuse to sleep early and went to his bedroom. He tossed

173

and turned in the night. A few times he got up to look out at the blank night through the window. Early in the morning Dhani knocked and came into the room.

Dhani sported a fur-lined suede coat, with a pair of gloves in his hand. "Reiner and I decided to go skiing today and we'll come back on the 23rd. Can you be an angel and look after the old man till we return?"

"Sure. Don't worry. Have a good time," Prem said without thinking.

He lay in bed, listening to the driver trying to start the engine. Soon he would know what it would be like to go from one empty room to another in this sombre place. When they had left, Prem dressed himself, and came downstairs, moving quietly along the dark passages, half expecting to run into Herr Helmut von Regnitz.

Someone presently opened and closed a door. It turned out to be the cleaning lady from the village.

"Hello", Prem greeted her, preparing to be most friendly and helpful.

But the fat woman walked away lopsidedly like a lame hen. No one had warned him to get out of her way. What was one to do? Covering himself with an overcoat and gloves, his escape was deterred momentarily by the arrival of a car. From the type of leather case the visitor had in hand, Prem guessed that the tall and thick-set man could be the doctor doing his rounds. Prem waited for the cleaning lady to let the caller in and when the two Germans went inside to see von Regnitz, he went out, following Königswieser Strasse in the opposite direction from the town. On this side of the estate, Herr Helmut von Regnitz did not have any neighbours and there were no car tracks or any sign of human beings on the snow.

He wandered from the road into the snow-laden forest, wanting to look for the mystery. One knew intimately the monsoonal rains, the desiccation, the croaking of frogs and the humming of insects of the northeastern plateau of Siam, but the strange shapes of leafless beech, elm, and birch trees in the mist and the young spruces hiding under the snow had to be treated with awe. The mystery and the untold beauty lured him deep into the forest.

The enormous lopsided woman who came to clean the house and to cook for the old composer opened the front door for him on his return. She coldly observed his shocking condition with a caustic cracking noise out of her narrow mouth. At the door, Prem took off his frozen shoes and the coat, and tip-toed timidly to a safer distance. In the bedroom he undressed and lay in bed to keep warm, waiting for the cleaning woman to go away.

She did go eventually, banging the front door to announce her departure, leaving quite a distinct smell behind to remind one of her presence and labour. Prem came into the kitchen to look for food. There was a bowl of 'Sülze' left out near the kitchen sink to be cooled and set. The brawn was made of pork fat, smelling of vinegar. A large plate of freshly made apple strudel seemed tempting, but then he saw a note saying something in German about Bratwurst mit Grünkohl supposedly for dinner. Checking the time, he decided to wait until old von

Regnitz invited him to lunch.

In his room, the composer was playing the piano. It was not a melodious tune, but repetitive. At some point, Prem thought, the old man must be hungry and come out to eat. So the Siamese set the table for two, then put the sausages and the sloppy cabbage in the oven under a low heat. He settled down in the living room to wait for the composer. For a long time, he sat, gazing out of the windows at the snow-covered courtyard.

The *gemütlich* hours had passed and there was no sign that the host would appear. Then the snow began to fall and darkness descended. He lessened the sharp edges of hunger with a glass of milk, and continued to wait, sitting in the dark so that he could see the snow falling and the glowing whiteness outside. But finally he ate the joyless meal alone, and after washing up, went to his room and closed the door. Good then, he thought, the silent night would be perfect for composing a song.

Setting down into bed with writing materials, he leaned on the pillows put against the top of the bed, listening to the murmuring of the great house. For a long time he listened and watched the falling snow. Words too descended like snow, flake by flake, word by word. He lifted up his expectant face and his hands to catch them:

> *In an ancient room*
> *in the monsoon country*
> *I lie in disuse*
> *while most lustrous laughter*
> *comes with the rustling of leaves*
> *from thieves in the night*

176

grown brave and fat in impunity
while I am weakened
cloying in connivance
in doldrums and claustrophobia
scheming for cures — the sunshine
and the sea's soothing sound
and the cunning of Manorah,
who, on her fated day, succeeded
with a tale to repossess
her sequestered wings.

Manorah was a mythological half-bird woman, a beautiful winged creature who resided among her kind in the woods of Mount Meru on top of which gods and goddesses lived. Manorah and her entourage came quite often to bathe and swim in a lotus pond, the home of fish and colourful water birds. One day a hunter came across the group of these strange and delicate half-bird people, and devised a way to make his catch. Equipped with an enormous snake, he waited for them at the pond. The sound of their flight made him more alert, and when the women took off their wings and glided into the water, the hunter rushed out from his hiding place and snatched a pair of wings. Most of the bird-women could fly away except Manorah whose wings had been taken by the man. She, with a large snake constricting around her to prevent her escape, was brought to the palace as a gift to the king, who became very attracted to her. But his love for the creature made the grand ladies of the court hot with jealousy. So they schemed to do away with Manorah to win the favours back from their king. It so happened that the king had to go to war. During his absence the courtiers condemned Manorah to death by burning. A pyre was prepared and lit, but Manorah asked for her wings to perform a dance before she would die. The wings were brought to her, and as soon as she had them, she flew away from the smell and vice of human beings.

That was a "once upon a time" story Grandfather had told him when he was the little Tadpole.

If Manorah had not succeeded, she certainly would have been immolated, watched by a cheering, jeering crowd. And in his nightmare, it was Dhani who was being led to the pyre. Poor Dhani. Some young Siamese men who were hysterical, broke the line and out they came slapping the victim's face, pulling his hair, spitting on him. The hateful people sang:

> *Make him cry!*
> *Make him beg for mercy!*
> *For what he's done to us,*
> *For what he could have done to us!*

Dhani begged for mercy, kneeling, sobbing. His skull was bleeding and his face dripped with blood and his clothes were torn and splattered with excrement.

> *Burn him, the dangerous alien*
> *Hiding under the Siamese skin*
> *Under a Siamese name, a Siamese face*
> *Yet its heart is bent upon destroying*
> *It is a deadweight on the land!*
> *Such a person cannot live on our land!*

Like unleashed fiends, many men rushed towards their prey rendering blows. One or two of

178

them pierced Dhani's heart with a stake. The body was then hoisted by the neck before they doused it with petrol. Prem saw Dhani's winged soul rise with the flames and smoke. Among the thousands of people watching the burning of Dhani, he looked as beastly and unfeeling. But he kept hearing the call of Dhani's soul, pulling at the heart, making him weep.

Prem woke up weeping still. Was his despair so refined now that he could cry only in dreams?

Unable to fall asleep again, he rose and put on warm clothes. Wiping the fretful sleep from his eyes and face, he began to draft one of his essays required for the Spring Term. He worked for a long period; writing and thinking in English had become almost natural now. But at the beginning, his lack of critical thinking posed a difficulty for his studies. In Siam, he had hardly been taught to question, to make criticism, to discuss. Most of the time one was spoon-fed, learning by rote. Therefore to write: 'In my opinion,...' was at first staggering. He worked on until nine o'clock. After having washed and dressed, he came downstairs.

Yes, now he knew what it was like to go from one empty room to another, to be left alone in this immense house surrounded by shivering leafless trees, isolated by snow. Yet all the while the mystery remained in the room in which von Regnitz stayed. They were both cut off from the outside world, left to their own resources. I should be able to confine myself in a room for a long time, Prem thought as he fixed his own breakfast in the kitchen. Not expecting the host to join him, he did not set the table. Coffee and toast would do. Ah, there were signs that old Helmut had come out during the night to claim his share of Bratwurst mit Grünkohl and the apple strudel. Sly old thing!

Yes, it was sly to come out like a thief in the night to nibble at sausages. Now, what could he be doing in that room?

Prem went to the door of the study, bent down to look and listen through the key-hole. As he was cocking his left eye, the door was suddenly opened.

"Good morning!" Herr Helmut von Regnitz greeted his house-guest.

Being caught in the Peeping Tom act, the guest seemed out of his wits.

"I..., er, I just want...to know," Prem stuttered.

One would be more at ease facing the sickly man in a brownish dressing gown rather than this gentleman of the old world 'en grande tenue'. For a moment Prem could not believe his eyes that it was old Helmut von Regnitz who was standing upright in front of him. Whoever this fearsome person could be, the blue eyes were alive, shining with excitement. And shouldn't the old man say 'Guten Morgen'? But it was 'Good morning' in perfect English.

"You're welcome. Welcome to my workshop," the composer invited, stepping back and opening the door wider. "Komm!"

Workshop?

It could be counted as a privilege to be allowed to enter the musician's private room in which the symphonies, operas, sonatas, concertos, and tone poems had been created. Originally designed as a library, the study was smaller and softer in tone than the lounge. During the owner's illness, the grand piano and a bed had been installed in order that the composer could work and sleep in his 'workshop' without having to climb stairs. For the ailing man, it was most convenient. Piles of papers lay in order under crystal paper-weights on the desk and on the secretary.

"I was just going out to look for you," said Helmut. "Sit down, please."

They sat in opposite chairs set around the low coffee table in the space reserved for receiving guests. The settee and chairs were upholstered with cured black leather.

"I apologize for leaving you to yourself so much," the grand old man was saying. "You must forgive me. Make yourself comfortable."

English put them on a neutral ground.

"What are you working at?" Prem asked.

The distinguished face became pensive and the lips pressed and twitched slightly. Helmut von Regnitz, looking towards his desk, said:

"A tone-poem. It's finished now."

Not that he knew anything about tone-poems, but Prem could see in the blazing blue eyes that the composer felt gratified with the work; the fire remained smouldering, the heart throbbed exultantly sending blood to his formerly pallid face. In Helmut von Regnitz, there seemed to be so much energy in store, making the scene Prem witnessed the other night through the windows just a nightmare.

"Are you likely to start composing another work soon?" Prem asked.

"No, I don't think so. This may be my last."

Helmut von Regnitz got up slowly, and went to the secretary from which he brought out two champagne flutes. Gently, Helmut set the glasses side by side on the writing space of the cupboard doors.

"We're snow-bound," Helmut said. "I expected a friend to join us but he could not make it from Karlshausen where it is snowing heavily. Well, we shall have a drink without him and celebrate the tone-poem."

"What's the name of your tone-poem?" Prem rounded his lips around the words 'tone-poem' to taste its delicacy.

"*Tod* or 'Death' in English,' Helmut said non-chalantly as he was about to leave the room to fetch a bottle of champagne.

When the composer had been working full-heartedly on this opus called 'Death', being aware of it in every breath he inhaled and exhaled, it had become an old familiar name. But to Prem who had been trying to conjure up the shape and form of the romantic-sounding 'tone-poem', it was staggering to hear that it could encompass such a stark theme. Seeing the dumb amazement on the face of his house-guest, the composer turned half-way at the door to explain.

"It's about a dying man who tries to grapple and struggle with Death which I've been trying to see as being...what do you say in English..."

"Tangible?" Prem quickly guessed.

The composer did not seem so sure; both realized the inadequacy of language.

However when the musician returned with a bottle of champagne, it appeared that they had forgotten all about their previous conversation.

"Zum Wohl!" Helmut toasted after having filled

their glasses.

"Prost. To 'Death' — your tone-poem."

Had his friend from Karlshausen been able to join them that day, it might have turned out to be a rather grand and exciting occasion, for obviously the composer was keen to discuss his recently completed work with someone who shared his interest and knew about composing and rendering a score.

"My friend who could not be with us today is a well-known conductor. What a pity he could not make it."

Was it also for his friend that the graceful old man was all dressed up? Prem sensed his own insignificance. His only comfort was to wish that champagne would be worthy of the event and he would not ask silly questions and act clumsily and spill the champagne.

"What did you want to know?" Helmut asked, tilting his head slightly.

Prem remembered then that he had seen Helmut's face in some of the photos in Dhani's albums. It was fifteen years younger then, a more fleshy face. Now the handsomeness had given way to distinction, the blond hair turned snow white; only the strong jaw remained quite the same, or became more prominent in years of recurring illness.

"When I met you at the door, you said you wanted to know something." Helmut referred to the incident at the door where the Siamese was caught peeping through the key-hole.

Really, he should have forgotten that by now, Prem thought to himself, trying to fumble for some remark which would cover him and at the same time explain his action.

"Oh, I wanted to know what's in this room, to see if there were photographs, books, albums, things of Dhani's childhood. I gathered that he and Reiner went to the same school and Dhani has made a home here."

Helmut von Regnitz did not answer at once, for it seemed that something deep inside him was stirring. "Childhood?", Helmut uttered as if he was mildly surprised by some association of ideas.

"Yes, Dhani's childhood. Or Reiner's. If I know something about his early days, it might help me understand him."

Old Helmut pressed his lips as if to commit to himself the understanding of his own. His eyes were out of focus and he murmured in German what could be translated as: "So it's childhood then, the recollection of it and the happy moments of his life, his memories of the loved ones. Death wouldn't take control all the time; there must be moments when Death relaxes its grip. The transfiguration would be possible..."

Prem watched in amazement a peculiar expression on his host's face. But for not understanding German, he took it rather badly.

Helmut stood up; he did not quite know where to begin. Agitatedly he said:

"Please excuse me. I want to do more work."

Perhaps he realized then that he could be misunderstood as being impolite but not knowing how to use English to lessen the severity of his tone, Helmut added only one word: 'Bitte' the meaning of which the guest had not yet learned.

Prem took his glass of champagne and quietly

184

left the room. The alcohol had made him dizzy, but he finished it off in the kitchen. Should have taken the whole bottle out here too, he thought morbidly. Every time I open my big mouth, the English and the German shudder for fear of what will come out next!

So he brooded in the living room. Looking out through the window panes, he saw how the day had deteriorated, now threatened by a snow storm. The eaves whined and the whole mansion shuddered and moaned. The trees shook and swayed with the fury. The storm was lashing everything in its path.

Prem tried to put his mind in order by using the techniques of Vipassana learned and practised in the *Wat*. He became aware of his own reaction and thoughts. With concentration, he channelled his mind to the thoughts of home, recalling faces of his people, the sound and movement of the herd, the mood of the plain and the rice fields, and the songs the herdboys had sung against the back-drop of the furious snow storm and the trembling house. In many ways, his people in Napo would be happier than he who had to go through cultural tensions and conflicts. But he dared to venture here alone, not in search or in pursuit of happiness. Instead it was, as Kumjai said, a *sacrifice* he was to make, following a dream. And now he had a dream of his own, that is the dream of being a poet! This private dream was not born when Kumjai gave him a book of poetry as a prize for being the first in the class, but it began when the first breath of a water buffalo was felt on his skin. The open plain had been for centuries heavy with layers of poetry, permeating the skin of the animals and the souls of men.

At this point, he reflected that von Regnitz had been able to pursue his *métier* not only because he was gifted and was supported and encouraged by his parents and teachers to follow his training and career in music, but also because the society to which he belonged provided the stimulus and the impetus which worked for him, not against him. Panya Palaraksa, the gifted flutist of Napo could have become famous, but in his village, he used his instrument crudely made of bamboo to play heavenly tunes only to the buffaloes.

Helmut von Regnitz did not appear for lunch or dinner. What could Helmut do in his room all these hours? Prem continued to wait in the living room, watching television after helping himself to sausages and boiled cabbage.

"Komm! Help me," cried Helmut from his room. Prem stumbled over a chair. The cry for help startled him. He entered the room in a flash and found the old man gasping for breath on the floor. Having seen what had happened through the windows one snowy night, Prem maintained full control of himself.

"I can't open that drawer," Helmut cried convulsively. "Please help me."

Prem went to the cabinet below the painting of a landscape and tried the handle. It seemed tightly jammed, but by forcing it, he succeeded in opening it. The contents scattered all over the floor. So he gathered the plastic containers, a few small bottles and a syringe onto a tray and brought it to the bedside.

With an incredible will and self-command,

Helmut tried to lift himself up from the floor.

"My pills, bitte..." he tried to indicate the small bottles and the plastic containers.

He stayed a while with the sick man, but since there was nothing else required from him, he left the room so that the composer could rest. On the way out Prem noticed the disorder of the writing desk and the scattered papers on the floor. He did not look back but kept the door ajar so that he could enter quickly if his host called out for help again. After turning off the television, he lay on the settee.

Gradually the dawn made the outlines of branches and snowy landscape visible. It was a bleak morning; nothing moved, nothing broke the silence. At about nine o'clock the telephone rang.

"Good morning," Prem answered calmly. "Sorry I can't speak German. Can you speak English? Yes, he told me that you would call yesterday. Can you come this morning? Please come as soon as you can and call his doctor for me too. Herr von Regnitz is dead."

Before people would arrive, Prem tidied up the house, putting the papers in neat order. Then he covered the corpse with an eiderdown. Standing at the bedside, he looked sadly at the body. Then he touched Halmut's forehead which was cold and brushed the snow-white hair so that the dead man would be presentable to the visitors.

"Goodbye, old man," Prem whispered and left the room.

The first person to arrive was the doctor. Prem watched him coming through the snow, carrying his small leather case. The man was tall and hefty. Gravely he stamped his feet to get rid of the

187

snow on his boots.

"In his bed," Prem offered the information.

Whether the German was thankful or not, it was difficult to decide; certainly, there was not even a grunt or a word of thanks.

After seeing his dead patient, the doctor made a telephone call, looking more stern and disturbed than ever. When Prem came out from the kitchen where he had put the tray with the champagne bottle and glasses away, the doctor stood warily at the other end of the living room, eyeing the Oriental with distrust. Prem saw the same silent accusation seen in the eyes of the cleaning woman.

The Siamese stood still as if hypnotized by the threatening look from the bulky German. Presently the door bell rang. The doctor turned and went to answer the door and let the caller into the house.

For some time the doctor and the conductor had remained with the dead man. When the two Germans reappeared, the doctor bore himself ape-like, his arms outspread and forceful, coming ahead.

"May I offer coffee?" Prem's voice trembled noticeably. I shall need the skin of a buffalo to cope with these people, he thought to himself.

"That would be nice. Thank you."

The conductor spoke, for the doctor as well, in English, with an accent of a foreigner accustomed to using English. They sat down side by side on the settee.

Prem was aware that the death of the composer weighed heavily on all of them. So he took time in pouring the coffee, keeping his hands steady. Should he speak first? It would break the spell.

"Was there any visitor to the house last night

188

or yesterday?" asked the conductor.

Now having put the steaming cups of coffee in front of the two Germans, the Siamese was ready to reply.

"After the doctor and the cleaning lady, no one called. Was he expecting someone? Who would brave the snow storm? No admirers or friends could have got through the snow, if they had even tried."

"The doctor believes that his patient died of an overdose of drugs," the conductor sounded suddenly quite impersonal.

Two against one, Prem thought as he observed how the two Germans sat so solidly side by side. The doctor shifted his heavy weight, preparing for any aggression that the Oriental might display.

"Really?" The Siamese looked up at the conductor.

"Did you give the injections?"

"Injections? No, I didn't.

While the two men held a conference in their language, Prem poured more coffee into their cups.

"In Germany," the conductor said in English. "It's illegal for anyone except doctors and nurses to administer drugs by injection to patients. You may have to be interrogated by the police."

"Very well then."

It was not only the foreigner's passive tone of voice that bothered the doctor, who fidgetted impatiently, but also the seemingly calm, inscrutable oriental face that aroused his annoyance.

Then three plain-clothes police arrived. While the five Germans held a discussion in the privacy of the room where the late composer was at rest, the Siamese took the opportunity to clear the coffee

189

table. Later he went up to his room to prepare to depart with the policemen. Silence would fall upon the house once again until Reinhard and Dhani returned. Till then Helmut von Regnitz would rest in peace.

Behind the conductor, Prem walked, wading through the snow with his hands in the pockets of his overcoat. The doctor said *Auf Wiedersehen* to his people when they reached the police car parked at the end of the accessible part of Königswieser Strasse. They bundled in, two in front, three in the back. Sitting between the conductor and the most senior looking policeman, Prem leaned back, his head resting on the top of the seat, seeking some comfort from this attitude and from closing his eyes after the longest, most strenuous night he ever remembered.

As the car approached Munich, Prem became alert. I'll remember this day, he thought, the 23rd of December 1975, riding into Munich with three plain clothes policemen and an orchestra conductor with the eyes of a dead man looking on. Of the city, he committed to memory, from fleeting glances: the streets crowded with people, the Christmas decorations, the frozen river in the middle of the city, the pair of bulbous church spires against the bleak wintry skies, statues and trees dappled with snow.

They took him to the Drug Section. Flanked by the tall and fair bulky men, the Siamese appeared relatively dark and small. Already Prem was made to feel as if he were some kind of a drug addict or pusher, or a drug trafficker of international repute. The eyes of men at the entrance and in the lounge area focussed not only on him but also on the musician. They entered a sombre office in which there was a desk, two chairs, and some steel cabinets; this disappointed Prem who expected to be taken to some grand Gothic edifice guarded by uniformed policemen. Two of the plain-clothes detectives disappeared, and the senior man invited the newcomers to sit down. The conductor and the Siamese sat with their overcoats folded on their laps facing the unoccupied desk.

Now that they were left alone together in the room, the conductor adjusted his armless steel-and-plastic chair:

"My name is Wilhelm Hagenbach."

He gave his hand for the Siamese to shake.

It never ceased to amaze the Oriental, this manner of shaking hands. You could touch hands not a moment too long or too briefly, squeezing it slightly, not too weakly or too hard, shaking it. What was it supposed to confirm?

"I tried to come to visit Herr von Regnitz yesterday, but it was not possible."

Prem braved the situation and looked Hagenbach in the eye, and reminded himself that he was dealing with a person of fame and an artist whom he had admired, therefore he should keep his big mouth shut, for fear of uttering outrageous remarks.

Hagenbach shifted and crossed his legs; the movement caused his hair to fall over his left eye, and he combed the lock back with his fingers halfway across his forehead.

"Was Herr von Regnitz very upset?" Hagenbach asked.

"Well, he dressed up for you, waiting for you

with champagne and all."

In the poignant silence, Prem tried to equate what he truly felt towards this man whom he had remembered since his first Prom concert at the Albert Hall in London. Was it Hagenbach's rarefied air, or the fame, the stature of an artist whose achievements caused envy as much as admiration?

"Is it necessary for you to be here with me?" Prem asked.

It seemed that Hagenbach did not expect this; he stirred and uncrossed his legs in surprise. For a moment he did not know what to say.

"Being involved might jeopardize your reputation. One never knows, there might be a reporter waiting outside."

"I would like to be involved," said Hagenbach and left it at that.

For now the policeman who had shared the back seat with them in the car came back into the room and politely briefed the conductor about the procedure, in the German language. Then he asked the Siamese to follow him. Prem obeyed and surrendered himself to the authority. In a small, brightly lit room he was photographed and fingerprinted. Returning to Hagenbach, he found that the new policeman, supposedly the owner of the desk, was there talking with the musician. This man, smoking a cigarette, looked mean; his face was narrow and pale, needing flesh and a touch of humour.

"Sit down, please," commanded the Commissar.

The Siamese delayed, standing next to the conductor, wiping his fingers with his handkerchief. The Commissar cleared his throat impatiently, and

Hagenbach shifted. However, Prem took his time, sitting down, and kept on wiping his fingers, hardly looking at anything else.

"So! We have caught up with you!" the Commissar decided to begin at once.

Though the policeman's decisive tone of voice was meant to be a threat, to the Siamese it sounded amusing because of the quaint accent.

"You think you are clever. Nein? Very clever. A little trick. Nein? Giving zie old man zie injections."

Putting his handkerchief away into a pocket of his trousers, Prem looked up at Hagenbach:

"I don't know what he is talking about. Do you? Ask him to speak English, please," Prem said, emphasizing each word.

Nothing seemed to ruffle the conductor who appeared polite and correct at every turn; he repeated in fluent English what the Commissar had just said.

"Tell him then, please," Prem said to the conductor, "that I came here to answer questions regarding the death of my host in a civilized manner, not to be threatened. If I am to be treated like this, I shall only answer questions in court."

For the first time in his life he wanted to be defiant, to stand up against the authority. The nature of a buffalo in him surged, rearing its dangerous head and sharp horns. To use his own devices, allowing the eyes of the buffalo to glare and the horns in readiness for an attack, he was in his own element. As a result, the Commissar and the conductor held a rather long discussion in their own language.

Meanwhile Prem came to his senses. Because for centuries buffaloes had been tame and docile, they had always been ready to submit themselves to their masters or to the ones who surpassed them in strength and in qualities. Therefore the glaring eyes and rearing head of the buffalo subsided. He felt ashamed of his recent conduct. He who had been an acolyte, had taken the Eight Precepts and the Vipassana should not have resorted to such a common practice in combating intimidation.

He glanced at Hagenbach and tried to fathom the damage he had caused. Since the musician had been maintaining his politeness and the air of the well-mannered gentleman throughout the interview, it was difficult to tell whether he would think unkindly of Prem after such a performance.

Prem was ready to surrender himself to Hagenbach so that whatever they had to go through in this predicament would be done with a degree of integrity and in a calm and thoughtful manner. Then I shall go my separate way, Prem thought to himself. Never to see this man again to spare him the memory. I know now that I don't deserve anyone's affection and friendship. It's better to be alone if one fails to behave decently and to cultivate friendship.

What could the two men be saying to each other for so long? Prem wondered. One had stepped down from his podium, condescending to get mixed up with the police in the drug squad and with a Siamese cad who could be as devious as a beast that poverty had raised, and the Commisar who had seen innumerable criminals and dealt ruthlessly with them.

As for Prem, this experience had not been what he dreamed of at all in deciding to come to Germany. All he wished for was a white Christmas, and the first touch of snow.

The conductor and the Commissar stopped talking. For a moment they waited, watching the crestfallen Siamese. Why wait? Prem asked in silence. I won't raise a hand to defend myself from the blows. Tomorrow the newspapers all around the world would be carrying the news. Would the bold headlines be: Great German composer died of overdose of drugs? Would it be said who did it? There were only two of them in the lonely house, cut off from the world by the snow. One was dead and gone, the other could keep a secret in the deepest region of his mind, be as mute as a tree or the snow.

"The Commissar wishes to ask you to make a statement," Hagenbach was saying. "It would be helpful if you can give details of the state of mind and the condition of Herr von Regnitz prior to his death. And you, please, state whether you made the injections or not."

Could Hagenbach be using the apparatus of the Drug Squad to obtain information for his own purpose?

Without looking up, Prem asserted that he would comply. So then the tape recorder was set. He began with his soft monotone:

"If no one had told me that Herr von Regnitz had been ill, I might not have known that there was a sick man in the house. To me he looked quite normal. He kept to himself a lot in his room, working on a piece of music till it was finished. I hardly saw him for he only came out once at night for something to eat, and not wanting to disturb him, I kept out of his way. Then yesterday before noon, he invited me to his 'workshop' or his study to celebrate the completion of the tone-poem..."

Prem stopped because his mind suddenly recalled the name of the work: Death. It came back to him like an omen of which he was not aware at that time. He trembled now thinking of it and goose-pimples ran over his whole body. Had Helmut been grappling with his own imminent 'Death' all along?

"He was all dressed up as if he was going to a gala premiere of his own concert, in black-tie but without any flower in the lapel. He was in a good mood, looking pleased for having finished his work. So we drank champagne and tried to make conversation. But then all of a sudden he wanted to be alone and said that he must do more work. I left his room and did not see him again till about eight o'clock in the evening when the door of his room burst open and he cried out for help. So I rushed to his room. He asked me to help open a drawer where he kept his medicines. He took some pills and after I gave him a glass of water, I left his room..."

"What did you see in that drawer?" the Commissar asked.

"Some small plastic containers and bottles. There was also a syringe."

"You saw a syringe," the Commissar stressed.

"Yes."

"Repeat the affirmative again."

"Yes, I saw the syringe."

Then Prem could not go on. It seemed as if

his own mind had jarred.

"Please continue," Hagenbach prompted.

Prem looked up at the humming tape recorder. To this machine he said: "I brought from the kitchen a glass of water for him then I left him, thinking that he might need rest. But after the news at nine I turned off the television, and quietly went to see how he was doing. He was leaning against the pillows propped up against the top of the bed, looking quite comfortable in his gown, half-covered by the eiderdown. He beckoned me to pull up a chair and suggested that I should fetch a bottle of champagne from the fridge to celebrate an idea."

"For a new work?" I asked.

"No for this one, *Tod* or *Death*", Herr Von Regnitz indicated the huge volume left open on the bed between us.

"But you told me that it was finished."

"No, it's going to be the UNFINISHED. How could one know Death for real till Death comes to take one away. So I will leave it unfinished and after I am dead, then I will know." Herr von Regnitz smiled at me, but I was not sure then whether the smile was sad or sardonic.

"But when you're dead, you won't be able to work!" I protested, trying to be humorous.

"That's true. But I think I would know when I shall die. I might have my friend, the conductor who could not be with us today, by my death bed. I shall tell him about it until my last breath," he said in the most serious manner. So to change the subject I went out to the kitchen and brought a bottle of champagne to celebrate the new idea. I don't like to drink, and I don't like champagne, but I drank it with him all the same.

"We toasted the *unfinished.*

"But Death had not left us at all; it seemed to be hovering around, in his mind. Eventually he said:

"Aren't you curious how I know when I will die? Doctors have given me three months to live," he simply smiled at his own remark. "And they have been so polite and kind about it, trying to keep it from me. I forced Frau Muller, the house-keeper, to tell me. Just to scare her and to see to whom she was loyal. It was fun to shake her up a bit. She has been coming and going here for over fifteen years since I returned to Germany. Have you met Frau Muller?"

"Yes, but we did not speak."

"That's her. But she's good at heart. Would you be so kind and take the tone-poem away to the desk?"

Now it was Hagenbach who stirred, turning to look at the Siamese. Prem became aware of their attention, but he still spoke directly to the tape re-corder. What did Hagenbach do, and where was he during 1938 and 1942?

"What would you do if you had only three months to live?" Herr von Regnitz asked me.

"I don't know," I said. "Maybe I'd write some-thing down so people might remember me, or just go home to my village and spend the last days in an utmost awareness of each minute passing by, in total appreciation of each hour, and in peaceful union with the surroundings and be happy with resigna-tion from life."

"Sometimes you do suffer from pain, a stroke or trauma. What would you do to cope with pain?"

he asked.

"I have a great capacity to endure pain. I have fallen from trees, from my hut, from buffaloes. There were wounds, bruises, burns, scars."

"You didn't take any pain-killer?"

"No, there isn't any in my village."

"I always thought the people in the East took to opium or drugs as a way of life. Maybe I am wrong. Well, right now I am beginning to feel an attack of it, in my heart. Here." Herr von Regnitz rubbed the left pocket of his gown. "Anyway, the pain might go away and I shall not take any more pills. Tell me, how could you cope with your pain?"

"One just has to, I suppose, and go through with it. For me, pains come and stay so long, but when there is an ounce of happiness, it goes through me so quickly like there were holes in my heart. Happiness never stays long there. Here." I rubbed my own heart.

"Well, right now I have both happiness and pain, and it seems that they are having a big battle here too. I am happy because I have seen another possibility in my tone-poem. Many thanks to you for asking about childhood. You might not know then what you have given me. You gave me an idea. And now I shall leave the tone-poem unfinished so that at the very end, my friend who could not be here with us tonight, will finish it for me. You see on the desk there is a letter I have drafted for him. He will know what to do with it. His name is Wilhelm Hagenbach. He goes a lot to London. Have you ever seen him? He's also a friend of Danny. Last season, Hagenbach conducted many concerts in London. Quite a great man now. You'll meet him later on. He'll come to see me when the snow clears away. And for Christmas he always comes for a drink. Right now, let's have another bottle. I can see your glass was empty a long time ago. Would you be so kind and go down to the cellar? A man who has only three months or less to live deserves something nice. There are a few bottles of Latour 1961 left there, at the far end of the cellar. Please bring a bottle."

"I went down the narrow stairs underneath the house and brought the wine up to the study, fetched new glasses from the cabinet and the corkscrew from the kitchen. This bottle must be something very special because he took care to direct me how to handle it and leave it open for a while before serving. Wine is also wasted on me and I can get drunk so easily on it."

The Commissar shifted with impatience. However the Siamese did not seem to see or to take the hint.

The tape came to an end, so he stopped there and returned to his fingers, rubbing them while waiting for the Commissar to reset the machine.

"Did Herr von Regnitz mention anything about Berlin?" Hagenbach asked.

"Berlin?" Prem asked the tape recorder which kept on humming, whirling on its course. "Berlin? Yes, he talked of Berlin saying that it was a waste, the way they tried to inject life and the arts back into it. Berlin would never be the same, the old Berlin which was almost dead or should have been dead in 1942 or thereabouts. Since then the city could only be transformed into something else. He also talked of the old Berlin, what it used to be. In front of me, he had built the city up and I could see it as the centre of German life and art, and now its death or *Tod* which was the word he used. He was trying to tell me that it was not so much the imminent death of a man that he had been trying to compose in his work, the last one — the tone-poem called *Tod*. It was also the death of Berlin, so it seemed, one superimposed on the other; each grappling with its own death, or Death comes to them, doing its identical work: The man and the city experiencing their transfiguration at the same time..."

Here Prem faltered; his voice became weak and it was apparent that he trembled. Was it only this reference to Berlin in *Tod* that Hagenbach needed, using the hand of the law to pry it out of him who was unfortunate enough to be with the composer at the hour of death? Hagenbach might have already pocketed Helmut's letter left on the desk to be read three months after Christmas. It should have been Hagenbach who sat at the deathbed, taking notes to finish off the tone-poem, and not him, who knew nothing of music.

"Then I made an excuse and said good night. I went up to my room and slept. In the morning about eight I came down, and because the study was on the way to the kitchen and the door of Helmut, sorry, Herr von Regnitz's room was partly opened, I went in and found that he was lying on the floor...No, I did not, repeat did not give him the injections or any medicine of any kind," Prem agitatedly concluded. He wanted to get away now.

Exhausted, Prem feared that he might lose control of the situation. His hands began to tremble, so he held his hands tightly together, hiding his fingers between his thighs.

Yes, there were two reporters waiting outside. Hagenbach declined to confront them; therefore, the Commissar arranged for them to leave the room by another way.

Walking along the street, Wilhelm Hagenbach had to stop a few times to wait for his charge to catch up with him. They entered Neuhauser Strasse from Karlsplatz. Shops were brightly lit and decorated with Christmas colours and gift-wrapped parcels and pines coverd with cotton wool to resemble snow. Outside, on the streets, the snow was real.

"This area has been closed to traffic, reserved only for pedestrians. It's quite an interesting place," Wilhelm Hagenbach said and took the lead again.

Farther along Kaufinger Strasse they came to Marienplatz.

"Are you tired?" Hagenbach asked politely.

"Not really. You've longer legs and so walk much faster than I."

"Walking fast keeps you warm."

"You see more things, being slow."

The conductor might be wondering about what he had done to cause this Oriental to be overly defensive.

In front of them stood the neo-Gothic Rathaus. Prem noticed the snow-covered gargoyles.

"On the tower there," said Hagenbach stooping slightly with one arm on the shoulder of his companion, the other pointing. "See there? The carillon plays at certain hours and the puppets dance."

In a second the bell struck to announce six o'clock.

"It's yet too early to eat. Let's walk farther. Then we'll find a restaurant for dinner."

Hagenbach led again, skirting around the Pillar of Mary, passing under the archway. At the beginning of Tal, they turned left, following a smaller street.

"I think this wine cellar is good. Like a glass of wine here to warm you up?"

They sauntered in and waited for a waitress to find a table. Prem could guess why Hagenbach chose this place; it seemed unlikely he would be known or recognized by the staff or the customers. He could be anyone here instead of a famous musician hounded by reporters. Here in this ordinary wine bar, Hagenbach appeared to be just another German taking his visitor around Munich. The place was crowded, but after a moment of waiting there was a table for them at the back. Hagenbach took off his overcoat for the waitress to hang up, and suggested that his companion should do the same. Then they sat down. How his voice flowed when he conversed in his German, so polite, even when he spoke to a waitress.

"I asked for a good bottle of wine," Hagenbach turned to tell his guest. "I hope it's agreeable to you."

"German white of course," Prem spoke as if he was world-weary, sophisticated, ironical and Danny-like. "Yes, that would be delightful."

And he hated himself for it; for intentionally trying to hurt Hagenbach.

Their bottle came, but the waitress poured the wine sloppily.

"I could teach her a lesson or two on pouring

wine," Prem said, but suddenly his facial expression changed from indifference to sadness. For he was reflecting on the previous evening when Helmut von Regnitz prompted him how to treat and open and pour their Latour 1961.

"Zum Wohl," said Hagenbach.

"Zum Wohl." Prem reciprocated and elegantly held up his wine glass, the way Dhani had taught him. You'd hold a white wine glass at the stem, with your little finger sticking out.

The waitress offered them the menu, but Hagenbach suggested to his guest that they should move to another restaurant for a good dinner after this bottle of wine.

"You handled the Commissar very well," Hagenbach said, smiling.

"Really? But if you weren't there he would have eaten me alive. I know he would. With those cool eyes and a sneer on his lips. He would. I am sorry. I behaved so abominably."

Wilhelm and Prem smiled at one another. They did not say anything for a while. Then, they moved off to 'a proper restaurant' the conductor frequented.

"It's near the National Theatre," Hagenbach was saying. "The food is excellent and it's not so noisy. We often go there after concerts.

Prem noticed the 'we' and took a deep breath before going into this new place which bore a French name but seemed Spanish inside. Herr Hagenbach was welcomed by the head waiter who helped with the coats and showed them to their table, while some diners whispered to remark on his presence.

In such a place, you'd take time reading the menu and carefully choose your food. Despite Dhani's training and the English suit from New Bond Street, he felt ill at ease.

"Let's see if they have a Latour 1961," Hagenbach said, glancing at his guest.

"I shouldn't drink too much," Prem pretended that he did not get the point.

"Why not? You don't have to drive, neither do I. I'm wise to leave my car at home."

Like Helmut von Regnitz, Hagenbach could have been devoting his life to music. To excel himself, to be the master of his craft, he had to be dedicated to it, putting a frame around his life — a boundary within which music and music alone mattered. Had Hagenbach ever ventured out beyond this frame? Had he allowed foreign elements or any involvement to disturb the orderliness of his dedicated life? If I could enter Hagenbach's private world, Prem thought, and wander through, like going into a Bavarian forest because one is attracted by the mystery of the snow-covered landscape, what use would it be to know intimately all his facets as well as being able to acclimatize oneself to the four seasons in a European country? Eventually I shall return to Siam to live a life of a mute, concerned only with survival. It will be too far-fetched to keep Hagenbach and von Regnitz as a frame of reference in trying to create works of art in Siam. A more realistic frame of reference would have to be invented after leaving Europe.

Meanwhile Hagenbach was politely giving their orders to the head waiter. It sounded charming — the German language spoken by this baritone. Then Hagenbach made an excuse to leave the table so as to make a telephone call. Prem surmised that his wife must be told. Were they very much in love, Prem wondered. She stayed home while he flew off to various musical centres of the world. But she knew that he would return to her. And if you got to know them, she would be the one who kept up the correspondence and signed the postcards or the Christmas cards saying how busy he had been. No I shall not have the pleasure of receiving a post-card from her. Prem was entertaining himself with the thought when his host returned and said:

"I've just spoken to Reiner on the phone. We agreed that I take you home by the S-Bahn and when we get to Heeringen we can ring him from the station and he'll come to pick us up there."

Prem yawned. But Hagenbach became busy with the sommelier who had brought a bottle of wine.

"Sorry, no Latour 1961," Hagenbach said to his guest.

"You'd be sorrier if you give me too much wine. We Siamese peasants are very jovial when drunk and could be very personal, saying awful things," Prem said.

"Yet you seem to have got on rather well with Helmut who was notorious for being terribly difficult to get on with. You should consider yourself lucky he invited you into his studio."

"And only to kick me out after one glass of champagne?"

Hagenbach smiled at the remark.

After the sommelier had poured the wine, the conductor raised his glass:

"Merry Christmas and Happy New Year."

As if Death and despair had not occurred.

Just on the tip of his tongue, Prem was about to say: 'What a pity, Helmut could not make it through Christmas. Otherwise'..., but he checked himself in time. Let the dead rest; he had suffered enough. Right now it was not the time and place to resurrect Helmut. Moreover, neither Hagenbach nor Prem himself was ready to discuss *Death*, the unfinished tone-poem. Let the police have the finger-prints, photographs and the half-truth statement and nothing more.

"Are you married?" Prem asked, fixing his eyes on his own wine glass.

"Yes," Wilhelm Hagenbach said mildly.

"Any children?"

"Three. Two boys and a girl. You'll meet them when you come over to have dinner with us. My wife and I would like to invite you to come to have Christmas dinner with us tomorrow. Reiner and Danny too. We live just about twenty-six miles from Heeringen."

Prem accepted the invitation. The red wine in his glass was disturbed with a tremor from his fingers. Frau Hagenbach would be well aware that thousands of music lovers around the world clamoured for him, and merely looking at you she would know that you were just another in the thousands who gazed at him with admiration or secret envy.

The secret admirer took a big gulp of wine and asked for more.

"The police would find my fingerprint on the syringe," Prem said off-handedly. "You see, I picked it up from the floor when it fell out from the drawer."

Wilhelm looked directly at his guest; his clear blue eyes beamed into sharp focus. "You have no need to worry about that now."

"But they will believe that I made the injections!" Prem said agitatedly.

Hagenbach put his knife and fork together and wiped his lips with the napkin.

"By the way," said Hagenbach. "Did you know that Helmut was left-handed?"

"No," Prem looked puzzled. "Why?"

"His left arm had a needle mark."

In silence the two men looked at one another. Prem put his elbows on the table, his chin resting on the folded fingers, looking into the eyes which remained clear and blue. To himself, he said: Politeness will never allow this man to tell me how he holds a distaste for lies. Well, truth from a distorted source would seem as crooked as the passages through which it came. Too bad for Wilhelm Hagenbach. He would think I make up things to suit my own imagination.

"Let's hurry and get away from here before the crowd comes out from the theatre," Hagenbach suggested.

Will this man hand me over to the German police? Prem asked himself, while Hagenbach was paying for dinner.

Sitting closely next to the conductor on the train, Prem closed his eyes, seemingly trying to sleep. Meanwhile he tossed slightly with the train, thinking: Hagenbach will hand me over to the police in the end, once he had taken from me what he needs.

When they were met at Heeringen Station and driven home, Hagenbach talked in German to Reinhard and Dhani. Arriving at the house, Prem made an excuse and went to his room. He tried to sleep but could not. How quiet had the house been. Had Helmut really been taken away? Once again curiosity and thirst made him get up. Putting on Dhani's old dressing gown which was a little too large for him, he tip-toed downstairs. He was surprised to see light coming from under the door of the study. Not wanting to be caught peeping through the keyhole again, Prem knocked and opened the door. At the desk, Wilhelm Hagenbach sat, still in his suit, obviously losing himself in the volume of the tone-poem. He did not look up to check the intruder until Prem had advanced right up to his side.

"You should be in bed sleeping," said Hagenbach.

"I came to say goodbye," Prem said.

Early in the morning Reinhard and Dhani took Wilhelm home, leaving a note to say that they would return within two hours. 'Away! Away!' Prem heard a whispering voice. Could it be a cry from the old man? He did not see any soul about. In the study, Prem sat at the edge of the bed in which Helmut had died and Wilhelm had slept. 'Away! Away!' he heard again. But having already packed and dressed for the departure, he could afford to linger in this quiet and sombre room in which death and despair had occurred.

He got up from the bed, and at the desk, ran his fingers along its top as a gesture of goodbye. Having tightened the belt of his overcoat, he picked up the small suitcase and left the house. He stopped now and then on the road to change hands and to rest. From Heeringen Station, he caught a train to Munich, then a taxi took him to the airport.

Right up to the last minute he still feared that the German police would stop him from boarding the aircraft.

Airborne, he huddled in the seat, feeling insecure because he was still above Germany. By now Dhani and Reinhard would have known that he had escaped. Having put himself up as the guarantor, Wilhelm would certainly be disappointed. Prem sighed: Yes, many things are better left unsaid. Many, many things.

The first time I spied Helmut from outside the house while I was standing deep in the snow, seeing how he suffered pain, I began to be involved in his life and death. Why must this experience be a painful one? I wanted only to have a glimpse of a German childhood and a summer day, and to follow the father and the son into the woods. It was a warm, sunny September day in 1948 when fir, elms, and beech trees began to turn autumnal. At Muthal there was a forest-house by the stream called Wurm. How the leaves, red, yellow, golden, green, caught the sun.

The flowering geranium on the window sills confirmed that it would be possible to reconstruct their life in Germany after returning from Switzerland. Of his wife, Helmut did not talk much except that she died in 1945.

"You must come here again, Prem, and stay with me one summer, and I'll take you along the track Reiner and I went that day in September 1948.

You'd love our forest in summer time, and the Wurm is cool and clear. Fritz, the owner of the *Forsthaus* in Muthal would prepare a typical Bavarian dish for you..."

But there would be no more summer walks through the forest to Muthal for Helmut, who in his last moment murmured:

"Who is outside? Gunther, Eschi, Leni, Erich? My wife must have gone out. She loves picking mushrooms in the forest on a day like this..."

You too could see them, blond, fair-haired, blue-eyed. You'd have done anything possible to bring him back, to give him once more a summery walk through the woods in September, to hear again how he says 'work-shop'. Helmut, poor old Helmut. What a tragedy to die in the arms of a stranger.

"...Why, why do you cry, boy? Smile. Komm, smile. My wife said goodbye to me with a smile on her lips. You don't know what it was like to smile in 1945..."

If Death could be made tangible, you would be tearing at it, protecting the old man from its approach. In Napo a witch-doctor would be throwing magic grains of rice all over the room to keep off Death, but here you had nothing except bare hands and tears.

"Listen, Listen carefully. Here he is. Look! Death. Death is exactly what I've perceived for *Tod*. Look! Die Verklärüng..."

9

April 1976

Spring was turning into summer. Another year had passed since his departure from home.

Prem had written a letter to Honourable Brother, the monk at the Wat, talking about his studies, of living with Dhani Pilakol, and of the way he and Dhani talked about many issues, especially concerning their country, of the conflicts and tensions he had been experiencing in coming into contact with the West. But now, Prem concluded, I somehow regret the discontinuity of observing the Eight Precepts and the practice of Vipassana. I have broken most rules of the Precepts: I lie, desire, and give way to lust, revel in comfort and luxuries, and consume intoxicating drinks. As for Vipassana, it would be perilous without your guidance. And now I crave to be a poet! My Venerable Brother, if only you knew how un-Buddhist and unholy I have been! As a result I am now suffering conflicts. You see, while Buddhism preaches detachment, the West encourages involvement, desire, conviction, individuality, and craving. It seems that one must crave to expand and produce, to make the world go round, so to speak. The whole of Western productivity rests on this. It pains me to stand in the twilight zone somewhere between the two worlds. More painful still when the temptation to drift towards the West becomes, at times, too strong to resist...

But Prem decided to continue when, in October, another year at University College began. Setting himself to the task, he produced the text of a long cantata, not entirely for practising his craft, but also from echoing the poignant Hagenbach — von Regnitz affair. Writing 'A Cantata', his most demanding and longest work, preoccupied him. It took his mind off other matters. Working on the poem, there were times when the frustration and the intensity of his feeling grew beyond his control.

When the opening for the New Poetry Competition was announced, Prem submitted 'A Cantata'. He knew why he had to give his German experience a form, but in entering the competition, he did not aim to win.

The completion of 'A Cantata', however, gave him a sense of relief. Time too helped turn the wound into a scar. He blushed a little, thinking that he, like Wilhelm, had been exploiting the experience, turning it into a poem. How had Wilhelm been doing with his *Tod?* A postcard from New York did not tell much: Mein Lieber Prem, I'm longing to return to Germany where summer is so glorious this year. I must get you back to Munich at once when I have a few free days. You will be most welcome to stay with us. My hotel is near Central Park, sometimes I can snatch a few moments to walk in the Park to 'set me up'. The Met is one of my favourites...

A few months later, it was announced that 'A Cantata' by 'Sontaya' won the First Prize of a thousand pounds. Having been aware of how much he owed to others who had been kind to him, the poet who had suddenly so much money in his pocket tended to be too eager to give, extravagant in gifts and entertaining. He bought a wrist watch for himself while the money lasted.

Having borrowed the car from her father, Stanley Durham of Bradford, Elizabeth drove Prem to the Brontë Country. In Haworth they stopped to visit the parsonage where the Brontës used to live. They also went to St. Michael's church in which Emily Brontë was buried. Looking at her grave, Prem said:

"Come, Lizzie. They've thrown the church on her, but her soul is still roaming the moors."

Crossing the Lower Laithe Reservoir, they came to Stanbury, a quiet and small moorland village where they parked their Austin and began to follow a footpath which led to the ruin of Top Withens, supposedly the site that Emily Brontë used for *Wuthering Heights*. Following the uneven path made up of loose stones, the two pilgrims gradually climbed the barren slope to the Upper Heights where a derelict stone farmhouse stood and where a few sheep grazed. Here Prem halted. He looked back at Stanbury and dots of farmhouses scattered all over the moors below. The vast landscape was of green against grey; heavy clouds drifted above and there was a gentle wind. Stanbury Moors and Haworth Moors were homes of heather, tussock, and gullies, where small ravines run and sheep roam.

"Imagine, the eternal lovers — Catherine and Heathcliff together, like you and me, now light-footedly skipping over these moors," said Prem.

"I don't care much for the Brontë sisters. Thomas Hardy is my man," Elizabeth brushed her hair from her face.

"Shh!" Prem silenced her as if the wandering

soul of Emily Brontë might hear.

"We made a trip to the Heights once when I was at Bradford Grammar," she softened her voice to suit the dreamy look that came across his face.

Her cheeks flushed from the sun and the wind; her long light brown hair flowed across her face. In sheer happiness, he stood looking at her, as mute as the moors, for she had given him a glimpse of her childhood. He could imagine Elizabeth Durham skipping over the heath and himself, Heathcliff-like, dark and demoniac, following her like a shadow.

He followed her now, heading towards Top Withens.

"I feel as if I'm coming back to a place I knew so well," he told her. "Listen. I can hear Joseph muttering!"

She turned to face him. Shaking him with both hands, she said:

"Come on, Prem. It's the sheep there. Baa! Baa!" But he refused to be shaken out of his reverie. He continued to visualize Heathcliff brooding in the most desolate part of the moors.

"Lizzie, let me tell you something. I'm like Heathcliff. Nobody knew his origin and thought he was a Gypsy because he was dark and vile. I'm dark and could be very villainous," he scowled and made a face at her. "When I was young, a tiny boy, I fell off our hut and lost consciousness, then a year later I almost drowned. Both times they put me up on the fire and gave me up for dead. My mother disowned me in our way of giving up one's baby to the spirit which wanted the child for its own and so brought death to it. But by giving me away to the spirit who has adopted me for its own, she let me live!" Prem threw up his hands to show how happy he was to be alive.

"To live and be very wicked," Elizabeth said.

"How am I wicked, my fair-skinned English lass?"

"By making people fall in love with you and then dropping them."

"Or making people hate me and then drop me?"

"Yes, very nasty and awful."

It was her turn to make faces.

He chased her up the hill till they arrived at the ruin. The wind moaned through the crevices of the deserted house of which the roof had come down along with Joseph's curses. On the other side of the building stood stunted twin sycamore trees. Prem checked the wind-combed branches and measured roughly with his eyes the length of the bough that had scratched the window panes of the room in which Mr Lockwood, the troublesome guest of Wuthering Heights had passed the night. In Mr Lock-wood's nightmare, he heard and saw Catherine Earnshaw-Heathcliff-Linton begging to be allowed in. *I'm come home,* she cried. *Let me in! I'm come home from the moors.* But being afraid of her hold on him, he cut her hands on the broken pane. Blood ran but still she persisted. For years she had roamed the moors!

Wuthering Heights had such a commanding view of the moors that Prem was held spell-bound looking over the barren slopes and valleys and farmlands where Emily Brontë had sought solace in desolate and unpeopled places. Yes, lonely and desolate places attract lonely people, he said to the wind. He exulted in the experience of having embraced and made communion with the location where she had found sustenance and peopled Wuthering Heights from the richness of her imagination and her craft of hewing from stones the characteristics of Heathcliff.

Prem picked a twig of budding heather, and gave it to Elizabeth, saying:

"Here, I give thee the token of my joy," in a Shakespearean manner. With his right hand over his heart, he bowed to her.

Elizabeth did not laugh, but she slowly approached him, receiving in the manner of a maiden of the middle ages, the gift of joy. Then together they sat on the ruin of a wall looking over the loneliness of the moors.

"A penny for your thoughts," she said, clasping her arms around him to be close and included in his world.

"Oh, to be in England now..."

Prem laughed; his laughter, blown by the wind, got caught in the tossing heather and tussocks. Once more the sun broke through the clouds.

On the way back they spoke very little; the rain clouds had drifted over the Pennines and the air turned chilly. She drove nonchalantly, her mind was somewhere between unfeeling and cautiousness, with her eyes fixed on the road. It had been raining slightly. What kind of childhood had this girl had? Prem pondered her life. Looking at Elizabeth he saw an English landscape with which he had been familiar, from which he would depart eventually on his journey back to Napo.

"Lizzie, do you have any idea what it was like

in 1945?" Prem asked out of the blue.

This was what she did not like in him; Elizabeth realized that most times when he was quiet, she was not with him for he could be anywhere far removed from the present.

"Where are you now?" she took her eyes from the road to look at him. "Why 1945?"

Helmut von Regnitz who had died in his arms said something about 'you don't know what it was like to smile in 1945' and that was over thirty years ago.

He turned his eyes away from her. To keep him with her she said;

"I wasn't even born. I'm not that old! Nineteen forty-five, eh? Weren't they jumping with joy for winning the war?"

"Who?"

"The Allies! Who else?"

"So what were the Germans doing then?"

"Why do you think of the 'Krauts' right now?"

"How many times have I told you not to call them that?" He glared at her.

"Now I can see a devil; it's lurking in your eyes," she said.

They continued the remainder of the journey in silence.

Among those with whom he had come into close contact, Stanley and Emma Durham of Bradford had shown him the world that Dhani Pilakol would not enter, the world of the working class. As for Prem, he felt that the Durhams were genuinely kind to him. Stanley Durham, a burly man, held qualities which Prem could recognize as those shared by his own people in Napo.

Emma Durham looked frail when she stood next to her husband; it was quite obvious that she had aged faster than he. A bundle of energy, however, Prem observed, not as frail as she looked.

He would remember the Durhams long after leaving England. They had been generous and hospitable. Prem appreciated his first-hand experience staying in a working man's home. At one point Prem visualized Mrs Durham as a mother in Napo, going through hardship and scarcity, coping with disease and physical pain without modern medicine, suffering from the heat and flies. When she moved, Prem followed her with his eyes, seeing her opening the refrigerator, bringing out food, turning on the tap, preparing a meal or making tea in a clean and well-equipped kitchen. At the same time, he pictured her doing the same in Napo, searching among baskets and jars of stinking fermented fish for something to cook, blowing at the embers to make fire till ashes turned her hair ash-grey. No refrigerator. Nor table or chair. Poor Emma Durham would have to learn how to squat! But here, in Yorkshire, revolving around her life and her person was the protection of the laws, the police force. There was a certain kind of decency and fair play and freedom which the English seemed to take for granted.

Prem tossed and turned in bed, in the house of the Durhams. That night he once more made a vow that he would not become a teacher in a city, but in a village where a dedicated teacher like Kumjai was most needed. But then he must create a survival scheme so he would not perish along with Kumjai.

10

October 1976

"Just as well you were not here," Dhani said broodily.

Prem, who had just returned to their flat in which a group of Siamese students had held a meeting, was not surprised to see the mess. It was obvious that the party had been lavishly provided with food and drinks.

"We can't run a tiny organization like our Siamese Students' Group without strife, disunity, deterring one another from doing things, without being at each other's throats. And these are the people who would one day become leaders," Dhani lamented.

Prem quietly lingered for a while, but then he went into his room so that he could read his mail in private. Piang had written:

My dear Tadpole,

When there is nobody else to write, I have to tell you sad news. Grandmother has passed away, and now Mother is ill. This is the time of year we need every hand to harvest the rice. Don't worry though. Sickness comes and goes, making us stronger. My second child, a girl, is a joy to us all.

The news reached us that Teacher Kumjai was killed in a clash with the troops. It has been said that he was one of the most wanted guerrilla fighters in our area. His head, dead or alive, was worth many thousands in money. But Toon told me the other day that Kumjai was still alive, that the news was false, that our teacher managed to escape. However, our village and several others near us have been declared a guerrilla-infested area. Police and troops come at times to take control and flood us with propaganda. So you can imagine how I sometimes feel about all this, about some men who speak of 'going to join Kumjai' or 'going into the forest', when they stupidly deliver themselves into the hands of the loan sharks and middlemen. How brainless some of us can be to lose their money and their land in a gambling den or by borrowing money without taking care when they sign a piece of paper. Only Teacher Kumjai could help them in these cases but he is no longer with us.

I am not supposed to tell you much about things in this vein, for Mother feared that you might be unhappy to know that Toon is now married to someone she did not even know. Please forgive me for telling you sad news. It is better, I think, that you should know now rather than when you come home.

I miss you a lot.

Piang.

Prem was dazed by the news. What could one do when one could not be there to share their seasons, sickness, happiness and unhappiness, good years and bad years? As long as he remained in England it would always be only a longing for a life to be lived close to the soil, to follow the course of a village life, to be content with the placidity of the plain, to rescue Toon from a marriage by proxy, and to bring up children away from strife, falsehood, chaos, and corruption.

He once boasted that all he wanted was to be able to help his country and its poor. What a silly boast now, made in a distant time and place. Here he longed to be a scholar and a poet!

Of Teacher Kumjai, in sheer despair, Prem shook his head: If Kumjai is dead, then they've murdered an innocent man, a dreamer.

Waves of pain came and stayed.

It was difficult to imagine that on his arrival in Napo, Grandmother would not be there to greet him. Would Mother survive this illness? Would it sound bitter to say to Toon: You couldn't even wait for me. Why did you think I left home for all these places all these years? And when my hands are strong enough to pull you out of the mud and the mire, you give yourself away to someone else. Poor Toon. I can't help you now.

When he looked at himself, he thought: In England, you are trying to embrace a European way of life, hobnobbing with lords and ladies, enjoying luxuries, thinking and writing in English. Like Dhani, you will return to Siam with an Anglo-Saxon mentality!

"Prem!" Dhani banged at the bathroom door. "Are you still alive in there?"

I have tried to get along with Dhani just as much as a peasant would be subservient to the elite of society. Have tried. Have gone through with it all along, meekly obeying. Made lonelier by the distance between Napo and London, between Beethoven, Mozart, Wagner and the wind-rustled leaves and the cries of crows and the croaking of

222

frogs over the vastness of the rice fields. Have tried. I have. Have gone through without a word of complaint the Munich affair. Buddha. God. Christ. I have tried to rise from the mud to catch some light. Let me fall back then, back to the mire, back to ignorance, subject to evil, to brute force, and damnation.

He wept.

"Are you still alive in there?" Dhani shouted again. "Hurry up! I need a bath too. We're having visitors this evening."

Dhani's voice rasped in his skull. Pain burned on and smouldered without any outlet.

The word *visitors* was a clue to be *presentable*. To avoid unnecessary remarks or reproof from Dhani, Prem took the precaution of carefully selecting his clothes and his shoes. The final touch was to don a cravat the way Dhani had taught him. Then he checked his hair and face. How presentable he looked! Nobody would ever suspect the torture inside.

Having helped himself to a glass of wine, he sat in an armchair in the living room, listening to a record, waiting for Dhani to be ready for his guests.

Seeing that his friend was having a drink, Dhani said, on the way from the bathroom to his bedroom:

"Give me one, too, please."

In the kitchen, pouring a glass of wine for Dhani, Prem weighed his losses and gains. Should he remain in London for two or three more years, he might become another 'Danny', another westernized Siamese. The difference between the real Danny and the pseudo-Danny would be that on returning to Siam the latter would be very poor,

223

lacking any support to maintain the princely aura and bearing. What use would it be to have one's name boldly attached to a few books of poetry when villages like Napo were still subject to scarcity, robbery, ignorance, and illness without doctor or medicine?

"Ah, thank you," Dhani said, accepting his glass of wine.

Then their visitors arrived. Prem lowered the volume of the music and prepared himself to encounter the situation in which social intercourse would call for charm and politeness. The ejaculation of surprise and joy at the door indicated that the visitors were a Siamese woman and the other an Englishman. They took their time to admire Dhani's collection of antiques and *objets d'art* in the hall. The scintillating and cultivated voice of the woman indicated that the prerogatives of the elite were hers. While they lingered in the corridor, Prem got a whiff of her perfume. And when she entered the living room, he stared at her in dumb amazement, at the shining Siamese silk of an evening dress and the glitter of diamonds and pearls.

"Prem, Mrs Salika Lloyd. And Peter Lloyd. All the way from the Heavenly City, Siam!" Dhani introduced the Lloyds to his friend.

The lady's beauty and poise were dazzling. A Siamese elite of Dhani's status, Prem observed. Of her husband, he reminded Prem of the *farang* who took his visitor to see the Wat and pushed aside the boy selling temple rubbings.

Offering to be the butler, Prem made and served drinks.

"Congratulations!" Dhani raised his glass to

224

the Lloyds.

Allowing time enough for his visitors to sit, the host turned to the lady and asked:

"How do you feel, to be Mrs Lloyd now?"

"Oh, Danny! Don't keep harping on it!" she protested. But with coyness, charm, and poise. Her diamond ear-rings shook with haughty, splendid fire.

For a moment the buffalo boy seemed to be enthralled by her beauty and demure gait and glittering jewels. Of her husband, Prem perceived the life of an expatriate, an executive in a commercial firm in Siam, now married into one of the wealthiest families, living in a great mansion teeming with servants and chauffeurs, owning a holiday villa in a beach resort on the coast of the Gulf of Siam.

Then their conversation was revealing more and more; they talked of the political changes which had occurred in Laos and Cambodia, of their concerns and resources, the rising political unrest and the lack of confidence in the security of their well-being in the face of change.

While the Lloyds' voices rose and fell, Prem could see Kumjai as the teacher was struggling bitterly to free the lowest human lives from ignorance, from being prey to corruption and injustice through the power of education. But then Kumjai had to take another course, being chased out of the village, a victim of thieves and murderers. Yes, it was Kumjai who said to the passing wind and to the unheeding ears and beady eyes of the children in the forlorn little shack called school that we would learn in time how to make sacrifices for the good of all, instead of the selfishness and the well-being of one's family and clan and the concern for one's power bases.

Prem saw Kumjai traversing the smouldering plain on a sweltering day, carrying his broken dreams.

"Let's go then. I booked a table for 8 o'clock." Dhani stood up in readiness to take his friends to a restaurant of his choice. "Come, Prem. Put on your jacket."

"I'd rather stay home, if you don't mind."

"Why?" Dhani cocked his handsome head to impose his prerogative.

"I have to finish an essay tonight.

Dhani recognized a stubbornness which on this occasion he did not deign to overcome.

"Have a good dinner and a pleasant evening," Prem politely bade them goodbye at the door.

Salika Lloyd's perfume still lingered, however.

Prem felt that he had been out of touch with what was actually happening in his country while Dhani did not care since he had successfully detached himself from being Siamese. Dhani preferred to live in England or anywhere except in the country where he was born. The Pilakols' Swiss bank accounts would enable the heir to live in affluence all his life, wherever he chose.

Yes, Toon, Prem thought, if you ask me now whether it's worth all the heartache and tears of parting, I begin to think that the ambition, the departure, the aspiration to earn a degree is becoming a sordid waste.

Then the telephone rang.

"No, Danny isn't home, Sir. But I'll tell him as soon as he comes in," Prem said politely to the Ambassador who had rung to break the news that

226

another massacre had occurred, on October 6, 1976 in Siam.

That evening the BBC television network broadcast the massacre which shocked him out of his senses. No, it could not have happened in my country, Prem thought as he was watching the television. It could not have happened in Siam. It must be a mistake. The BBC mistook a killing field in Cambodia for Siam.

At about eleven o'clock Dhani returned to the flat. Prem checked Dhani's face and realized that Dhani had not heard the news.

"His Excellency wants you to call him right away," Prem said.

"Is it that important?" Dhani checked his watch.

Still smelling of wine and the good time enjoyed with the Lloyds, Dhani allowed his person to be physically pushed to the telephone. However, the telephone conversation was brief and Dhani's good humour still made him bright and cheerful.

"Well?" Prem looked at his friend.

"Well what? What do you want me to do? Shed my tears? It's your country, not mine."

Cynicism augmented by too much wine carried Dhani too far.

"As far as I'm concerned, I don't give a damn. The July Revolution! The October 14 bloody turmoil! And now the October 6 massacre! Christ! All I can say is get on with it. Kill each other off!"

Suddenly the sorrow caused by sad news from Napo and the bitterness in the depth of his heart came forth. He hit Dhani in the face.

"Say you're sorry for saying such a thing,"

Prem threatened to hit Dhani again. "Siam is your country too!"

Dazed with pain and blood, Dhani said:

"I'm not sorry, but you will be."

Blood spoiled his grand attire now. Picking himself up, the wounded man went into his bedroom and closed the door.

Becoming aware of what he had done, the buffalo boy unclenched his fists. From his own wardrobe he took his coat and left the flat. Outside, the autumn air surged upon his murderous face. The Victoria, a local pub around the corner had closed its door, and the last few drinkers were making their way to their cars. He walked quickly past them, bending his head to hide the anguish which might burst upon his face. Where was he heading for? He did not know or care.

A blow on the nose and a few drops of blood from Dhani was nothing in comparison to the October 6, 1976 massacre, and the news of Kumjai's death. The faces of the murderers and the murdered blown up on the television screen revealed the primeval cruelty and the nature of the beast which were embedded in the hearts for centuries.

Of Kumjai, Prem thought: Why must you go against the fierce current? And now your eyes haunt me, testing me whether I will keep our dreams going. No, I will not keep them going, Kumjai. I shall have to murder them too. Here and now I decide to return to Napo to forever be a native son not so different from any other man of his land. I shall return to Napo and relive my life as if I had never been away.

The hurriedly found room in Earl's Court offered a narrow bed, a threadbare carpet, a naked bulb for light. Here most tenants were young people. They spoke with cockney-like accents which, Prem learned later, was Australian.

No, he would not serve. But how could he rebel? How could a mentally deformed person, who had been maimed and crippled for life so as to be meek and manageable without a mind of his own, stand up against such a powerful mechanism?

Then one day he recalled what Dhani had warned: "Don't do anything which will jeopardize your scholarship." What? Things like being involved with Elizabeth Durham and negligence towards studies? The indenture of the scholarship stated that the scholar must pay double the amount of money granted in case of a breach of contract. Having carefully examined the contract of the scholarship, Prem saw one way out. He would not complete his courses, and therefore fail to win a degree. Without a degree, he would be of no use to *them*.

So from now on he would read only books which interested him, and go to lectures when he felt like doing so. Since October 6, 1976, there had been some commentaries, criticism, and reviews in the press and on television. When one's country was in focus and criticized, one either turned a blind eye or took an interest and made careful studies of the criticisms. Prem went further and read the essays and books of Robert Halsworthy, D.J. Enright, and of several English scholars and writers who had lived and worked in Siam.

Should I be ashamed of some of the Siamese qualities? Prem asked himself. Every time he saw a look of contempt in the eyes of the Europeans, he told himself that in Siam there was at least Kumjai who was honest, dedicated and incorruptible, that there were qualities which he cherished as well as some which he wanted to change.

11

September 1977

A vow to renounce my passport to an office which could be used to create power and wealth was not enough, Prem thought. I might do more than that. Being mentally maimed for life, I must learn to overcome my intellectual shortcomings, and look deep within myself for certain abilities which might have escaped crippling, and then develop them to their full capacities.

It seemed justifiable to return to the beginnings. If you, like Dhani, would not go back to the old, you would be forsaking it; thus you would travel on into the new, a homeless, lordless, friendless man, forever a foreigner, an outcast, reluctantly tolerated as a different being. To be an alien was to be more than an outcast, remembering old times and weeping over fond ones left behind. But then he might be miserable in Napo, knowing that there were the Pilakols, the Phengpanichs, the Lloyds and their like, and in other countries people more fortunate than his own who had to dig up roots and catch frogs and insects for food. Oh, why had he ventured away from Napo at all? What had he done to have to go through these tensions and conflicts?

His mother had said to him when he was a little boy: One day you will be taken from home to live in a far-off place because you have taken the little birds away from their mothers and their nests. You have been cursed by the mother birds! You will have no home of your own, travelling from place to

231

place all your days. Wretched and fearful you will be, like the little fledglings you took away from their nests.

How right she was. He was paying for his misdeeds, destined to live the life of an exile even in his own country, an alien without a sense of belonging and permanence, without fixed abode. There was, however, the perpetual memory of childhood, of home, of the herd and the plain. But now that small sunburnt boy existed only in dreams. This one was different and spoke a different language, while the Napotians were still bending over the same paddies where rice was yet thriving, and life there remained almost the same as ever...the wind blowing the golden sheaves, the laughter of the reapers... noisy warblers carrying off seeds to their nests... crabs busily digging their holes before the water dried away. These were the same as ever; only he had changed.

Now above all else he heard: Listen! If you return, everything will be fine, and everyone you love is waiting for you. The village is still peaceful, and you will soon be calm and unfretful. Don't cry. Don't be weak. You're stronger than you think. Come home and allow the sick to see you for the last time and then help take them to the pyres.

The spirit of the dead and of the living who were dear to him passed before his misty eyes. The wrinkled face and the calm eyes of his old father, the wizened face and weary eyes of his old mother, the stern face and questioning eyes of Kiang, the beautiful face and soft eyes of Piang and the loving watchful eyes of Toon and the dark faces and pleading eyes of the Napotians and other villagers in their forlornness broke through the haze and walls of this towering city, watching him, moving nearer and nearer, but suddenly far, far away.

Forgive me, Prem cried out to them. Forgive me for not being there when the land needs ploughing and the rice needs to be reaped, when the monsoon did not come. Forgive me. For I'm a stolen nestling. I too am suffering.

The air seemed thin. From the north bank of the Thames, he watched gulls poised on the lips of the wind. Bridges, ships, St. Paul's, age-old edifices, the curve of the Thames, leafy sycamore trees on the north bank. All the while he was saying good-bye to London, to a brief spell of freedom, to writing and reading, to poetry, to the shabby little room in Earl's Court, now that the departure must be planned.

He arrived at the Royal Festival Hall where he would meet Dhani and Wilhelm. The occasion would mark the first meeting with Dhani since moving out in October 1976, almost a year ago. On approaching Dhani, who was dressed in his usual immaculate evening suit, Prem was aware of his jeans, his suede shoes, and his long hair.

"Sorry I'm a little late," Prem said awkwardly. Since the October 6 incident in the flat, they had once more become strangers towards each other. The blow on the nose had caused not only a flow of blood but also damage to Dhani's dignity and their relationship.

"Wilhelm wants to see you after the concert is over," Dhani said. "Let's go in. It's about to start. Here's your ticket."

The coldness of the voice and the manner in

which the words were spoken were like those of a polite stranger whom one had asked for directions. Should Dhani want revenge, Prem would gladly receive the punishment, knowing that this could be the last time he would ever see Dhani.

As for Wilhelm Hagenbach, time had healed the pain. The effort to create 'A Cantata' and its completion had turned the wound into a scar. Now what remained would be the last distance he and Hagenbach had yet to travel together along the road on which *Tod*, the last work of Helmut von Regnitz, would be finished.

Wilhelm Hagenbach, the conductor, was bowing from the stage to the capacity audience. This movement caused a lock of his hair to fall over his left eye and he combed it back with his fingers — a gesture Prem remembered so well from the Prom Concert in August 1974. Would Wilhelm, like Dhani, act as if we were strangers? Prem wondered. Wilhelm had good reason to give him the cold shoulder, the politeness reserved for the public at large. Against that politeness you would be just another outsider. After all, you ran out on him after he had promised the Munich police to keep you in Germany for further questioning. When Dhani rang from Hagenbach's where they were sitting down to Christmas dinner, you simply put down the receiver and did not answer further phone calls. A lot of water had flowed under the bridge; yet it was difficult to forget the Hagenbach affair. It was useless not to respond to the postcards, letters and phone calls. Frau Hagenbach had not been asked to write the postcards to say how busy her husband had been; he himself had had to write from

Karlshausen, New York, Berlin, Stockholm, and even from London itself when he came to conduct concerts. After October 6, 1976 you saw no one except Elizabeth Durham and a few Australians who lived in Earl's Court. Months had gone by; and in 1977 Toon had a baby boy, and Piang and Kiang added a child each to their families. Yet you slogged along the streets of London, season after season, longing for the departure for home, keeping alive in your heart the strength and determination to create and complete two books of poems which came under the titles *Poetry of the Rains* and *Poetry of the Plains.* These poems were no longer born out of bitterness and despair. By looking back from England, the distance gave truer perspective, and you were no longer blindfolded by unthinking nationalism. Now that the contact with the West had ceased to cause so much tension and pain, the conditions and living in England had become neutralized; and being independent of Dhani, on his own once more, helped him to finish the poems.

Wilhelm was conducting Dvorak's Cello Concerto in B Minor. Whether Wilhelm was truly a great conductor as the record covers and some critics claimed, the ears of the buffalo would not be able to tell; but the music moved him, giving him joy.

Then the Cello Concerto came to an end, and Dhani applauded energetically. "Splendid! So superb!" Dhani said. Hagenbach came and went, bowing and sharing the ovation with his guest artist, the female cellist.

After the interval, and having sat down to Beethoven's ninth symphony, once more Prem made Wilhelm a centre-point of his concentration. Deep into the first movement Prem reached the outer region of Hagenbach's sphere, but moving internally. However, like being attracted and drawn to the snowy landscape of a foreign country, he dared to enter, only to become afraid of the vastness and the mystery of the unknown territory. Yet he would not turn his back on the mystifying land-mass, so he remained revolving in the outer strata, far enough to be above mediocrity of thoughts and feelings. When the bass came forth in the 'Choral' movement with its very profound and tremendous: 'O, Freude!', Prem's whole being shook like a small aircraft in flight caught in a storm, shattered by the thundering voices of the hundred members of the choir. He was swirling in an endless space.

Yes, it could be partly secret envy of the success and greatness of Hagenbach that kept one away from handing oneself over to him — not the fear of being handed over to the police later on! At the end of the symphony, Hagenbach reaped another success amid the cheers and applause. He was generous with the soprano and the tenor and the bass who came to the fore, all holding hands and bowing together to their clamouring admirers. What an inspiration!

"Let's go back stage to meet Wilhelm." Dhani was saying.

Prem followed like an obedient child. It would be useless to resist other forces which were much stronger than his own, now that he had seen and heard what dedication and greatness could do.

In the artists' room, Wilhelm was talking with a few musicians, wiping his face with his handkerchief. Seeing his visitors, his face looked brighter;

236

and he beckoned them to enter. However, Prem stayed behind with self-effacement and humility.

"We'll take a taxi," Wilhelm said to Dhani, politely declining Dhani's offer to drive them to the hotel.

"Give me a tinkle some time," Dhani said to Prem on his way out of the room.

"I will," Prem answered.

He realized that their relationship had been a fragile one, broken easily with a blow on the nose. Any attempt to repair it would be superficial.

When they got into a taxi, Wilhelm put his books of musical notes and an attache case between them and said:

"You should pay us a visit. We'll show you some beautiful parts of Germany. I know that Christmas was hard on you. Everything is all right now. The autopsy ruled that Helmut died of a heart attack, and as you knew, his condition, with excitement and some drinks..."

That Christmas seemed like yesterday. And now he was walking alone along the track into the forest of fir, elm, and pine trees to Muthal where Helmut and Reiner had their lunch in the open by the Wurm in September 1948. Would there be another September for him in Europe? He did not want to look Wilhelm in the eyes, though what needed to be spoken years ago must be spoken. Tremblingly Prem said:

"If I ever set foot in Germany again, it would not be for a better visit, but to remember everything of the past, to revitalize all the memories, so that I would never forget them."

Having delivered this remark, he looked ahead

to where the taxi was heading, and was surprised by the discovery of why he wanted to hurt this man. Was it possible to wound Hagenbach? Great men might be too big and too important to be hurt by such pettiness. However, Prem did not turn to observe his target, for he was trembling deep inside. He was then clinging to the lifeless body of Helmut von Regnitz, gazing at the gate of death and the airless distance through which a soul would be taking an endless journey.

"I want you to join us for the premiere of *Tod* in Berlin this November," said Wilhelm in his usual polite tone of voice.

Outwardly Prem seemed becalmed now, so that his stubbornness would remain covered in some form of sober disguise between no and yes. He offered to carry Wilhelm's briefcase and other things while the taxi driver was being paid.

In the most famous hotel in Mayfair, courtesy and the trained eyes of the hotel people forbade them to notice the long hair, the jeans, and the unbrushed, old suede shoes. The lift confined them. The passage became a maze. Where would it end, this journey? Prem sighed.

"Since you've already completed Helmut's *Tod*, why do you want to see me?" Prem asked as soon as the door was closed behind him.

Wilhelm seemed to be too occupied with putting his things on the desk to say anything for the moment. If he had not acquired understanding of human behaviour and nature, he might be wondering why he bothered to be involved with this young man.

"Please sit down," the host turned halfway to

be polite, after he had taken off his bow tie and unbuttoned his collar. Then he talked on the telephone with Room Service to ask for a bottle of champagne to be sent up. After putting down the receiver, he said to his guest:

"I'll take a quick shower, so please let the man in if he comes while I'm in the bathroom."

The room service waiter came with a trolley of champagne in a bucket and a tray of glasses.

"Shall I open the bottle now, Sir?" the man asked.

"We'll wait for Herr Hagenbach to come out from the shower," Prem answered in his proper English well-learned from Dhani.

Before leaving the room, the man carefully adorned the bottle with a white napkin.

Then Hagenbach appeared, wrapped in a large white towel.

When will it end, this journey? Prem asked himself, looking at the conductor who was putting on his black rollneck pullover in front of the dressing table. The black trousers and the black pullover emphasized the fairness and the blue eyes. After combing his hair, Hagenbach joined his guest.

"Sorry to have kept you waiting," he said.

The shower and the change of clothes had obviously freshened him. He smelled of fine eau de Cologne. Taking the champagne bottle from the ice bucket, he skillfully uncorked the bottle.

"Cheers," Hagenbach raised his glass.

"Cheers."

Champagne still tasted as bitter as ever to the Siamese. Its quick, sharp dryness took him back to the time Helmut had opened a bottle to celebrate the tone-poem called *Tod.*

"About *Tod,* Hagenbach turned half way to address his guest. "I didn't complete it. After consulting with my colleagues, we think it would be better for the time being to leave it as it is. You may know there are several 'unfinished' works of great composers. Some of these unfinished pieces have their own structure. The unfinished symphony of Schubert for instance has been left as such though several composers have tried their hands at completing it. As for *Tod,* I may try my hand at it later on. And I'm still interested in more details from you."

Hagenbach paused, and remained standing tall, looming in his dark clothes. But Prem was silent, thinking: I am here, not quite at your mercy, to give all that you need from me.

So he stood up. In an effort to speak, he behaved more like a hooded man upright in his own shadow.

"It may seem I am a liar; but in truth, I have to resort to imagination," said Prem. "Now I myself don't know for sure what is what. I'm afraid I might give you an inaccurate account."

He turned away from the blue eyes to face the windows looking on to the roofs of other buildings, thinking of putting into spoken words a certain lonely understanding of his own nature. But it sounded lame when he tried:

"I have too powerful an imagination to retain facts. Yet stronger than imagination is my private logic."

Having thus spoken, the poet agitatedly moved as if under torture. So then the conductor had to go

240

back to his chair and sit down, asking his guest to join him at the table.

"You were like a snowy Bavarian country scene at which I looked in awe and admiration, knowing that it's a place impossible to make a home and stay. I have to react to you the way I do."

Now it was Hagenbach who was at a loss for words.

So the poet swallowed a big gulp of champagne. Trying to steady himself and control his voice, he ventured to add:

"I can see beauty in most things. I've loved a girl, a herd of buffalo, have loved my teacher who might be dead now, and a northern boy who lost his life by facing an army with his bare hands. I could hold their love within me for they are within my reach. But yours is impossible. Besides I tend to agree with Helmut when he said that human involvement is a waste of time. May I have more champagne, please."

Under the cover of a self-commanding air, it was difficult to tell whether the conductor was taken by surprise or not. But as smooth and as polite as ever, Hagenbach said:

"Before he'd become a recluse Helmut had behind him fifty years of human involvement as his resource."

And poured the champagne for his guest.

"Did he tell you how I managed to enter his enclosed life?" Hagenbach asked.

"Yes, he did. Was it in 1958 when you were twenty-six? He said a young up-and-coming composer called at his house wanting to conduct one of his operas. The young people of today, Helmut said, were so eager to accomplish something in a short time. But that young man claimed he wanted to rebuild the musical world of Germany. After the war, everybody seemed so busy building or rebuilding what the war had destroyed. If it was not for the fire in your eyes, Helmut would have thought you were boasting. Luckily you asked for his work composed before the war. This is what he said: After 1945, what I heard sounded brittle. I fear I've lost heart in what I do. I wondered whether these young musicians, especially Hagenbach, would notice how brittle everything I create could be. Maybe he only pretended that his interpretation was guided by my earlier works."

Wilhelm smiled at the remarks and the recollection of his own.

Then it was time for the host to suggest dinner. The guest declined.

Hagenbach had to apologize:

"I usually eat late after a concert."

But Prem, covering himself with a mask, could smile mildly. What could unmask a hooded man? Lines from 'A Cantata' came flooding back to him. He tried to flow with the tide. He knew this would happen: what he had imagined for his prize-winning poem was to be imitated by the actuality.

Prem got up and left the table. With his wine glass in hand he went to the window. Wearily he said goodbye to Europe, to the pleasure and pain of coming into contact with the West, to London. The sound of goodbye rang through his brain, echoing.

Below, the streets of London seemed indifferent as always whether one was to pace them in daylight or late at night.

12

December 1978

"Is he here yet?" asked the Student Officer as soon as Dhani opened the door for him.

"Not yet," his host responded bluntly.

"What has become of Prem?" How could he become a different person almost overnight. I thought he was an exemplary student, and he did so well in the past. You and I have seen how well he behaved. Then he failed his examinations and disappeared for a long while without telling anyone of his whereabouts. He must think he is here on holiday, being paid by the government to do what he pleases. One day I went to see him at his flat and caught him in his room with a girl, both stark naked, drinking wine from beer glasses. And your friend had the cheek to invite me to join them! Since then I refuse to check on him at his place. And he refuses to come to see me in my office," said the Officer, and blew his nose.

Dhani served coffee in the living room.

"For all I know, your friend may lose his scholarship if he doesn't turn around and make good again," the Student Officer declared. "He could not be tolerated should he fail one more year and behave badly the way he does."

"Cognac?" Dhani asked and opened the glass cabinet. The Officer sucked his teeth.

To Dhani, it had become a habit to ignore what he did not want to hear or see. He poured the cognac for himself and for his guest. Meanwhile, the visitor appeared rather agitated. Pacing the floor, the Student Officer spoke in a tone which he generally adopted to impose his authority and importance.

"I've been compelled to make a report on your friend. My recommendation could influence the decision whether, in the case of misbehaviour and failure in his academic performance, the scholarship would be terminated."

"Would you please sit down," Dhani pointed to a chair near the window.

The Officer dropped himself onto the chair to emphasise his professional despair.

"Do you have any idea where he went and what he did when he took off without telling anyone?" the Officer said peevishly.

Dhani went to his desk and produced from the top drawer an envelope:

"From the horse's mouth," he said, handing Prem's letter to the Officer.

The Student Officer opened the envelope and began to read:

November 24, 1978

Hotel Gotty
11, rue de Trevise
Paris

Dear Danny,

I've just found a cheap room to stay for a while in Paris. Rue de Trevise is not exactly off rue de la Poissonniere but it's near to the Folies-Bergeres.

From here, it's just a short walk to the Louvre where I have been spending hours looking at the paintings and sculptures which seem to come to life when you stand there contemplating them. Knowing no one here I discover each day many places on my own, mostly by walking. Not being able to speak French, I can hardly communicate with the people, who seem to be willing to leave you alone. So you end up walking along the streets of Paris for days without speaking to anyone. A few words of greeting exchanged with the concierge of the hotel are enough to cure the weariness on returning at night to sleep.

At eight o'clock in the morning the maid knocks at the door to bring me coffee and a croissant for breakfast, which comes with the price of the room. I let the coffee and the croissant go cold, lying in bed to go over once more the thoughts and scenes which occurred during the last few months while I moved about Germany, Sweden, Norway and Denmark before ending up in Paris.

Let me start from the beginning of this journey: Accepting Wilhelm's invitation to attend a concert at which he was a guest conductor of the Philharmonic performing *Tod* in Berlin, I left England for Germany. We met in Berlin, and having the day free, I joined a group tour to East Berlin so as to have a glimpse of the remnants of the old Berlin which to a large extent is now in the East.

Our bus tour entered East Berlin through Checkpoint Charlie where two uniformed officials, a stern looking man and a corpulent woman, entered the bus and asked for our passports.

And from this checkpoint, an official tour

guide took over, starting to tell us in an 'official' tone of voice which sounded like a recording about East Berlin. I tried desperately to recall Helmut's voice as he described the old Berlin to me.

Then I saw the tall churches, the stately houses, the university buildings, the opera house, the museum, and government buildings — some of which have been left unrepaired as reminders of the defeat and the devastation of the War. What I hoped to find was the Berlin to which Helmut dedicated *Tod.*

The calm and gentle voice of Helmut returned to me as the images of the old Berlin conjured up for me on that wintry night in Heeringen loomed over the real City.

As a guest of Wilhelm in the Kempinski Hotel, I enjoyed a few moments when he was not wrapped up with his concert programme and the company of his musicians and admirers. We have long passed being totally serious in our conversations, for now he seems to have revealed another element of his character: his sense of humour. Watching him dress for the evening of the concert, you would think that it was his very first conducting experience because of the way he made a fuss about his handkerchief, the cuffs of his shirt, and a button that came loose. I had no idea that a celebrity could take so much care about his appearance. I began to wonder whether the lock of hair over the forehead and the emotional expression on his face while conducting the orchestra were parts of the show.

Performing *Tod* in Berlin might have a special significance. Whether it was Helmut von Regnitz's intention to have its premiere in Berlin or whether it was Wilhelm's own ambition, I was not so sure. However, the concert was well received, and Wilhelm would count it as another success in his career. The programme included Mozart's Piano Concerto No. 21, followed by Richard Strauss' Last Songs, then *Tod* came last. The house gave a tremendous ovation at the end.

Then there was a champagne party in the hotel to celebrate Wilhelm's success. About ten or twelve musicians from the orchestra and several of his admirers, not to mention a few bejewelled ladies of charming wit and elegance, crowded into the suite. This crowd seemed to rival the highbrow clique in London. The only difference to me is that here they spoke in German. While the party was going on and the champagne was flowing, I saw two Hagenbachs: one was the public figure of the acclaimed Conductor, and the other was a man with whom circumstances threw me into intimate contact. Between the two there was an interplay of the severely disciplined, hard looks with the warm, sunny smile. It was to the Conductor I was saying the last goodbye.

Should I be grateful to have opportunities to observe how the talented Europeans are rewarded, how they strive to achieve their ambition, and how they conduct their lives? What could I make out of the intimacy with Wilhelm Hagenbach and the moments we shared walking through the forest of Heeringen on an autumn day? Despite some weak moments in which I could be envious of his stature, his success, his fortune and his friends, I could not lead a European life.

What I want now is to return to my home village, to the peasant life and to my beginnings. While it seems so natural to you to be a part of the European community and to enjoy the European way of life and culture, it would never work for me; it would seem false.

One day I shall tell you about a primary school teacher named Kumjai and about a young student from the north called Rit and of nameless old men and women and of peace from the rice fields and poetry and songs which heal and soothe troubled hearts. Then you might understand why I have to act this way and return to my roots.

Having said goodbye to Wilhelm Hagenbach, I boarded a train to leave Berlin for Sweden. Where was I heading? There was no real purpose in this, except to keep on moving. As soon as the train left West Berlin, two East German police officers came into the compartment. They checked my passport and wordlessly went through my luggage, then having handed me my passport, they left. In darkness the train sped on through some unidentifiable towns of northern East Germany. At about 2.00 a.m. the train reached Sassnitz, the point where it went into the bowels of a Swedish ship connecting this port to Trelleborg on the Swedish coast. While on board the ship passengers from the train could go into the ship's restaurant for snacks and refreshment. A cup of strong coffee cheered me up somewhat so I remained in the restaurant among sleepy passengers until the ship reached Trelleborg at 6.00 a.m. From here the train picked up the rail for Malmo, where it stopped. Changing trains, I took another, the first one to depart Malmo. I noted that this part of Sweden is of low farmland, sparsely populated. Later on the flat landscape gradually became sloping pine forests. There are some small, quiet seaside houses scattered among out-crops of low hills and stunted pines.

That day the ride ended in Oslo where I stayed the night. Norway, home of Ibsen, Bjornson and Gustave Vigeland, looked not so foreign to me. I walked around looking for a place to have dinner, ending up in a small pub in Stortingsgate. I stood there among the Nordics with a glass of beer, trying not to give any sign of being totally lost. Then I moved on after having dinner in a restaurant of the Continental Hotel. The air turned chilly and biting. The night crowd became thin and the footfalls sounded loud and echoing. I walked on along the quay, gazing at tall ships and dark shadows of sea-farers still moving about on the ships. I wished to intercept the tales and the gossip which the ships were passing on to the host city, to be told of ice-bergs and dolphins and albatrosses. And I longed to know what the city would tell in return.

From Oslo a driver gave me a lift. We took the E18 route to Karlstad, a small but stately city, in the heart of Sweden. The driver, Nils Danielsson, a florist of Karlstad, talked of his sunny holiday in Siam some years ago. Obviously he fell in love with our City of Angels and with a seaside resort. For his love of our country, he offered to put me up in his 'vonung' at Vanernsgatan for a few days. Though it was not the first time that I felt grateful to old Siam, I appreciated the good feeling that due to the pleas-ant time some nameless men and women gave to Nils Danielsson in the Heavenly City and in the resort, he, in turn, was kind to me. Obviously he had a rather vivid memory of his experiences during his short stay...the names of bars, beaches, people and restaurants. No doubt, one day he would see his travel agent and ask for the same tour.

During the day, when he worked in his flower shop, he gave me the key to his car. And I drove along country roads to Sunne, Torsby, Stollet, down to Hagfors, and Munkfors, stopping at lakeside places and enjoying the fresh Swedish air. At one or two places, I walked away from the car, into the pine forest, and disturbed a herd of elks. I stood still on the soft carpet of moss and asked myself: How could I go back? How could I overcome my crippled mind?

It was getting cold and misty. The lakes looked empty and placid. Nothing moved. Small boats were taken ashore, laid to rest, keels up.

By the shores of these lakes in late autumn, the loneliness and serene beauty reminded me so much of Jean Sibelius' music. In Karlstad there is an excellent library in which I spent many hours in the music room to listen to Sibelius' *Tapiola, Valse Triste,* and *Finlandia* conducted by Wilhelm Hagenbach from a DG recording. I walked along uncrowded streets and sensed the loneliness of a small town; I watched Nils Danielsson through the glass pane of his flower shop and saw him quietly trimming long stem roses and arranging them in a large vase. Then I went back to his flat, packed my bag, and wrote a note saying 'Thank you for everything and your kindness' and left without saying goodbye.

In Stockholm I found a room in a hotel near the railway station where you can have a smorgasbord breakfast of pickled herrings and bread and coffee for seven Kroner. I walked around the famous Opera House and heard Wilhelm's voice: "I love working at Stockholm's Opera House and enjoy a dinner at its restaurant". Without Wilhelm, I would not dare to enter the Opera House, its restaurant and its bar. Farther, I gazed with absorbed admiration at King Carl Gustaf's palace across the water on which a Finnish ship was leaving for home.

Then I fled from city to city, from Copenhagen to Amsterdam before ending up here in Paris. I have spent nights in lonely train stations, keeping awake and watchful in fear of my personal safety among the drifters who roam at night.

Now, at the mercy of this city, I long to be told by a kind and understanding person that I could be on the right track, that there won't be any regrets, in leaving Europe for home.

Meanwhile I'll stay on in Paris for a while, and if the Student Officer wants to get me, he will have to come over here to drag me back. Maybe it's about time. I can't hide any longer my contempt for this insignificant-looking man who holds a significant job. All he could do now is to quickly get me back to Siam.

Prem Surin.

Having come to the end, the Student Officer clutched the letter, waving it with desperate, speechless agitation. Finally he managed:

"Can I take this away?"

So then, without delay, he got up and prepared to go.

"If you promise to return the letter to me," Dhani said smilingly.

It was past ten o'clock but Prem, who was supposed to join them, had not turned up.

13

April 1979

"Please come in," said the First Secretary of the Royal Siamese Embassy, leaving the door to his office wide open.

Despite his high rank, the First Secretary had a rather dogged appearance as he stood there waiting for Dhani to enter.

"And thank you so much for coming to see me. Please sit down. I won't take much of your time. There are only a few questions I would like to ask you regarding your colleague, Prem." The diplomat sounded apologetic.

He gently closed the door and glided back to his chair.

"First, besides that English girl, has Prem any other close associates?"

The First Secretary had to clear his throat after his rising thin voice broke from his effort to control the situation.

"As far as I know," Dhani said firmly, "there are about three persons, namely Charles Tregonning, an Englishman, Wilhelm Hagenbach, a German, and Bruce, an Australian whom I know only by his first name, a neighbour in Earl's Court. And now would you have the decency to explain to me why I was called here?"

Dhani's face seemed an inch longer. For a few moments the silence between the two men was almost unbearable. Nevertheless the diplomat managed to smile, saying:

"It's not an easy matter to send a student back. The decision requires careful consideration. We're led to believe that Prem has become estranged."

Here, he paused as if to weigh his words. "Yes, estranged. There is no reason why he could not study and pass the examinations, but now it has been obvious that he has turned into a dissident. He drinks and acts waywardly. He shared his room with a woman, and he gets involved with homosexuals. Besides, our information indicates that your friend has been linked with a former primary school teacher in northeast Siam. This teacher was a leader of a group of insurgents."

"Am I involved in this, too?" Dhani interrupted.

The smile disappeared from the diplomat's face.

"Your father is. He is vulnerable because he has signed as the guarantor for Prem's application to renew his passport. How did Dr Prakarn agree to sign?

"I asked him to."

Dhani knew that his reply was curt, yet he maintained his attitude.

"I see," said the senior official. "Then, those poems of your friend. Are they really written by him?

"Sir, are you insinuating that Prem is not the author of his own works, or are you trying to discredit him?" Dhani stood up then.

They were interrupted by the arrival of His Excellency the Ambassador.

"Danny, pop in to see me before you dodge

254

away."

The young Pilakol remained standing, turning half way from the First Secretary.

"Perhaps you should not keep His Excellency waiting," the senior official suggested.

"Thank you so much," Dhani responded quickly, and went out of the room.

The First Secretary did not resent the pre-rogative and the close relationship the young man held with the Head of the Mission. He, who was from an ordinary family and had had to work himself up to his present position, could only admire high birth and wealth. However, Dhani's rudeness left a little mark on his mind. His annoyance rose but he kept himself in check, applying the usual regression by acting rather childishly as he went out of his office to ask a secretary for a cup of coffee. His thin voice rose and floated as he laughed, teasing her and complimenting her on her choice of dress for the day.

In the next room, Dhani could lean back now with ease and comfort in an easy-chair next to the Ambassador.

"So your friend is leaving us," His Excellency remarked. "How about you? Wouldn't you like to go back to Siam? It's about time your knowledge, your degrees, were put to use. Your father could arrange a top job for you. I believe he and your mother are keen to have you with them. From what I can gather they've already built a house for you. Maybe they have an eye on a girl for you too. How about that!"

The old man chuckled. But because Dhani brooded, the Ambassador said:

'Come, come, Danny. What's the point of going from one school to another when you are needed at home? One thing I don't like about your father is that he lets you please yourself too much."

Dhani became more depressed after he left the Embassy; there seemed to be a threat to his sense of permanence when the question of having to return to Siam was raised. For now he had established his European life to such an extent that to say goodbye to Europe would be disastrously painful. He could not see himself living with his parents in their home, for once there he knew it would be most uncomfortable to see, day in day out, servants kneeling when taking orders. He also remembered quite well the scene in his father's office in which men and women came and went seeking his favour. Some of these people behaved as if they were spineless; some were sly and many came with subtle offers.

14

June 1979

From the descending aircraft Prem gazed upon green fields and scattered villages and towns and swollen rivers which coiled glitteringly towards the Gulf of Siam.

Soon the Heavenly City came into view. Amid the shambles of wood and concrete, the gold-dappled pagodas of the Buddhist temples reflected the sun. On landing, he took a taxi to Wat Borombopit.

The temple seemed the same as he remembered it. At the gate the two guards carved out of the gigantic teak trees were still there as stern as ever, reminding him of the guilt of having to sneak in and out with Rit.

Prem hastened towards the monks' living quarters. The heavy suitcase, however, slowed him down. At the door of the old quarters, he knocked and paused and knocked again. Then a young boy opened the door, suspiciously eyeing the stranger.

"No, the monk whom you have just mentioned does not live here now," said the young acolyte.

Prem did not believe his ears, so he tried to look inside.

"Do you know where he could be?" Prem asked.

The acolyte shook his head and quickly closed the door.

As if stunned, Prem did not know what to do. Turning and looking around in a daze, he knocked again. The same acolyte responded. Looking at the youth, the memories of his early days in the temple ebbed back.

"I used to live here," he tried to explain.

The acolyte remained silent, allowing the stranger a moment to linger.

"Where, what part of the country do you come from?" Prem asked.

"Srisaket", the boy said timidly.

"I come from Burirum. Not so far from your home." But then, the door was again closed against further intrusion.

Within the city, Prem walked for hours along the busy streets, trying to recover from the weariness and numbness, but it seemed the heat and the fumes and dust exhausted him. The teeming faces of his race evoked neither the sense of being secure in their midst nor the pleasure of a home-coming. In the end he returned to his room in the Swan Hotel.

Towards the evening the cumulus clouds darkened and hung heavily over the city. Half-awake he heard the thunder. Thinking of the rain-echoing country, he pieced together some half-recollected phrases:

> *Rain,*
> *here comes a monsoonal rain*
> *but there's only a handful of grain.*

It was a song heard years earlier on that well-remembered landscape of endless plains at this time of the year, when the newly-ploughed soil lay partly flooded under the clouds in which a young peasant girl could read auguries.

Laughter was often heard then.

The flight had ended, making him a stranger in a familiar city. A soft thud at the tarmac landing. The first embrace of the heat and humidity on coming out of the aircraft. And being told that the monk whom he had served did not live there any more. Srisaket. Another boy uprooted from the rice fields. Rit was not to be seen ever again.

Prem consoled himself with the prospect of having his first meal, a genuine Siamese dish and a bowl of noodles. Clusters of neon signs were already flashing out the tempo of the night. He paused, wondering which way to go. On the pavements the hawkers set up stalls selling food, flowers, rubber goods, stationery, utensils, lottery tickets, and cheap jewellery. Through it all came the hullabaloo raised by each vendor shouting for attention. Soon he found a noodle shop which he entered and sat at an unoccupied table. He ordered beef curry on rice and a bowl of noodles with meat balls. As the words left his lips, the waiter shouted the order over the noise of the diners so that the cooks could hear. At the next table sat six young men with several half-eaten dishes laid out before them. Their faces looked reddish from the local whisky and beer. Their ribald language proved that they were close friends. How carefree and happy they seemed to be. Wasn't I once like them? Prem observed. Fun-loving, gregarious, pleasure-seeking, without caring for serious thoughts. Looking back now, he could see why Kumjai and Rit had to suffer. Prem hoped that Kumjai was still alive, that his death was only a rumour. Should Rit have survived the October 14, 1973 Uprising, he might not have made it through the October 6, 1976 Massacre.

The waiter brought the curry and rice and a bowl of noodles. Prem ruminated, trying to project in his mind the old, overworked, insect-bitten water buffaloes which had been slaughtered for cheap meat, whose peculiar taste recalled the texture of the earth made tender by the rains.

The air was still sultry. Bars, restaurants, nightclubs, massage parlours, and brothels were in full swing. The streets were busy with cruising cars and taxis. Two Negro sailors a few paces ahead halted, and a door of a bar was opened for them. The cool, smoky air surged out from the bar along with the blast of music. Prem was still reluctant; the door stayed open, so he allowed the sensual forces to take him by the shoulder. The crowded room was a swarming, palpitating world of its own. Twenty audacious young girls in scanty costumes were dancing on the stage of lights while a colour television on a wall was turned on. On top of everything else a movie was also being screened. He was seated at the bar, and when his sight became accustomed to the dimness, he saw the grinning, painted faces and the beady eyes of the women. How they pinned themselves to the customers. The way they leered and offered themselves. I'll understand these things one day, he thought. The beat of the music and the near-naked dancers lulled him to stay on. Well, it's the last stop, then home, he reasoned.

The bar girls somehow did not bother to lavish on him their professional charm and friendliness to get a drink or two. Whether he was seen through the eyes of these experienced prostitutes as a frustrated university student who would sit over a drink for hours or a male prostitute who would compete with the girls in a straight bar, it was difficult to tell. Then his eyes focussed on one girl whose badge carried number 66, a very young and pretty looking person. Being aware of his attention, she averted her gaze, tilting her head in a haughty fashion and moved away towards a European client whom she began to caress. The bulky *farang* fondled her in response and she laughed a girlish laugh, teasing him because of his hairy chest and the 'beer' belly.

Prem tossed his thoughts about as the lighted stage turned green, red, blue, green, red, blue, to the non-stop music, as the television presented violence, death, crisis, through the late news, as the projector flicked another kind of drama upon a wall.

As an observer, he preferred to watch the faces of the women more than the other attractions which the bar had to offer, wondering from what walks of life could these people have come, from which rice fields could some of them have emerged to reach this stage and the status of the women with numbered badges as their identity. He recalled having seen several Siamese women who had been taken to Germany, and he had wanted to know the extent of their involvement and the cultural change the women must have gone through; their losses and their gains, whether they might have experienced cultural conflicts and tension similar to his.

Sitting next to him was a middle-aged *farang* whose features could be described as being mild and pleasant, an honest open face with a well-tanned complexion. His hair was neatly cut.

261

"How do you like our women?" Prem heard himself say, trembling slightly from the effort to force himself to emerge from the depths of his thoughts.

"Sorry?" said the man, bending his head to be closer as if the din prevented him from hearing.

Prem repeated his opening line.

"Most beautiful," the foreigner answered, smiling.

For a moment the two men glanced around the bar as if to seek proof. They saw girls cajoling their clients, playfully fondling and teasing. Those women who had not yet made a contact for the evening had that sharp look about them; their predatory eyes glittered intently.

"East and West, the twain have met," the man said.

"In the flesh," Prem responded.

He smiled to himself at his own remark, thinking of the involvements he had experienced in Europe.

"My name is Bruce, Bruce Grange," the *farang* offered his hand.

"How do you do?" Prem took hold of the hand and shook it warmly.

"Are you Siamese?" Bruce Grange asked.

"If you please. But I don't come here often!" Prem laughed. How he outrageously came out of himself. "And you. Is this your haunt?"

"I'm a tourist. Arrived this morning."

"Then how could you remain alone, without these girls going at you? They'd certainly smell a tourist out and go at the guy like flies to honey."

"I told them I like boys," Bruce said. "Then

you came along."

"Thank you very much."

"Another beer?"

"Why not. Let me get it for both of us."

How solid he felt then, realising also that it had to be a *farang* who put an end to his stateless-ness upon the home-coming. Feeling grateful for the company, Prem paid for the drinks.

"Before dropping into this bar, I tried to find a place recommended by my travel agent, but I could not find it." Bruce produced a piece of paper on which an address was written.

"I don't know the actual spot, but I can help you look for it."

Another round of beer confirmed that the two men were no longer strangers to one another. Having left the bar, they sauntered along the street of Pat Pong, then a horde of men accosted them with their offers of live-shows, blue-movies, nice girls, boys, and massage. As the *farang* and his Siamese friend tried to ward them off, the horde followed, repeating what they tried to sell, competing against one another while they worked as a team in preventing their victims from getting away. Because of his height Bruce Grange loomed among the hustlers like a bull surrounded by attacking hyenas. Then Prem said something in Siamese but they ignored him since their prey was the *farang.*

"Taxi? Hey! You! Taxi?" shouted one taxi driver from the middle of the street, stalling his vehicle while making a rude, suggestive sign with his fingers by way of a tempting invitation to a pleasure. Bruce tried to disengage himself from the mob but was not quite successful. Again Prem said something in Siamese but then he came up against one thick-set man who meant business when he pulled Bruce aside and began to tell him in a serious tone of voice about the *Adam and Eve* shows performed every hour right in front of you. Because he had no way out, Bruce listened and then politely rejected the offer. Suddenly there was another new member of the gang pushing the others aside to get at the victim. This person was outwardly a woman, commonly known as a *krathoey* — a man dressed as a woman. The *krathoey*, gay and loud, immediately flanked the *farang*, promising him a good time. As an onlooker, Prem saw in a flash that she was picking Bruce's pocket. Instantly he snatched the wallet away from her hand.

"Your wallet," Prem said to Bruce. "Let's get out of here." Thwarted, the *krathoey* glared at the man who had intervened. Then the thick-set thug signalled his colleagues. One of them hit Prem in the face.

"This is a lesson," said the thug. "You are a Siamese, yet you betrayed us. Why do you love a *farang*? Is he your father?"

Prem was dazed with shock and pain. Tears blinded him. Were it not for Bruce who was pre-pared to take action to defend his friend, the thugs might have done him more harm for he was Siamese as they were, and was not helping them to rob the *farang*. However the thugs relented, seeing that the scene began to attract much attention from passers-by. They spat and blamed the betrayer for their failure. Prem could still hear the damnation as they moved away. Blood oozed from his mouth and his brain still echoed with their curses.

He felt ashamed of what had just happened. Was it wrong to protect the *farang* against his own countrymen? Would he encounter more curses, damnation, and receive blows for trying to do what his conscience dictated?

"Thanks. You're very brave," said Bruce.

Prem could not speak; he was nearly choked by the blood inside his mouth. Instead of spitting, he used his handkerchief to soak the blood.

Prem wanted to say: Ah, it is nothing. Nothing at all. I have taken many blows before.

But he kept quiet, for he remembered that Rit had suffered more. Much, much more.

He said goodbye to the tourist, and went back to his hotel.

On his way to the village the next day, Prem told himself that kilometre by kilometre he was undoing the journey which occurred in 1965 when he left Napo for the capital. Leaving the city behind, the bus sped through Rangsit where factories had taken over the rice fields in recent years. Then the Central Plain of Ayuthaya spread out as far as the eye could see. The monsoonal rains had already brought floods to the plain. Grey outlines of hills which divided the northeast and the Central Plain appeared on the horizon towards which the bus was heading.

After the township of Saraburi, the land began to rise. Gentle hill slopes had been cleared for farming and plantations. Cotton bushes and maize and other cash crops were in their prime, fluttering darkly in the sun. Beyond Klong Pai, the land dipped and boasted only a few hills marking the beginning of an arid lee. From here the plateau started; it seemed mesmerising in the haze. The rains had not yet reached this part of the country.

The bus took over six hours to reach Muang where Prem got off. He lugged his suitcase and bags from the main road to the shade of a raintree under which a small group of men were squatting on their heels. Having joined the men, he asked in the local dialect about the bus which would be leaving for villages in the vicinity of Napo.

"There'll be a bus to Payak. We're waiting for it," one man told him.

So then he gathered his suitcase and bags and squatted among the men to wait for the bus. Time was of no importance now.

The sun, which had travelled deep into the west, had left a trail of lethargy. There seemed to be very little activity in Muang. An ice-cream vendor pedaled his trishaw cart along the road from shop to shop, his broad dark face full of hope and optimism.

From the shade of the raintree Prem scanned the rows of houses and shops and the market place of Muang. From what he could remember, there had been several new shops built of concrete rising to two storeys and boasting television antennae. Trucks and long-distance buses passed at high speed, raising clouds of dust, but when the dust settled, life too seemed to resettle into lethargy. Shopkeepers waited in the cool part of their premises for customers. Only a few hawkers moved, carrying their goods in baskets or in small pedal carts.

The raintree which gave a shady shelter did not stir, nor did the squatting peasants. Time seemed to stand still for an eternity. Dust settled on their dark hair and the dark cotton shirts and baggy trousers. Subdued by weariness, the waiting men seemed rigid and small. Somewhere in one of Prem's poems, he had portrayed them as being:

Some dark quiet figures,
ornaments of the bare earth.

Many a time his father had walked along this edge of the main road, bending his head to the ground, trudging with his mild doggedness after having made a sale of a year's produce. Kumjai, too, must have come to this spot to wait for the bus to take him back to Napo. He would sit on his heels like a peasant, patiently waiting with dreams in his eyes.

The bus came, raising great clouds of dust, blasting its horn. It stopped at this junction and immediately the conductor shouted the names of villages along its route. The peasants came back to life, and moved towards the bus. One of them stayed behind to help the stranger with his suitcase.

"Get in! Get in!" the conductor ordered as he rounded up the passengers. "Just squeeze yourself in somewhere for now, then when we get out of Muang, you can sit on the deck." The conductor pushed the last peasant into the bus.

Outside Muang the gravel road became bumpy and partially eroded. The driver took some care in steering the old vehicle to avoid pot-holes and loose stones. He asked his passengers to get off his bus when it reached some wooden bridges which might

267

give way.

The passengers, young and old, obeyed and let the bus go first, crossing the shaky bridges. Only after it had crossed safely did the driver halt and allow the people to get back in.

Prem climbed up to the deck and sat on bundles of goods, securing his ride by holding on to a kerosene barrel. Flanking him were the men with whom he had shared the shade of the raintree. The bus rocked and jostled and halted in negotiating the rough country road. The wind which carried the fragrance of the sun-baked soil brought exaltation. On fallow fields water buffaloes grazed peacefully. Their skins had taken on the colour of the sun-burnt country. Everywhere there was an expectation of the monsoonal rain.

Bridge after bridge, village after village, the old bus droned mournfully on. Sometimes it protested vehemently and went out of action. Then the driver got out, opened the hood and did some checking, before clanging the hood down nonchalantly, wiping sweat from his face. And reluctantly the engine started. On the bus went again, tilting to left and right, as the road dictated.

"You get off here to go to Napo," said one of the men who sat close to Prem.

This part of the forest had been thinned beyond recognition. He remembered it now. Here he and his father and Kumjai had waited for a bus to take them to Muang. A peasant who had helped him with his suitcase shouted for the bus to stop, and when it did, it became lost in clouds of dust. Then it was gone again, protesting against human beings who would not let it rest in its extreme decrepitude.

After the dust had thinned. Prem discovered that he was not alone on the road. The man who had helped him with his suitcase was standing meekly with a grin on his face.

"I'm from Napo," the peasant said.

Dusk was falling.

"Let me carry your things for you," the man volunteered. And before Prem could do anything, the man had already shouldered the suitcase and begun to stride forward.

Soon the moon appeared above the treetops, casting grey shadows. Cicadas hummed and owls hooted. At one point on their journey, the man stopped and put the suitcase down to relieve himself. He turned his face towards the bushes. Then after having covered himself, he turned to give his travelling companion a meek grin.

"Sorry, I didn't recognize you," Prem said.

The track had become narrow, walled by thickets and briars. The man politely coughed and took the lead. He shifted the burden to another shoulder before he could speak:

"I was born in Baan Wa. When I married a Napotian girl, I moved to live with her family."

The man's bare foot hit a protruding root and he nearly stumbled. Putting the suitcase down, he checked his toes, and quietly nursed his wound, spitting on it, and without a word, he lifted up the burden and strode on in front.

Then the man cleared his throat:

"Snakes. There might be snakes on the track. If one makes noises with a twig, they will get out of the way."

Prem smiled at this indirect suggestion. He

understood why the man remained truly humble and laconic. If someone appeared well dressed in shirt and trousers, like the Masters, then the poor man adopted the role of a peasant.

"Perhaps I knew your wife, if you tell me her name."

"She's Toon, the daughter of Ta Sa."

The conversation did not last. Calls of cicadas and the night birds took over once more.

Grandmother died at the age of eight-one. She enjoyed to the end of her life her status as the most senior member of the family after Grandfather, who had entered his eighty-sixth year. Grandfather had moved away with Kiang who had gone to live with his wife in Baan Wa. Because the father of his wife had recently passed away, Kiang felt that Grandfather should become the head of his new household.

Kum Surin had become hard of hearing and he stooped slightly when he was on his feet. Boonliang, who was a few years younger than her husband, did not want to believe that he was actually going deaf. She said time and again that he just could not be bothered any more with what was going on around him, whether it was love, hatred, loss, gain, injustice, hunger, pain, or riches. He would not allow himself to be brought to the boil.

After the death of her mother, Boonliang slipped into the role of Granmother. She had always been an anxious person who cared very much for the welfare of family members and for the traditions which the young should observe. She nagged at everyone to do their chores and to behave in the manner of old. Time, hardship, cares, and frugality touched her deeply and she had become wizened.

Piang too had become an ageing woman. Prem could hardly believe his eyes when he saw her. It seemed only yesterday that she had won the first place in her class, that she had laughed gaily and her hair had been full of sunlight, that she had read auguries from the formation of clouds and told him not to point at the rainbows. Now Piang was a mother of three, with a baby tagging at her side as she squatted on the wooden floor of the hut, preparing a meal.

At first Bae Charoenpol, Piang's husband, was a total stranger, and it was difficult to treat him as a familiar figure in the family. Bae had obviously replaced Kiang as the man of the house. Like most men of the village, Bae went about his daily life, busying himself with the tasks of providing food and protecting his dependents. Observing how Bae gently looked at his wife and children, Prem was aware that the love was there without having to seek words and kisses to convey it.

It seemed that the children found the stranger in their midst rather awesome. They dared not approach the man whom they were supposed to call 'uncle'. Perhaps it was the first time in their lives that they were made aware of the shame of having a running nose or a wound on a knee because this stranger might not like a boy or a girl who looked unclean and reckless.

Visitors called on the Surins after the news of Prem's arrival had spread. They came one by one or in small groups, and not wishing to intrude, they squatted on the ground and asked a few simple questions.

The majority of visitors brought small gifts of fruit or food. Tongue-tied, they preferred to sit quietly, blinking their eyes in a kind of dumb acceptance of what Prem told them about his life overseas.

Below the hut, the water buffaloes were penned. They had increased in number, for Bae had bought a few more and he had taken good care of the herd.

As Prem was preparing for a short journey, one morning, to Baan Wa where Kiang lived, putting on his clean trousers and shirt, Mrs Surin spoke:

"On your way, drop in on the headman. Pay him your respects. He has become our very powerful Master now. His new house is next to the shop of Chinaman Ching."

The headman's two-storeyed wooden house was protected by a barbed-wire fence. At the gate a signboard indicated the name of the village, the district to which the village belonged, the province, and the name of the headman followed in bold lettering. From the gable a national flag was fluttering. Timid villagers dared not enter uninvited and brave the imposing authority which the headman represented. And the pack of fierce dogs which now threatened the visitor acted as terrifying deterrents to anyone who tried to approach the house. The headman's wife appeared on the porch to check the intrusion. She wore a sarong and a loose blouse which did not attempt to hide a gold necklace.

Cornered by the dogs, Prem waited for her to take command. Meanwhile she ordered someone in the house to chase away the barking dogs. A man appeared clad in an old pair of trousers and nothing on top, grudgingly throwing objects at the animals, kicking the air and loudly scolding whatever had caused him to get up and exert himself on such a hot day. Then the headman's wife asked the visitor the nature of his business. On learning that the caller was Kum's son who had just returned, she let him enter the house.

Prem remembered her as a young woman of simple beauty toiling in the fields, darkened by the sun. Now she looked fair and well-nourished. Not having to suffer the drudgery of a peasant life any more, she complemented her husband's status and power with newly acquired confidence.

And the man who had saved the visitor from the dogs was Peng, the former head of the herdboys, who had slapped Prem in the face for reading a book of poems. Peng had now grown into a tough looking man. Having chained the dogs, he broodily went back to the porch where he had been cleaning a pistol.

"These damned dogs. I could shoot them dead," Peng muttered as he squinted, looking through the barrel of his pistol.

Prem did not tremble to see that the weapon was pointing at him. Once he had offered his face to be slapped to appease the brute force, and now he might have to offer his life. It was Peng who dropped his gaze and then spat. Armed, the former leader of the herdboy gang had become a hanger-on of the headman.

The headman's wife explained that her husband had gone to the District Office in Muang for a seminar which headmen from other villages also attended. "I'll come to see him when he returns," Prem said.

Before leaving he caught a glimpse of the inner room in which there was a writing desk and a chair. "That is the office," the headman's wife explained. On the walls several framed photographs, old and recent, were hung, depicting Masters of various ranks in their uniforms, and the headman and his wife — a portrait made by a city photographer. The so-called office was where the headman held receptions. Villagers in difficulties or involved in litigation would be taken there for *consultation* — a word which Peng had been hearing and had adopted to impose his own influence over intimidated peasants.

Once outside the compound of the headman, Prem stood still for a moment, looking for a direction. From there he could see a part of Chinaman Ching's shop where some naked children were playing. He used to hang around the shop too in the old days, tempted by the sight of candies and colourful goods and the smell of raw sugar. How old would the Chinaman be now? He seemed old then when Prem was a naked boy watching him with longing for charity that a piece of candy might be thrown his way. There was a time when Chinaman Ching threw coins and sweets out of his shop to the children of the poor. That was the day when he, as a suitor, knew that a village girl who was two decades younger than he, would become his wife. Ching had been very lonesome since his old wife had died many years earlier, and the prospect of having a woman again made Ching call for a celebration. He gathered around him several men to share his joy. Because Ching rarely threw a party or gave things away for free, it seemed hard to believe the news. Therefore some village males decided to see for themselves, and they joined the party without being invited when they saw that food and drinks were free. Men with red faces guffawed and sang odes to bid farewell to the loneliness of Chinaman Ching. Servants brought more food and more whisky. Laughter mingled with songs and the sounds of praises of the girl who would be the wife of Ching. Children who hung around were asked to dance the 'rumwong' and Ching rewarded them with coins and candies.

Now, twenty-two years later, Ching's wife had grown old and had delivered a horde of children, and Ching himself had become half blind with age. The village street had changed very little, however. Farther down the lane, gardens of mulberry trees spaced the huts; tall mango trees and coconut palms partially hid and gave shade and shelter to the houses. Massive bamboo groves surrounded Napo. Beyond, the paddy fields spread out as far as the eye could see.

At the edge of the village, Toon appeared. Two children were with her; the older one was riding a water buffalo but the baby clung to her. Toon herself carried two pails of water. The yoke on her shoulder bent with their weight. Somehow the encounter with a stranger made the baby cry; it wriggled frantically too, as if to urge the mother to get away fast. The water spilt from the pails as Toon tried to maintain her balance and cope with the situation. Meanwhile the older child did not wait, and steered the buffalo away from the stranger.

Toon said hoarsely:

"Be good now. Don't cry in front of our Master."

And she tended to the baby's crying face.

As if Toon had never been to Kumjai's classes, she seemed to believe, like most peasants, that the one who had been to a far-off place and had some learning could have the power of the Master. Could this be Toon Puthaisong who had won third place in her final year in Napo Primary School? Slightly trembling, this ageing woman could not stop her child from crying.

Toon trembled the more for now she felt utterly ashamed of her appearance, of the dirty blouse and sarong which were dyed black to cover age and dirt. She lost her balance and staggered, causing more water to spill, yet she would not put the pails down or change the yoke to the other shoulder to ease the weight.

"Where are you going?" she awkwardly asked, spilling her words.

The weight of the yoke on her shoulder made her lopsided and on the other side the baby hung on to her, pulling her blouse. Toon's wiry arms were tense, and having uttered some customary phrases, she moved on like a beast of burden.

Traversing the fields which had begun to collect rain water Prem arrived at the place where Peng had slapped him in the face for reading poems and where Kumjai had sat and rested one smouldering afternoon returning from his visit to Baan Wa where he could buy planks for the floor of the school. Now standing on that very spot, it was not difficult to recall the day when the teacher happened to come across the gang of herdboys as they were playing a game of dragging dry palm fronds over the stony soil to simulate the sound of a monsoonal rain so that the frogs hiding in holes would croak with joy, fourteen years ago. Where were they now? Peng might still be cleaning and admiring his pistol in the house of the headman. In his heart, Prem felt that Kumjai was still alive, hiding in the depths of the jungle. And the rest of the herdboys had grown and become peasants. Was it truly worthwhile to have gone away to places so different and so far? Then he heard a voice: You had to go away and learn so that you would not go through your life believing that your Masters and leaders became richer and more powerful, alienating themselves from the inhabitants, as a result of their benevolent fate or of good deeds done in previous lives, that when the middlemen enjoyed great wealth, it was because they were blessed.

The vision became clearer as he heard Kumjai's voice. The image of Kumjai in his khaki uniform of a primary school teacher appeared where he used to sit sharing the shade of the tamarind tree with the gang of herdboys on that sweltering afternoon.

"I wanted you to experience the way of life in a world so far removed from Napo, to be aware of changes and so be prepared for them, to know that poverty, ignorance, and corruption are human conditions which can be corrected..."

"Yes, yes, I know all that now, but then what am I to do or what shall I become?" Prem wanted

277

to ask, despite the fact that he had already found the answer.

Kumjai seemed to smile in encouragement.

Rising from the plain, a whirlwind brought a swirl of dry leaves.

Later Prem resumed his trek to Baan Wa. The immensity of the open land bore heavily down on the moving figure. The wind carried no voices now, but the fragrance of wild flowers. Clouds seemed to promise a good rice planting season.

On the horizon a dark moving figure appeared. Who could it be? Fourteen years ago Kumjai had shown up like that one sultry afternoon coming back from Baan Wa, crossing the plain. So then Prem stood still, waiting for a miracle to happen. As the speck grew larger, he trembled in anticipation, remembering the familiar gait. Soon Kiang Surin came into full view. So then walking towards each other, the two brothers met on the plain of their childhood. In seeing his brother, there was a glint of happiness in the eyes of Kiang, but then he could not express emotionally or verbally his joy. Like most villagers Kiang lacked a conventional means of expressing his affection; however, he took hold of his brother's hand and began to lead the way back to Baan Wa. After a while Kiang said:

"Actually I was on the way to see you at home."

Prem was moved, not so much by the humility in Kiang's voice, but by the haggard looks and well-worn, mud-coloured clothes Kiang wore. They could be his best clothes, put on specially for the visit to Napo. Moreover, what struck Prem most was

Kiang's mild doggedness which replaced the youthful pride and sternness he had seen in Kiang before the departure. What had happened to Kiang? What had beaten him down to this doggedness? Perhaps he too felt, like Toon, ashamed of his condition in the eyes of the brother who looked clean and well dressed.

They approached Baan Wa through the gate of the village temple where a ceremony was being held in the sala. Kiang explained:

"That's the rite of farewell for the teacher of Baan Wa Primary who's to be transferred to another school. I've made an apology but now let's join them."

Kiang took his brother up to the sala. Both brothers joined the gathering, sitting down on the wooden floor like the rest. The monks had come to chant prayers and bestow blessings, and then had gone back to their living quarters, leaving the laymen to share their food and drinks. The drinks were rice wine and home-brewed rum which were passed around among the men. At last a bowl made from a coconut shell containing the rice wine was passed on to Kiang. And Kiang accepted it with both hands, holding it with utmost care. So he took his drink from the coconut shell with a stern countenance which Prem remembered so well from boyhood. Kiang handed the shell to his brother. The rice wine was milky, slightly sweet, leaving a rather tangy after-taste. But the wine and rum did not lessen the air of solemnity which the rite and the blessing from the monks had created, for this was the gathering of the sage and the old. Men whose hair and goatees had turned white with age eyed solemnly the young man who had just joined them. Old women chatted among themselves, chewing betel nuts and leaves smeared with lime.

A very old man nearest to Prem stretched his trembling bony arm to touch the native son who had returned, and in a wavering voice remarked:

"O, child, you must be so healthy. Your skin is so cool." The old man's narrow eyes became moist and shiny with curiosity.

Those who were nearby turned to contemplate the stranger.

Then they looked at him in wonder, unable to turn their curiosity into questions. Their grey heads shook with age. What should one tell them to satisfy their dumb looks and unborn questions and explain the inconceivable concept of Europe and the ways of the West?

Then the teacher of Baan Wa cleared his throat, to thank his well-wishers for their support in the past and for their donation which he said he would not put in his own pocket but would spend on a football for the school so that the school children would remember him after he had been transferred.

There was not a murmur since the audience seemed to be prepared to accept in silence whatever had to be said.

Then Kiang and his brother made a move, begging leave. They circumvented a group of novices and temple boys who were raking and sweeping the temple ground.

"Grandpa wouldn't believe that you're here. He wouldn't believe his eyes, if he could see you at all," Kiang said.

"Has he gone blind?"

"Almost," said Kiang.

After walking through the village, they arrived at a stilted hut, crudely walled with hand-hewn planks, thatched with corgon grass, and boasting a few water jars and a pack of dogs. The dogs barked at the stranger, until Kiang managed to disperse them by cursing and throwing sticks and stones at them.

Having taken his brother up into the hut, Kiang called out loudly for his wife and children. His call, meant to be heard several huts away, conveyed that he was the master of the house, that the absence of his wife and children displeased him. Kiang continued to exert his status in front of his brother by ordering a group of youngsters who began to gather in front of the hut to take a good look at the stranger.

"Go and look for my wife," he commanded them.

Whether the children wanted to remain there feeding their eyes on the stranger or whether they were simply stubborn, it was difficult to tell. They moved slightly, however, to come closer to each other, still staring at the man of whom they had heard rumours. Prem too looked at them, seeing his own childhood: nakedness, malnutrition, scars, wounds, running noses, and fear of what one did not know or understand.

Because they feared the eyes of the man who appeared to be a Master, they slunk away and disappeared.

Meanwhile Kiang fetched a bulrush mat and spread it on the floor inside the house and invited his brother to sit down. The floor was made with large coarse planks on which Kiang seemed to notice for the first time the dirt and dust. He might have been afraid that they would be uncomfortable to sit on. So he looked bashful and began to be apologetic.

"A poor man's home," Kiang mumbled and sucked his teeth and waited while his brother took off his shoes to enter the hut.

And now perhaps Kiang might be aware of his bare feet too. All his life he had never had a pair of shoes. Looking down at his feet then, he saw how wide and coarse his feet and toes were. He saw too that some nails were broken and smeared with mud and grime.

But he was pleased to observe that his brother took off his shoes, following the Siamese custom.

Then Kiang went into a corner of the hut and picked up what appeared to be a heap of rags, taking it into both arms. It was only when Kiang turned and carefully stepped forward with the bundle that it was plain to see the head of grey hair protruding from the rags. Kiang lowered himself and placed the emaciated Grandfather Hod on the mat in front of his brother. Having put a small kapok pillow under the head of the old man, Kiang gently removed bits and pieces of old cloths from the face and shoulders and legs so that the old man might feel some cool breeze from being in the open part of the hut. However, it seemed that the skin and bones had not come back to life. So then Kiang had to bawl into the deaf ears of the old sleeping man who was drifting along the dark current of dreams.

"Wake up, Grandpa. We've a visitor. Guess who."

Kiang smiled at his brother.

"He hasn't been well." Kiang attempted to explain the condition of their Grandfather.

It was difficult to believe that this was what remained of the man who for so many years had ploughed the land and shouldered great burdens. Yet there was that familiar odour one could recollect from childhood, having slept so close to the old man who once sang:

Boy, where have you been all day long?
What have you done wrong?
Come, child, and rest by my side.

It was so nice to be called 'Child' or 'Boy' by the old man then; the words sounded so soothing, so forgiving, making one feel wholesome once again. But now the poor old man had been reduced to skin and bones and a bundle of rags.

Meanwhile Grandfather Hod seemed to open his murky, watery eyes; the lips moved slightly, producing a soft murmuring sound. Barely visible, the pupils shone between the narrow eye-lids, like hands of memory reaching out from the dark passages of the past. Then they faded and the glimmer of lights went out; and the eye-lids closed again as the old man returned to his great distance and the soft cocoon of dreams. Neither the cries of children nor the neighing of the horse could now bring him back to the present.

Kiang's children were loud with excitement because they were eager to tell their father about the adventure they had in bringing back the young horse which had broken loose, but when they saw a stranger, they became shy. Meanwhile Kiang's wife took the animal to the pen and locked it there. The woman seemed determined that she would master the horse and finish her task of keeping it safely in the pen before she would answer the shout of her husband. She was a stout woman with a dark complexion and sullen countenance. When she became aware of the visitor she looked embarrassed, forcing a meek smile.

Kiang seemed quite happy that his horse was safely penned and his wife and children were home. Once again he took the old man in his arms and lifted him to his usual corner to sleep. Having done so, Kiang said:

"Now then, children, what have we got for your uncle to eat?"

The boy who was the oldest showed the whites of his eyes, and the girl crawled up to hide behind the mother. They were afraid of the stranger. The mother sucked her teeth, embarrassed for she knew that there was hardly anything in the house to make a decent meal, that the question her husband asked was in fact directed at her. She had to say something.

"Perhaps you can catch a chicken, and I'll make a curry," she said, looking quizzically at her husband for approval.

Accepting the suggestion from his wife, Kiang asked his son to help him catch a hen. Following his father down from the hut, the boy became alive, chatting away, saying that the easiest way to catch a chicken was early in the morning just before the flock would get up and get out of the barn.

The boy's voice rose and entwined with that of his father as they were discussing the best way to catch a chicken now that they were all out and away from the barn. Meanwhile the hostess shifted and said to her little girl who was still hiding behind her that someone must look after the baby.

She gathered pieces of clothing and cloths which were hung nearby and made a nest for her baby to sleep on.

"I'll go to pick herbs to make curry," she said hoarsely. "Be a good girl and take care of your brother."

But the little girl shook her head and clung to her mother. Meanwhile the baby boy began to wail, being laid down on the floor. He waved his hands and feet in the air to protest.

"Do you know how to take a baby in your arms?" the mother forced herself to ask her brother-in-law.

She knew that she must make a move to prepare the meal or face abuse from her husband for being slow. So she tugged her baby, lifting it, and delivered it to the arms of the visitor. Then she crawled away and at a respectful distance, stood up, tightening her sarong, and left the hut to dig for a root of *kha,* cut a few sprigs of lemon grass, and pick a handful of lemon leaves. Her daughter quickly followed while her husband and the little boy raised such a din and dust in chasing the chickens all over the place.

When Kiang finally caught one he immediately killed it by twisting its neck. Then he brought it to the hut. Like a ritual the boy knew what to do. He fetched a bowl for his father and with boyish solemnity, he sat and watched how the chicken's throat was slit and how the blood ran into the bowl. For a moment there was a silence intense and concentrated, till Kiang let go of the throat. Then he kindled a charcoal fire in the stove.

Death did not come easily to the chicken; it spluttered vainly, spraying the last drops of its blood, till the boy got hold of its wings and lifted it into the air. Kiang then placed on the stove a pot half-filled with water, so when the water was hot, he scalded the chicken and plucked its feathers.

When the wife returned from the garden with a handful of roots and leaves, she washed and sliced them and put the prepared herbs in the wooden mortar. Adding garlic, little brown onions and chilli, she pounded the ingredients to a fine paste and the little hut shook with the rhythm of the pounding.

Throughout the commotion, the ailing great-grandfather slept, enveloped in the grey infinity of his silent world. Meanwhile, in the arms of the stranger, the baby fell asleep.

When the chicken curry was ready, it was dished out and the steamy bowls were placed on a large bamboo tray on which other dishes such as fermented fish, fish sauce with ground chilli and some vegetables were arrayed.

"Come. Let's eat," Kiang invited his brother.

The hostess retrieved her baby from her brother-in-law. Turning herself sideways, she lifted her blouse and began to breast-feed the child.

"Go ahead and eat," she mumbled softly to indicate that she would not share the meal.

"Eat now," Kiang said to his children.

So the food was thus consumed.

When the visitor eventually left, Kiang took his horse to water at the village dam.

"Ma, that strange man, I don't know him," said the boy.

The child wanted to ask the same question again, while his mother was finishing off the food which was left for her on the bamboo tray. It seemed she did not bother to answer the child's babble, then having spat a chicken bone out of her mouth, she said:

"That's your uncle who has been to many strange lands far away. So far you cannot go by walking. And he's a Master whom you must obey."

"Are you afraid of him, Mum?" the boy babbled on.

"Yes. People say he's been adopted by a ghost."

The mother burped and drank some water from a large bowl.

"Is Pa afraid of him too?" the boy asked.

"Sort of. To protect its adopted son, the ghost is always with him. And we are afraid of ghosts, aren't we?"

"Yes, I'm afraid of ghosts," the boy said and snuggled up to her for protection.

On the plain between Baan Wa and Napo, the herdboys from each village were rounding up their water buffaloes to return home at sundown. Flocks of minas and crows flew to their nests. Here, many years ago, naive little boys had tried to deceive hibernating frogs, grating the stony earth with palm fronds to simulate the sound of rains, singing:

On ancient stones
and ground dry as bones
we drag fronds to make grating sounds
of pelting rains and thunder...

But now a song of a more sophisticated lyric learned from a pop tune on the radio was being sung by a buffalo boy:

I have been following, watching
you jump and jostle, light as the air,
after the wind-carried thistles.
Look! Look! you cry, I caught one!
And then you let it go, blowing,
giving it back to the wind.

What is there but an object of desire
chased and conquered; while I suffer
every rise and fall
you make with love's rhythm.

And that buffalo boy sang it over once more as the herd moved homeward. None would know that twenty years later, another song would be composed to lament:

For now these rasping deadly palms
drawn across the skies
grating the air
deceive us
as their thundering bolts
wound the land and shatter
the ancient solitude
and men run, falling,
screaming and parting.

The mist spread and shrouded the marshes while in Napo smoke rose from wood fires, seeping through gaps in the thatched roofs. Meals were being prepared; weary farmers rolled their cigarettes while the children waited to be fed.

In the hut of the Surins, the children were playing on the porch, amusing themselves with a large lizard which they had caught that afternoon. The reptile was tied with a jute string to a leg of the cradle. Tired of trying in vain to escape, the lizard closed its eyes and remained thus despite the jabbing little fingers and sticks nudging it to be active again. After a while it opened its mournful eyes to bid farewell to the moon for the last time, and then died.

Once in a while dogs barked to keep the village vigilant and awake. Sometimes a burst of laughter echoed; sometimes a mother would be heard scolding her child; a baby wailed, and buffaloes sighed.

Having left the dead lizard alone, Piang's boy and girl amused themselves by becoming more daring. Taking their uncle's hands, they cajoled:

"What's that?" the boy asked.

"My watch," Prem said. "It tells time. Time."

The children giggled, not that they understood what 'time' was but because smiles and laughter came readily to them. And they liked the sound of the man's voice. This man whom they were told to call 'uncle' wore shoes and a funny thing called watch or time which the Napotians did not have. He's strange, the boy and the girl agreed and laughed.

I must get rid of this time instrument and the

shoes, Prem thought, to be like everybody else in the village.

"I want to grill the lizard and eat it. I am hungry," the boy said.

"I am hungry too," said the girl.

Without waiting for their uncle, they picked up the dead reptile and went down to the ground, to where their father had made a fire for the buffaloes.

Putting on his shoes, Prem followed them.

And I shall throw my shoes into the fire, Prem thought as he silently watched while the children were putting the lizard on the burning wood. A pair of English shoes created for elegance is out of place here when everyone goes about bare-footed. There is no need to be elegant in the European style when one has to wallow in the mud and roam the woods for food. The same goes for the watch bought with the prize money won by 'A Cantata', a poem composed out of the tension of another time, another place. It would tell only unneeded time when the sun, the moon, and the barking of dogs and the crowing of roosters would do. A taste of luxury, once had, is difficult to resist. Kiang too had a taste of it. Kiang and his asking for a few pairs of underpants! Now he goes through life feeling that he has been missing things which he might be able to have if he had money or opportunity. And this afternoon there was a gleam in his eyes when he looked at my watch and shoes and trousers. The same gleam I recognized fifteen years ago when he saw for the first time the underwear which Kumjai wore while taking a bath in the lotus pond outside the village. How many seasons would Kiang have to toil to produce enough rice and jute and tapioca to turn them into cash to buy a watch and a pair of shoes? Hagenbach could so casually ask for a bottle of Romanee-Conti at Claridge's. That bottle cost at least fifty years of father's labour, money earned from his sale of rice, which amounted to 280 baht a year, the figure I carried in my brain like a trauma to suffer with every mouthful of smoked salmon and sirloin steak and wine. Tears welled up in my eyes and the trauma of 280 baht a year throbbed painfully. I was a mere boy when father took me with him to Muang, and I had watched how the fat Chinese traders weighed and valued our yearly produce, had seen, heard and yet could not do anything when the illiterate old man, my father, turned to me for help: Is it correct, Tadpole? I nodded, yes, take the money and let's get out of here and return home to the village. I, who had learned from Kumjai how to add, multiply, and subtract, knew also something of shrewdness and meanness. Year after year, it was the same: a pitiful gaze at my face for help, his sad eyes on my boyish innocence — Is it correct? A nod, nothing more. At the time I began to sense the primeval bitterness and the futility in all things but pretended to be as dumb as a tree or the rice fields. I was nine, and on another trip I was ten, and later eleven. Still I gave him just a nod, but took his hand more readily each time to pull him away from the market place at the end of each sale, away from the merchants who, at the slightest sign from the peasants to plead for higher pay, would yell: "Take it or leave it!"

I wanted to spare Father the insult. He has always been so gentle, quiet and easy to appease, a dignified man when he is in his own environment.

I would not allow him, in my silent way, to fall on his knees to beg for kindness from the middlemen. For kindness is never in the book of trade, and one thing I did not want was for them to laugh and mock him, showing their upper hand.

Meanwhile age and drudgery lay heavily on him, making him stoop humbly. Silence surrounded him more thickly than before and he sometimes coughed to disperse the eternity of silence and gazed at what was going on around him with an air of detachment. I wonder whether he knew how I mourned the loss of the water buffaloes, my old friends, sold for a pair of shoes, a suitcase, and a suit. Yes, children, let's throw everything I have from abroad into the fire, and you shall take part in the act to pay homage to my friends, the water buffaloes. And one day we shall light another fire to pay homage to Kumjai and Rit.

Rit did not succeed in teaching me how to hate and how to disobey, not even when I learned of his death in the afternoon of October 14, 1973. At the time we did not expect the wrath and the murderousness. Rit had been waiting impatiently at the temple gate, having said: "Come to Thammasart University and you will know what the word 'Liberty' on the foreign coin means." I did not know then that marching peacefully from the university into the streets would cost hundreds of lives. The Honourable Brother the monk said he knew what was going to happen and he forbade me to go with Rit. He sat solidly looking at me to test my obedience. Like a dog, I obeyed. Later in my little dark room something in my blood throbbed for the first time resembling a yearning to revolt, but then it seemed there was an immense metal lid that would not let such a feeling expand and find a vent. At least Rit could spit in the face of his adversary. Rit, the fair boy from a northern hill tribe, had slid down time and again from a river bank to bathe and to swim in the cool, clear water of the hills, to die from a machine gun fired at an arm's length on October 14, 1973. I, a survivor, had to understand only years later the meaning of 'Liberty' written on a silver coin a foreign visitor gave to me one afternoon in Wat Borombopit, and years later the news of Kumjai's death brought that word back to me again. Meanwhile I had to learn the language of sophistication which Dhani tried to drum into my head, and for a while I obediently followed, apeing the mannerisms and mimicking accents, memorising names of composers and their works, names of wines and vintages and chateaux. Kitchen glasses would not do when the crystal and silver could do a better job in upholding a sense of good taste. Dictated by fashion and Dhani's set of values, I spent so much time and effort to acquire fashionable and expensive clothes, to learn how to drink coffee or tea with my little finger daintily sticking out, to learn the mechanism of social grace, only to come back now to the old set of values, to the mud of my beginnings.

Perhaps Kumjai was more of a dreamer than I could have ever been. For now I have begun to heed a strange voice. This voice gives me no peace; it whispers in my ears every time a child recoils from me, seeing me a stranger, someone they are afraid of; every time I look upon the ruin of the school where we were happy once, reciting by rote verses and mathematical tables. I roam the plain of my childhood to seek peace, but in vain.

Where is the peace promised to me during the years in Europe? Yes, Kumjai was more of a dreamer than I could have been, a dreamer who had never become aware of wrath and murderousness. Kumjai is perhaps dead now.

At that moment the children claimed him once again after they had eaten the grilled lizard. They got hold of his hands as he was loosening his watch. They pulled him away from the fire, and laughed.

"Don't be a nuisance," Piang shouted at them from inside the house.

She was spreading mulberry leaves on a tray for silk worms.

They obeyed by keeping their mouths shut. But not for long. They screamed at the top of their voices, when their uncle threw the watch into the fire.

He put the palms of his hands over their mouths. "Don't cry. It's nothing. Nothing of value to us at all," he told them.

Looking silently at the fire, Prem thought: Has Piang already handed down the ancient heritage and the fear of the Masters and the Lord of Darkness to her children? You, little ones, must not dare, must not speak against the evil and the powerful. Has the little boy told his sister of taboo, a code of survival: the eyes that do not see, the ears that do not hear, the mouth that does not speak? Shall I also be an instrument passing on these messages to my own children when one day I shall have them, and allow the older to pass them on to the younger?

15

At the approach of the Buddhist Retreat, the Napotians learned that a young man in their village was becoming a monk that season. The monk-to-be was the native son who had returned from foreign lands.

When an auspicious day had been fixed by the abbot of the village temple, both Kum and Boonliang Surin went from hut to hut confirming the date and inviting their relatives and neighbours to the ceremony and the feast.

One late afternoon Kum took his son to the village temple to have his head shaved by the abbot. In front of the old venerable monk, the father and the son lowered themselves and prostrated three times. When a bowl of water and a razor were brought, the benign monk cleared his throat and signalled to the young man to move closer to him. Prem readily moved up to the abbot, whom he had known since childhood. With his eyes closed, he submitted himself, arching his neck so that the abbot could get hold of his head and wet his hair.

When the abbot spoke, the timbre in his voice finely vibrated: I have been waiting to see how many young men would decide to become *Bhikkhu* this year. Well, at least there will be one. I am glad. Last year there were none. Young men go away. They go off somewhere and leave the old people to work in the fields; monks too like to go away to

295

reside in city temples where they can study and make connections. I ordain them and then they leave me. A few years in the city and they study foreign languages and receive degrees and get themselves promoted to high order; some of them become well-known as makers of magic, amulets and talismans, having thousands of followers. I am glad, child, that you will be the third monk in this temple, and I hope you know that this is not a rich temple; it's a temple of frugality and of peace where you can detach youself from the worldly concept of value and pleasure; where you will follow the steps the Buddha has made to reach the cessation of 'thirst' or craving which is the cause of all our suffering. Don't mind me preaching at you, child, for you will know of all the teaching of the Buddha in the course of your ordination. O child, I am glad for you now that you shall learn how to stop all that is causing suffering in the world today, that you will make the first step in removing the hindrances to joy and peace; you will be in the battle of freeing yourself from lustful desires, ill-will, hatred, anger, torpor, languor, restlessness, worry and sceptical doubts. It is not easy, child, though it sounds so, and it may require all your strength and will to win yourself over to this path. Should you find the monkhood too severe to go on, you have the freedom to put aside the robe and return to the life of a layman any time you so wish. But once you liberate yourself from those hindrances which I have just mentioned it will be easier to keep the 227 rules to which every monk should adhere. Child, how one could easily suffer displeasure and unhappiness at losing honour, and people's respect, from gossip and worry and the lack of sensual gratification. Such is the way of the flesh whose thirst can never be satisfied. It always craves for more and more. Can you see, child, that the fall of every strand of your hair, or every stroke of the razor brings your renunciation closer. This renunciation does not mean you are running away from the world, but learning to live within it with detachment. In time you will realize that honour and dishonour, praise and condemnation, love and hate will equally have no effect on you. You who have travelled far and wide would have been attracted by some beautiful charming people; you like them, enjoy seeing them, being close to them, having pleasure and satisfaction from them. This is enjoyment, an enjoyment which is not permanent, just as those to whom you are attracted are not permanent either. When you cannot be with the loved ones or when the situation or the attraction changes, you suffer disappointment or sadness, or in some circumstances you might become foolish or behave unreasonably. If you can detach yourself completely from sensual thirst, from physical attraction, you will be free; this is freedom or liberation, a tiny slice of the total liberation which you, as a monk, will experience. For the territory of lust, hatred, anger, greed, illusion, false views and ignorance is vast; and you are tempted to them through your eyes, ears, sense of touch, nose, and your whole body. Careful now, and do not move. I must be steady with the razor as it has to go over the hair around the scar. You must not be bitter, child, and you must forgive the man who gave you this scar. You did not know that I saw him throw a stone at you that day when you were only six years old. I was sitting under the banyan tree to rest for a while after a long trek from Baan Wa, and I said to myself I must pray for that boy who did not raise a cry while blood was running down his face. I never knew why he threw a stone at you. What did you say to him? You must forgive him all the same, now that you are going to be a monk. In monkhood there is no room for hatred, bitterness, and jealousy. There is no need to raise a finger to revenge yourself, because each of us suffers his own *karma*, those who commit bad deeds will suffer bad results. Kumjai must have taught you this at school. I am sure he did, for I remember seeing him put up a little board proclaiming that goodness prevails forever. When he disappeared I went to look at the deserted school and found the board there, so I took it to keep here in my room. One day, when the school can be opened again, you may want to put it back on a wall.

I have already forgiven him a long long time ago, Prem thought, though I know that the scar will remain with me till I die. It is the scars in my mind that I do not want to have, the English scar and the German scar which remind me of the joy and tension and conflict experienced in countries so far away from home. They assault my mind when I am most vulnerable, or they remind me of my longing to win renown as an artist though I have already burned two books of poems, 'The Poetry of the Plains' and 'The Poetry of the Rains', along with suits, shirts, trousers made of fine material. I will not forgive myself for making my father sell our buffaloes, my old friends, for a sum of money to buy a suitcase, a suit, and a pair of shoes before leaving for England, for not returning soon enough to save Toon from a marriage by proxy, for not having fulfilled any of Kumjai's dreams, and for becoming a stranger in my own home. A year has gone now since my return to Napo, yet conflicts follow me, giving me no peace for which I have searched high and low all over the plateau where I was happy once. And I will not forgive myself for failing to reopen the Napo Primary School, no matter how hard I try. So now I turn to your temple, hoping that as a monk, I will be allowed to teach the children in the old *sala*.

He prostrated before the abbot after his head was shaved. Kum too prostrated and begged leave.

The next day, Kiang rode his horse into Napo. He alighted in front of his parents' hut, but seeing that the party was almost ready to leave for the temple, he did not go inside. He announced his arrival with a loud greeting, and then busied himself with grooming his horse for his brother to ride to the temple.

No one suspected the gravity in Kiang's heart. He decided to withhold the news of the death of the grandfather until the ordination ceremony was over. Kiang had discovered the death of the grandfather only that morning.

Prem emerged from the hut in white shirt and trousers; his tonsure exposed him to the morning sunlight. The horse shifted and shook his beautiful mane. Then he mounted the horse as his parents and relatives and friends began to walk towards the temple.

Inside the Wat, a panel of four monks and senior members of the village waited. Sitting separated from the others, the abbot faced the door through which the monk-to-be would enter. Behind him were gilded images of the Buddha in various sizes on a nest of wooden tables in front of which bronze urns stood to receive votive offerings of flowers, incense sticks and candles.

Columns of light slanted through the windows, enhancing the contrast of the monks' yellow robes and the golden images of the Buddha and the bronze against the dimness and the austerity of the chapel.

The abbot cleared his throat now for the sound of music and footsteps told him that the procession was within the temple ground. The village sage and religious men, who sat on the floor in relaxed attitudes, straightened their backs preparing themselves for the solemnity and the rigour of the rite.

They all looked towards the door when Prem entered, carrying on his forearms the set of saffron robes, measuring his careful steps as he approached the abbot. He gently lowered himself, put down the set of robes on his left, took the tray of candles, incense sticks and white lotus flowers and offered it to the old monk. Then he prostrated himself three times before the monks. Sitting with both of his knees touching the floor, again the set of robes on his forearms, joining hands in token of respect and worship, Prem began chanting the plea in the Pali language — the official language of Buddhism:

"I take, O Venerable Bhikkhu, for guidance the Buddha, his teaching and the order of monks. Grant me to be ordained as a novice, and then as a Bhikkhu in the Buddha's doctrine. May you take these robes and kindly have me ordained."

He repeated the plea three times.

Then the abbot received Prem's robes, put them before himself and made an instruction of the basic knowledge of the structure of Buddhism, the Triple Gem, namely the Buddha, the Dhamma (his teaching) and the order of monks, telling him how he could take them for his spiritual guidance and how he could benefit by being a Bhikkhu.

Acting as Prem's Preceptor, the abbot took the small inner robe out of the set and put it on him, and taught him how to put on the rest of the robes. He then asked another monk to assist in the change of clothes.

Having allowed a moment of ease among the gathering, the abbot called for another period of concentration. As the Preceptor of the new Bhikkhu, he would now bring to his attention the most crucial points in the general practices and rules of conduct for monks. He began with the Four Resources on which the ordination was based, and then included the maximum Misconducts.

"You, the new Bhikkhu, shall not commit sexual intercourse, even with an animal; for if you practise such, you will no longer be allowed to continue the fellowship of the Order, a follower of the Buddha. This, you shall not do for the rest of your ordination.

"You shall not steal, or entertain an intention to steal, or take anything which is not given to you. When a Bhikkhu takes to thieving whatever is not given to him, being worth very little or not, he is accordingly no longer a Bhikkhu.

"You shall not kill or cause a life to be extinguished, even though that living creature is only an ant or a tiniest living thing in the water. When a Bhikkhu deliberately deprives a being of life, including a manner of causing an abortion, he is accordingly no longer a Bhikkhu.

"You shall not lay claim to super-human qualities, even in the manner of saying, 'I take delight in a deserted place'. When a Bhikkhu, having evil desires, overwhelmed with covetousness, lays claim to the non-existent, untrue super-human qualities, he is accordingly no longer a Bhikkhu, a follower of the Buddha.

The old religious leaders and senior laymen in the chapel raised their cupped hands so that the fingers touched their foreheads to indicate their joyful recognition of the ordination. Thus the procedure was ended.

In a small room allocated to the new monk, a young acolyte had been polishing the wooden floor with a wet rag. He stopped this activity when the monk entered. Crawling to the door, he left the room so that the monk could be alone. Pundit Bhikkhu sat down on the floor and relieved himself of the begging bowl. He saw that someone had prepared for him two bottles of drinking water and a glass, a mat, a pillow and a few candles. Nothing more. Having renounced his home and all the worldly things, he hoped that he would be safe, for he wanted to survive, waiting for the day when Kumjai, who might still be alive, could return to Napo.

"Will you require a mosquito net?" The boy asked later.

Looking at the acolyte, the monk recalled his

own past, his life in a city temple. He looked kindly at the boy and said:

"Will I need It?"

The boy went away without answering, and a few minutes later returned with a mosquito net which had been previously used by other monks. He did not enter the room this time, but remained kneeling at the door.

"The abbot calls for you, Venerable Brother," he said.

The old monk, waiting in front of his room, said when the new monk came to see him:

"You have blessed your parents with great happiness by becoming a monk. It is one of the highest acts of gratitude towards the parents who share the merits gained from your ordination. I could hardly believe that you, who have grown up from a quiet child — I remember having seen you as a little boy whom everyone called the Mute — would be sitting here today as a monk. I remember also the day I visited the school after the storm and the flood had destroyed much of it. I had to move the classes to the old sala. It was nice to hear the children's sing-song voices, reciting mathematical tables and chanting some verses. I enjoyed being among the school children, though they seemed to be frightened of me. Come, we must bestow merits on the deceased, to Kumjai and Hod, your Grandfather, who died this morning."

Handing a bowl of water to the new monk, the abbot asked Pundit Bhikkhu to pour little by little the water from the bowl on to the ground while he would lead in chanting the *Yatha* to send the merits to the deceased. He began:

"Just as an ocean is filled by rivers and streams, so the dedication dispensed here is received by the deceased. May whatever is wished and desired by you be immediately realized. May all plans be successful like the full moon or like a brilliant gem."

At sunset a novice beat a huge bronze gong to announce the time of evening prayer. A pack of temple dogs howled, as was their habit every time the gong was sounded.

People of Esarn
By Pira Sudham

Pira Sudham brings into the light lives of some of the
ordinary people who live in obscurity in remote villages. With
the skill and craftsmanship of a sensitive writer, he conveys
the inner voices of his subjects regardless of how illiterate,
timid and insignificant they seem in their daily lives. Their
simplicity and sensitivity come through his direct and clear
prose, yet moving and touching. He writes with understanding and compassion for his people.

Foreign writers writing about the Thai people look at
Thailand from the 'outside', but Pira Sudham writes about his
people and country as seen from the 'inside'. This is one of
the things that makes them so fascinating.

Shire Books
GPO Box 1534
Bangkok 10501
THAILAND

Pira Sudham's Best
Siamese Drama and Other Stories from Thailand

An outstanding Thai writer presents an insight into Thai life, particularly that of rural Thailand.

Shire Books
GPO Box 1534
Bangkok 10501
THAILAND